IN
SEARCH
OF THE
BLUEBIRD

By Franco D'Rivera:

In Search of the Bluebird: Vol 1
In Search of the Bluebird: Vol 2

IN SEARCH OF THE BLUEBIRD

MELANCHOLY STORIES ON LOVE & TERROR
VOLUME TWO ✝ BY FRANCO D'RIVERA

iUniverse, Inc.
Bloomington

In Search of the Bluebird
Melancholy Stories on Love and Terror: Volume Two

iUniverse books may be ordered through booksellers or by contacting:

iUniverse
1663 Liberty Drive
Bloomington, IN 47403
www.iuniverse.com
1-800-Authors (1-800-288-4677)

ISBN: 978-1-4620-0185-9 (sc)
ISBN: 978-1-4620-0186-6 (hc)
ISBN: 978-1-4620-0187-3 (ebk)

Printed in the United States of America

iUniverse rev. date: 03/19/2012

For Dad, Paquito.

If your parents begin to like your work . . . . it's getting bad!
—Charles Bukowski
from the documentary *Born Into This*

Lo que vale es la intención.
(The value of a gift is in "the giving," not in the gift.)

—Old Cuban proverb

But if in your fear you would seek only
 love's peace and love's pleasure,
 Then it is better for you that you cover
 your nakedness and pass out of love's threshing-floor

—Kahlil Gibran
Excerpt from *The Prophet*

CONTENTS

Introduction: Rhapsody, and Chaos

Shark attacks are very rare, they say—whoever they are . . . these people who know the score and how everything goes . . . . As rare as anything else out here that's quite horrible, I'd suppose, yet rarity never stopped things from happening, especially certainly not freakishly horrid things that suddenly explode or bite or fall and make it to front pages of dailies and where the participants in these events would take little refuge—I'm convinced—in the rarity factor of their misfortunes.

Once, as I experienced a hysterical onset of panic in shallow water at some beach in New Jersey, a friend was attempting to calm me down by spewing some very wise statistics at me: "Don't worry!" he barked. "Shark attacks are very rare," he said, grinning and gripping my collarbone firmly between his thumb and forefinger as a kind of reassuring anchor-clutch between himself and I, who stood only feet away and who was regardless frozen in an indefinite panic suspension. "As rare as being struck by lightning, my friend! They say."—Hmm . . ."They say," he'd said as an afterthought, the kind of under-breath utterance that classically rouses nothing but doubts in me. Well, this could have very well been perhaps a welcomed appeasement were I at all aware of the statistics of lightning strikes . . . which, of course, I was not.

But I was then further educated generally on that matter as I was standing still on that bank and in the epicentral cold unrelenting grip of this paranoid and aquatic terror: It is said—again by them—that apparently lightning doesn't strike the same place twice! Now . . . how is this measured? Precisely what man is responsible for standing in the lightning-stricken area for some long-enough window of time to attest to such a theory—that, in fact, lightning has not struck there again!—I do not know of this kind of person and would be tempted to question his existence. And I say "his," only because it is clear that women are naturally too clever to fall for such a foolish prospect. Despite all this nonsense, and if anything serves or says anything at all about this fact-drawing parallel my friend was grudgingly arriving at, it is that whichever shark will attack you will not do it twice! And this is probably—I'm assuming—mainly due to the high probability that, during that first attack, he will most likely kill you! And you certainly cannot be killed twice. Right? (My sources communicate to me that except for zombies and mummies, the latest information above is, in fact, accurate!)

Look, your guess is as good as mine, and I don't know what all those half-smiling people who habitually squint toward the horizon are thinking about—what with that look of approaching epiphany and bizarre and profound satisfaction, and perhaps this makes me a somewhat incomplete person in a manner; I don't know . . . insensitive in some way, maybe—but neither have I ever pretended to have found anything spiritually resonant in me hidden within the waves or the mystical marriage of sunlight and water, but I do have and always will have a strange and somewhat ridiculous love for the sea. I do. But most certainly and above anything else what I have is primarily an unwavering distrust, ice-cold terror for that which lingers within it—and most especially, above anything else, sharks. It is a fact that sharks have no capacity to empathize with your terror . . . none! . . . and that is precisely what, if nothing else, makes these animals so troublesome to me. That, and the fact that their teeth can go through a grown man's femur like an electric nutcracker through a macadamia, and with the same easy mindlessness you crush your salad's croutons over brunch, too. They are unsympathetic dumb monsters that have no business living in the twenty-first century along with creatures that have already made it to the moon, for Christ's sake! What kind of crazy planet is this, anyhow? Is God for real or is this his "all sorts" drawer? I think we are not God's creation . . . I think we are the Son of God's science project—and he got honorable mention in that competition.

Anyhow . . . they insist that given the statistics, my fear of sharks is unfounded and thus unreasonable—deemed of course by those who determine what's reasonable. So . . . at any rate . . . to cope with this persistent, unbecoming paranoia or phobia and perhaps to work my way to an eventual and total recovery that will result ideally in one pleasant, worry-free, and glorious plunge and swim in the ocean, having total faith that I was not born to be a statistic but born to trump my terrors, I wear a particular T-shirt that bears a graphical imprint from the movie *Jaws* as a sort of therapeutic primer, a symbol of defiance of some kind that pokes at my panic gland fearlessly and repeatedly—I wear it often, and even now, as I type this, I wear it. I breathe heavy, but I work through it, and as I wear it, I often think that I can be my own best psychologist, but as my psychologist says, these are no more than manifestations of my ramifying delusional character, to which I respond that psychologists, better than anyone, should understand that people are way too complex to be understood by psychoanalysis (or at least dominated or steered or changed as a consequence of this understanding), because there's this little thing called "urge"—or anything else closely galvanizing to our primal design—that will invariably get in the way of that understanding as well as in the way of your better judgment, and next thing you know, you are back to snapping into that rampaging argument even after fifteen long years of therapy for anger management or leaping at the sight of shadows or arachnophobia or being inexplicably horrified of porcupines in top hats or whatever the heck your particularly persisting problem or hallucination may be.

I often wondered, Who analyzes her? Huh? Who? Do psychologists go to other psychologists? Do they take turns on the couch? Is this how their party goes? It seems awfully cannibalistic to me in some intellectual form, you know, if this is the case. Unholy in some way, even. Also a bit—or a lot—like having a remote control for your remote control—sure, it's possible, but still very odd. I don't even know what I'm . . . saying anymore. All I know is that if psychoanalysis worked well, shrinks should be ruling the world by now, no? I mean, if they know all the tricks of the noggin, they should certainly be able to sneak all the way to the top of the food chain! They are like Jedis with diplomas or something, mind-tricksters who know what we are going to do, weeks before we even think of doing it. They probably think we are all fools who live our lives like baby cavemen poking in the dark.

But my psychologist seems the type that owns a pig that will eat only bacon. But since it's an awful strange thing, she won't tell anyone about it—of course. Because . . . umm . . . the ramifications are way too weird! And the moral questions are impossible to answer with any degree of certainty, that's for sure. Though you will often find her gaze leaping out the venetians into an imaginary horizon as—I'm sure—hellish daydreams of cannibal pigs with revolvers and chaps raid her thoughts. Rabid porcines rampage the streets in her mind's eye and take over America á la *Birth of a Nation* in hoods and Confederate flags as infernal squeals fill the square with a godless, incessant screeching! Strips of Canadian and hickory-smoked bacon sling irreverently from the corners of their salivating mouths, clenched in their oinking smirks just below their little tusks, their eyes beady and red like embers, smoke shooting out of their soot-crusted, moist, round nostrils like cannonballs. Little black un-cannibalized piglets run for their lives, their cute little misfortunate ears flapping in frantic terror as one grotesque boar corners one in a cul-de-sac as his two six-shooters point straight into the piglet's pleading, shiny, large eyes. Above the poor little soul, a maniacal, emphysemic laughter; a demonic, hairy amorphous thing of a head—his black horse neighing on its hinds against the gold-hot sun that burns on the red, dried earth that too scorches the piglet's pupils to blindness and horror . . .

TO BE CONTINUED

Psychologists are often there to tell you why you poop your pants . . . and what you can do about it so you don't care about pooping your pants, since there's nothing you can actually do about pooping them. You will never be "fixed," I might as well tell you now, but you will become educated quite acutely on how exactly it was that you became a spontaneous explosive defecator, and such a bat-shit neurotic pinball machine! I'm not sure that understanding ourselves will take us to a better place; our nature indicates that we'll only become obsessed with all this new information and will subsequently all require therapy later on in life to deal with our inability to cope with what we have now found out about who we are. In essence: to forget all that junk we just discovered about ourselves! We could never know how something we didn't make, works. You take your broken wristwatch to a watchmaker . . . because people invented wristwatches. You don't take a UFO to the local mechanic, do you? And that's another reason why you never see space aliens driving around in old Chevys. Period. While it is in fact a much more effective way to remain incognito—which is what space aliens are all about: anonymity. Space aliens simply do not possess the understanding to find their way around American automotive engineering. It's not indigenous to their reasoning. And those are some facts of life, Bucko. There's a type of jellyfish out there that can generate its own light . . . something we, as human beings, will never be able to do. But can a jellyfish play the saxophone? I've never seen it.

But sometimes living blindly like a baby caveman poking in the dark is the best medicine for sanity. Look at old cowboys, for instance. I mean, it is true that they shot each other dead in saloons every single day, but so damn what? They were jovial—or something like that—and sure as heck they had a firm sense of who they really were. Not even a persistent, unrelenting alcoholism was an affliction for cowboys. That's how solid their foundation and self-image was—not that there was even such a thing as self-image to cowboys: self-image was simply the glimpse they caught of themselves in the dusty old window as they sauntered into that saloon.

Being a drunken gunslinger back in the era of dust and rolling tumbleweed was not any more newsworthy than being a helmetless cyclist these days. And I'm not promoting public drunkenness here, nor gunslinging . . . or even unprotected cycling, for that matter, but what I do promote, I suppose, in the form of a cheap bumper-sticker, is "BE THYSELF," no? Let circumstance be the architect of your ever-shaping character and identity, and be not you the forceful architect of that strange and contrived—and lastly restricting—vision of what your identity should be in accordance to how you wish to fit into the world somehow; because . . . well, because that would be a falsehood, wouldn't it? Besides . . . you would be robbing you of yourself! And you don't want to do that. You are a gift to everyone who surrounds you . . . including yourself! And it sounds New-Agie right now, I know, wow, but so damn what? Huh? Besides, I'm wearing Pumas, not Birkenstocks! And if the shoe makes the man, well, that makes me a runner, not a lounger. But even that is inaccurate because I loathe exercise! It's very tiring, if you've tried it . . . and most people do it for vain reasons more than health reasons, anyhow. Not that I'm not vain . . . okay?—simply not vain enough.

Old-time cowboys rode big horses and sweated into their long-johns and played Texas Hold 'Em and drank whiskey at the saloon and grabbed the waitress's ass as she passed by with a tray of shot-glasses and were wonderfully obnoxious and sometimes got very upset over poker and occasionally murdered someone over the table . . . but that's about it. They did this, day-in and day-out—until of course that one unlucky afternoon of our cowboy's "natural" demise in the midst of a cyclone of smoke and flying lead and bad bets and hidden cards and loud cursing and glass and whiskey and screaming prostitutes upstairs and toppled tables when the whole world at once goes black right after that mirror behind the bar finally explodes in front of Ol' Jimmy West making that shatter the last thing he ever hears and sees! And as the image of the world fractures apart in a single explosion and into a million broken glass images rolling and spinning in space, small moving portraits of a crucial instant in time, thus so comes crumbling to the ground, in a sudden and final shower of reflective crystal memory, too—like in a million flashes of joys and sorrows, triumphs and disappointments—each day congealed into a single mosaic moment, the entire life of this crazy old cowboy. The end.

There was never a cowboy out to "find himself"—and that is a fact of the animal . . . and if there was, it was probably one of those gay cowboys the type that are suddenly surfacing nowadays mostly for the sake of our entertainment and confusion. This very idea of "soul-searching" would be meaningless and bizarre—even depressing!—to the classic cowboy. Your soul found you way before you thought of that question, Compadre. But that's only in the event that you asked such a pansy, senseless question to begin. If you have to ask, "Who am I?" the answer is likely going to be, "A fool." It's a question that I don't advise and can only take you downhill—down, down, down, all the way to the psychoanalyst's sofa! And next thing you know, you'll be streaking naked down the avenue against oncoming traffic doused in maple syrup hungering for human flesh in a snarling frenzy!

If you didn't ask the question, then you are probably a cowboy, or something just as careless and honest, and your mama taught you right! You're one of the lucky ones. "Be a simple fellow who can manage complex things," my mama used to tell me all the time come breakfast. Umm . . . Ah, I'm lying! My mama never said that. But you have to admit it's a pretty cool thing for a mama to say, huh?

The only good place to go search for yourself—let's pretend there's such a thing—is in you. And let me not get sentimental here but it's true we're full of crazy surprises. Some bad, some magnificent, and we sure as hell should stick to the good ones! Remember all the crazy shit you have done along the way, and that's pretty much who you are. That's you! Feed it. Water it, like a plant. Wow!—this is getting good.

But people go to strange places to find themselves these days, I've noticed. Places like . . . Tibet. And I say to myself, "What the hell is this guy from Trenton doing in Tibet finding himself? That's never gonna happen, clearly." I mean, it's only common sense. Man, you can't suddenly decide you might be Tibetan no matter how cool it may seem! Tibet is great! Fantastic, even, I'm sure. But some guy from Trenton has a soul from Trenton . . . sorry, pal. And vice versa too—a Tibetan monk prancing around Trenton looking for his soul would be kind of silly.

But I have found that there are some rare souls out there that are strictly universal. And they really do exist. They belong to every people. And this is true, for I've come across many of those now . . . many . . . and they seem to be growing! Yes, they were born somewhere, but they belong to the entire human race. They have the facility to naturally understand and sense that we really are all the same animal. Our clothes may change. Or our color. Or the way we speak. But at the end, we all fall in love, and in love we all find the same truth. And I can't imagine anything more promising than that in this point in history. And I'm not talking some drug-induced euphoria here; I'm talking kindness and respect and enthusiasm for one another. Shit, this is beautiful!

How the fuck did I get here? Where was I going with all this? Oh, yes yes yes! Twice! Shark attacks and lightning bolts! Rare occurrences and natural disasters! Plane crashes and alien abductions. And luminescent jellyfish playing saxophone while E.T. cruises down Santa Monica in a cherry-red Chevy Impala with the top down, hitting the breaks for a thumbs-out, hitchhiking monk, destination Trenton in search of his soul—none of which are actually in this book (except maybe the Impala), but I assure you: it's out there. Volume 2 of this collection of short stories is the culmination of a string of tales that are related only by the invisible fulcrum of love . . . or terror—love by theme or love of mine for each one of these stories.

This volume is the second, a closing shell to this oyster of a rare pearl that is more deformed than ideally beautiful, and perhaps to be beheld—as someone else once put this prerequisite, albeit in a fine and distant context—"with the right kind of eyes," since though it may be imperfect, it is still, after all, my pearl.

In vino veritas, and words are my wine. And it is as I mentioned too, in Volume 1, that what collects these into a unit is not a specific theme or topic around which these stories will orbit, but instead, they are vignettes on the general phenomenon of love or terror in settings of the whimsy! Love and terror as the shape-changing chameleons that they are. These are the central and only true unifying presences in the two volumes; though explored, indeed, and as I later found out upon closer inspection, not through the conventional avenues often transited—but instead, they take a bit of a detour through the pebbly lands of the absurd, as pointed out to me, much to my dismay, and which, too, propelled me to reconsider once again the status of my sanity.

"A little . . . dark, huh?" Gigi said to me after reading just one of these. And I thought about it. Dark? I pondered. I think it'll bring life to a kind of—swelling perfection, by contrast, you know. You know how it goes; you become a philosopher suddenly. Then I thought some more. Or maybe dark, because . . . because . . . because it's too reminiscent of it . . . of life, I mean. I kept thinking this way to myself, you see, and feeling rather profound and incisive and all that . . . but I didn't have a solid answer for her just yet, to be totally honest. No no no, that can't be. I thought again. The stories are nothing like real life!—Ah, I was at a loss . . . so:

"Well, I didn't plan it this way." This just came blurting out of me like a semiconscious squid being blown out through hollow plastic piping, and I wiggled my fingers a bit and my mouth turned into a strange shape, like a gizzard for like a second or some kind of troubling grimace. "Damn! Am I depressed again, you think?" I muttered—paranoid, aligning my mouth back into regular configuration.

"You don't look depressed," Gigi said and for some reason put her hand on my forehead as if that does anything in regulating (or detecting) depression. So I squinted confusedly as she went down to my cheek and squeezed my face tightly into a bubbly fish-mouth that took away my dignity slightly. I rolled my eyes sideways to divert attention someplace else but it was useless.

"I'm not!" I insisted, swinging her hand away from my face as it had begun flipping and flopping all over it like she was a blind gypsy woman trying to get a look at me. "I'm not depressed at all actually, now that I think about it," I said sharply, but her expression turned slightly demented after this, and I stayed immobile in the event I would upset her further.

"Well, why didn't you write funny stuff instead, you fool?" Gigi said through a grin that relieved me somewhat, so I put my hands on my hips to play it cool and nodded while she spoke. "You're always being a damn fool, so I was expecting . . . maybe—"

"Maybe that's it!" I realized I was ignoring her for I could not recollect any of her words at that moment. "Maybe the serious fool writes about clowns and zombies instead, you know!" I said defensively and arched my eyebrows like the Joker from Batman, or something. "Did you ever think about that? The serious guy writes about wanting to save prostitutes from perilous scenes, all right? Who knows, Gigi? And about ghosts that spook the hell outta you at night, and other ghosts that you want close by—right? And the end of the world, damn it! Why not? And surviving cruel abuse, and survivors of torture?"

"Je—sus—"

"Or science fiction! Or close enough . . ."

"—Christ!"

"That's right!" I jolted up like a rat-trap. "It's like a gift-basket . . . only with words instead of booze and apples and scented candles."

"Hmm, I think you've lost your—"

"But it's light," I shrugged and suddenly pushed a stick of Wrigley's gum into my tongue.

"—mind."

"I mean, it's nothing heavy or crazy, or anything." I chewed. "I don't—think." I ran my tongue through my teeth nervously; they felt unusually smooth. "It's just a book, Gigi."

"Okay," she said, deflating and sounding very doubtful. But I was resolute! This was important for some reason, so I looked away and handed her the rest of the papers anyhow. "Here!" I said like a soldier, and then I sneezed.

"Gesundheit!" she said to me, flipping unceremoniously through the pages like someone looking for the letter H in the phonebook.

I looked all around but there was no waste basket . . . and I was prematurely disgusted by the gum I'd been chewing. It had been a bad idea to start anyhow, but I had popped it in my mouth out of some atavistic instinct, or something like that. I looked at my Pumas then and realized my right lace was untied. *Damn it!* I thought—and that's when I decided I would only wear boots from now on, or at least laceless shoes. Because it is a fact of life that no one respects a man with his shoelaces untied no matter how well he's dressed. It's a deal-breaker! You see a well-groomed shiny-haired man in a fine pinstripe suit and fine Italian wing-tips and with a fine briefcase walking down the fine shiny marble floor of New York's Grand Central Station with one of his shoe laces untied—flipping and whipping along like two dead baby snakes attached to his feet—and you will say to yourself, "There goes a fool."

Screw it! I thought, *I'll just swallow this gum,* and down went the Wrigley's. I looked up with slight tears in my reddened eyes as the small and amorphous rubberized ball made its way roughly down my esophagus, and I suppressed a rather powerful cough before speaking.

"Thanks!" I said to Gigi flawlessly for her thoughtfulness not to mention I was too very pleased and full of satisfaction since I got her to at least say she'd read the book!

She's that kind of girl, the kind that has terrible vision and very poor taste in clothing, and the type some would report to have a slight and peculiar body odor, the type of scent that to acute noses could maybe be discernible as feminine armpit when mixed with the fibers of old secondhand store garments—the kind of smell you would swear mimics the scent of young women in the mid—to late sixties in America when the sexual revolution was at its peak. This is the type who uses gynormous words even when just giving instructions on McDonald's drive-throughs, which can only mean when added up in its totality that she's a highly intelligent young woman!—one who will most probably read my book if for no other reason than to critique it!—which is, too, what I'm after and what I will appreciate, because I like spicy food, and hot chili pepper is to foods what criticism is to books: it enhances really nothing of the original flavor but it surely adds a magnifying dose of pain! And I think it was Lou Ferrigno, or one of those guys, who said, no pain, no gain! So even though I don't understand this phrase at all, since nothing good ever came out of my freak and horrid knee injury in the third grade—and I assure you, there was pain—I will take his word for it and accept that perhaps God had that in as part of his grand master plan for some reason, and also that God and Lou Ferrigno, probably . . . I say probably Facebook each other.

I surely would not be the same exact person today had I not suffered that sudden and horrible and painful and bloody and nearly permanently crippling injury at eight years old when I jumped over the bench in pursuit of love that afternoon. Perhaps this is likely too the reason of my fear of it (love), but also, I would not have this scar on my knee the shape of one of those pennies you squeeze to a copper oval at boardwalks and fairs with an imprint of the local landmark, wasting away both the coin and the quarter it costs for the machine to roll once around and squeeze your penny worthless, making Abraham Lincoln roll over in his grave, knowing that each time this happens, his compatriot, Ben Franklin's memorable slogan "A penny saved is a penny earned!" is thrown and discarded to the void of gross impertinency to be revised—and reduced—to "A penny squeezed to the shape of a razor-sharp slug with an unflattering likeness of the Statue of Liberty is a penny totally wasted!"

And so the stories of physical agony and X-rays and therapy and wheelchair-bound adventures during my months of recovery after the accident would also not be part of that quilted and dis-equal and somewhat stained tapestry that has become the mismatch collage that adds up to the days of my life.

And like someone once said to me, that he'd heard that there was a rumor that Lou Ferrigno once said at the gym one Sunday in a rare moment of illuminating epiphany, when he'd gotten up too fast too furiously after benching a monstrosity of metal repeatedly, that "there are few things in this life that are hard to come by, and those are real valuable and wise advice, aliens, and old albinos—but the hardest thing of all, has to be old albino aliens with great and wise advice! You get your hands on one of those, and I'll have to tip my hat." These were supposedly the words uttered by Lou Ferrigno just before he got up from the bench and hit the showers.

I sat on the couch with a bounce and tied my shoelace when Gigi wasn't looking. "Umm . . . Just read it all, all right?" I said to her then in a tone kind of like a geography teacher, and I thought to myself, *Where the hell did that come from?*—but I gave it no further time and went back to business, so before I went ahead and excused myself to use her restroom to check on the grip status of the other shoelace of my Pumas, I threw her this pitch right as I cut the corner. "It's got clowns in it! And zombies. Jesus Christ! Zombies, Gigi!" I gave her an intense look, and then I winked and made a clicking noise with my mouth, which I'm nearly certain helped to persuade her.

And it was then, as I was turning that very corner toward the restroom, that I caught the "look"—one of those rare glimpses that immediately confirms you have a woman's attention: an eyebrow arches upward while her gaze drops down like billiard balls all on their own, evasively, and you just know she's been disarmed! She'll clip down softly at the corner of her bottom lip, which indicates invariably she's having a real tough time keeping herself together. God damn it, this bastard will find me out! She'll probably think to herself while you relish this moment and think yourself very picaresque. Then!—she'll release the bite, but it will be by that point truly too late. This look flashed all at once across her semblance right at the precise moment I was done uttering the word: "Zombies." I knew then that she was mine!

Several minutes later, I came out of the restroom with freshly washed hands and tightly fastened shoelaces, and I looked at her dead in the eyes as she stood there blankly or impatiently—she can be very ambiguous sometimes—and I said confidently, "McDonald's?"

There was a brief moment between the word and her forming response. "Indubitably!" she muttered under her breath but without messing up, and putting my manuscript in her hemp bag, she grabbed the keys firm in her fist. "You have any gum?" she said, turning to me in a tone that denoted weakness for me now, and I chuckled, relieved, but wondered how long it would last.

"Nah," I said dismissively and happy—for some bizarre reason—that I couldn't accommodate. "I swallowed my last piece."

Happy, probably because I liked her; because it is a fact of life that there's nothing that a woman will find more attractive than being displeased or ignored . . . but within measure—of course.

We walked out the door, and she locked it behind us while I looked down the hazy gray hallway, my hands inside my pockets, rummaging through my coins and keys and my Long Penny I got at the Empire State Building when I was fourteen. And I thought how sometimes ignoring what old dead presidents have said is also a sign of progress; after all, it's nothing more than the opinion of a trickier dog with fancier pants, idolatry, anyhow, in other words, and many a time—this tendency we got to take whatever anyone else that has managed to stumble upon iconicity says as an absolute infallible thought, gigantizing them, sure is a good way to get stuck somewhere within their brains; and that somewhere can easily go against us at the end. Tenets are rigid! And in its inflexibility lies its fault—fear and hatred for other ways of conceiving another possible vision or perspective from which to see the world are often attributed to tenets' attitudes. Tenets that often claim they have found the impossible—and what's scarier, more constricting, than that?

So it's healthy to question what you're hearing and to remember that things will not be true forever. But even without any of this cynicism, maybe we have to simply move beyond the dreams of the past and accept that so long as we keep those slogans vital for too long, it can only stifle today, no matter how good and true and relevant they may have been in their proper time. Life runs its course and so do the course of causes. "I have a dream," for example . . . keeping that tenet pertinent is dangerous, because I believe Martin Luther King's dream already came true. At least that's how my generation feels; we see it all around ourselves. It's best to part with the vitality of the phrases—though never with the kind of spirit that gave birth to it—since the phrases can do more harm than good today. It can make some believe—on any side of the spectrum of colors—that we are still separate as a people. Keeping the slogans is keeping the need is keeping the barriers. Lift it and do away with it! People are more willing to embrace unity—in fact, become united—when there's not even a mention of these false distinctions any longer. Focusing too sharply on imaginary divides can only make them stronger.

Gigi and I made our way down her building's staircase, and in the distance, a dog barked, and a woman screeched in horror of it. A car then beeped, and another one accelerated with a fading booming along with it. And the day went on, very much like this, for the rest of it—with its sounds and its dimming, and its strange conversations.

"It's good to be alive, isn't it, Gigi?" I remember saying to her through a mouthful of French fries when the sun was gold and falling. And the world, too, went on . . . with its eternal hum and without ever standing still—not for a second . . . blue and round . . . till the last day of it, when the sun swallows the earth, and all history goes on to not matter anymore . . . and with no warning, nor time sufficient—except for a few minor and random explosions of terrible love—to redeem our pending ills.

The End

In Search of the Bluebird comprises two volumes of stories in which, through these sometimes senseless and heartfelt suppositions, we plunge into the world of the bizarre—and this is, of course, often even more so, when we come dangerously close to our reality! These are tales of friendship, love, beauty, and terror—stories of the long trip toward the horizon, stories of the imaginings of a dreamer, stories about endurance in the face of irreparable things, stories about fighting the iron grip of constrictions, real or imagined, stories about the battle for freedom by a person trapped in a cycle of vice and cruelty, stories about that happiness that lingers even in someone's grayer days. An ode to the resilience of the human spirit, a celebration of the never-ending human longing for beauty and awe and truth, about the pricelessness of friendship, about the upside of madness, about breaking free of afflictions, about freedom of mind and spirit and certainly of person. Meditations on simple fears, about solace in odd things, and about the fragility or resilience of love: an explosive ode to the beauty of people and on the invaluable material of childhood, as well as the monstrous warping that occurs when this is permanently offset by violation and cruelty.

Reality is at times sidestepped here . . . suspended, but without ever discarding that essential element of the total truth that is the fundamental, intangible motivator and provocateur to the human spirit.

Most of the stories are told through the searches and chronicles of Max (or Sam). This man (or woman: Samantha) would be the same in every story but only that he (or she) is instead—unbeknownst to him (or her)—what he (or she) would be in different places, different times, and different ages. The protagonist is the same person in each story. Only his (her) world will be different each time, each tale. His (her) memory too, washed clean of any other of his (her) other incarnations.

It certainly is a departure at times from what's around us—but within itself, whenever, and in every page of the book, it's all real.

The two volumes, if they were combined for a single purpose or aim, point to and serve as tribute to the undying yearn for truth, a humanist ode—albeit dark at times—but it is in darkness that light can have any meaning—to the search for the one fundamental, though elusive, thing that would have our completeness . . . our total betterment! And it is this love, with that intangible, imprecise focus, which points us the right way and drives us there, and it is only with this love that we can defeat all of our terrors.

The Bluebird and I: A Brutal Note on Pacifism and Other Wraths

The bluebird is the Russian mythological symbol for happiness.

The Blue Bird was a film I saw in my early youth, also the very first film to touch me deeply. It was a Slavic film (I believe) and I saw it when I was still quite small—around five.

There was a short scene in the movie about separation that affected me the most out of all the scenes in it, so much so that it has stayed with me till this very day. Incredible, yes, but it was—I suppose—the first time I came face to face with the power of empathy by way of art, of film-making—an art form that enthralls me and that I love and am in awe of to this very day, an art form that gives so many so much participation: writers, actors, directors, musicians, dancers, stuntpeople, set designers, lighting specialists, makeup visionaries, garment designers, pyrotechnics experts, sculptors, cinematographers . . . all these (and more) joined for a single piece of magic! And it was through film that I first came to face a synthesis for empathy. Strong emotions brought about by something other than life, a premeditated synthesis (a scene)—like a mirror—that can shine back at us, to bring about from us a hint, a reminder of what and who we are. Empathy, that innate and resonant thing in human beings that manifests so early on—nearly immediately—in life, and too, powerfully enough to be even recognized, chiming through and into our very souls so indelibly through the projections

17

on a mere piece of cloth. This is how sensitive, how beautiful we have become.

I was oblivious back then—of course—that I was feeling for someone else in the film, regardless of the fact that they were not my struggles, not my losses, and not my separations I was witnessing on the screen. Or were they?

Looking back and pondering on the scene when these two children were broken apart gives me but a measure of the capacity—even great need—for close unity in people, perhaps, too, serves me as a small testament that confirms how straightforwardly singular the human spirit is across vast geographies. This need for unity, and the anxiety, even grief, at separation—as I witnessed/felt back then—was so much a relevant human concern, as the movie surely confessed, all the way in Eastern Europe where the movie originated, as much as it was in Havana, where I watched it. And maybe this fact was what began to forge—even if in small, little, rudimentary ways to start—the sentiment of kinship and true understanding and closeness that immediately forms between myself and people of nations so fascinatingly distant from my own today. This little film had brought the hidden message of universal fellowship and opened a door in me. The reassurance that on the other side of the globe, very similar hearts to my own would be found, was a glorious notion beyond my capacity to contain the excitement for it—or to express my discovery clearly. The landscapes will surely be different—as I noticed the snow and their coats and their horse and sleigh and their snow-covered trees—but their emotions, their humanity, oh, those will be indistinguishable throughout the whole planet! And that was tremendous news.

What gives me greatest felicity and hope as I witness the world perhaps moving toward a more homogenous and global culture—in the sense of understanding one another more than in the sense of forging a universal traditional identity—has been that in having the fortune of meeting so many people from so many parts of the world (not because I have traveled quite a bit, because I have not, but because I have lived in a city that has given me that chance), I have found more similarities than I have found differences! But the differences, themselves—as it turned out—have been, thus far, nothing short of enriching to me, and I hope the other way around. I confirmed in the flesh, decades later, what this movie had proposed to me.

Early surges of strong emotion are often indelible, and what the film *The Blue Bird* provoked in me was in fact powerful, even though I remember only three things of it: the separation (emotional conflict!), the jewel in the boy's hat (a yearning in his mind), and the bluebird (hope and, later, happiness), I immediately understood these things clearly without even knowing that I understood them! Apprehension, then longing, then fulfillment. These things are part of the essential material of our humanity, and from the start. They are not taught like math; they are attached to the finest sense of them all, a sense more delicate, more inexplicable and mysterious than sight—our heart, our metaphorical heart. For through what organ do we feel emotion? And to say the brain is to defeat that beautiful reluctance of our race to reduce our greatest virtues to mere biological mechanics, no matter how true this may be in the greater schemes of our logical understanding.

Love is so essential to human beings that our symbol for it has universally become the heart—the primary organ without which there is no life! And that's how important love must be to us, in everything that we do and in everything that we are. Love is life's way to show gratitude, to appreciate itself—to glow in the magic of living.

The images on the screen are all vague, yet the emotional memory of it is lasting.

This was all about the same time I was separated from my father when he first defected from Cuba to ask for political asylum in Spain, and this is likely too why even though I was only five years old, I understood the power of such an otherwise seemingly simple scene in the film. Separation had no real meaning to most of those kids around me just yet, and that's why none of the other children in the theater wept. The dictator-imposed separation between my father and I would run for the better part of ten years.

As the film progressed, the bluebird came to the screen, and as tears ran down my small cheeks, this bluebird was enough to restore, inexplicably, all hope and ease in me. My gaze squeezed forward, and my face and eyes dried; my cheeks tightened into a smirk. The bird and the color alone were enough to give me faith! I had found strength in beauty. The small bird's color, glowing neon blue in this sort scene, was an odd defiance! He was small, yet he was not camouflaged—hence open to lurking threat, to the logic. He could be seen from anywhere! And that's when I felt awe for the first time, and when I came to see courage and to know what it meant—which has nothing to do with fearlessness, as I later came to understand more fully, for what is so courageous about having no fear? Instead, courage means to stay, to be and remain or to confront, regardless of your vulnerability, and despite your fear.

Courage means to be free and grounded regardless of what surrounds you. To dare to be small and blue in a world where this might be a disadvantage. To dare to feel misplaced—if you are—and know that your refuge is in you and often nowhere else. To dare to have your own color despite the misunderstandings of others toward you, and to know that your strongest ally is authenticity! To abstain from a manner of thought that is not your own, or following some of the world's ill designs, is another form of protest and a way to claim with good measure of courage your personal freedom. Many a time your negations are your affirmations—you are not obligated to join anything by way of hypocrisy. You need not explain to anyone, as no one explains to you. The world takes care of your life and death, so it's best to be thyself, no? Take criticism as envy, for often that's exactly what it is. People who criticize you are often furious that they can't see what you do, or are frustrated they can't make you see what they do. But don't pity them either, for evil deserves no pity, and envy and ill-form is an evil. Remember that truth is always truer when spoken with compassion. And we should try to be angered at nothing except evil, which surely deserves our wrath. And beauty, nothing but our love. Seek. Seek in your own direction. That's courage.

Have I found what I seek, yet? Right now, if I'm to be truthful, I'll have to answer, no. But like someone else once said, all my life my heart has sought a thing I cannot name—and that sounds just about right for now. Have you found what you seek?

And when speaking of courage, I'll never speak of savage carnage, for there's nothing honorable in killing in my estimation, nor is any cause where human beings' utilities are to die and waste away—rather than serve with their life and vitality and constructive contributions—worthy to be recognized as a cause rightly fought, and there's nothing that disgusts me more nor disgraces our kind more extremely than war. Nothing that earns the wrath of the masses more! And it's not that I show no respect toward the soldier—because indeed it is precisely because I respect and value his life above all that I oppose all persuasion into war, and with that, the possibility of his very life prematurely put to waste. And if this is not respect in its utmost, then I will try harder. And forgive me if in my haste and careless honesty I insult the few with a conflicting view on this, but in my eyes a hired murderer is no different than one who does it for his own personal reasons, with the exception of the monetary gain in the latter no matter how much he deludes himself with faux-moral justifications—no different at all if you consider the pricelessness of human life an absolute, which I do. Think—before it's too late, before you realize someone else with other plans other than your own, not to mention evidently evil, when killing is part of that attempt to obtain, has made you squeeze a trigger toward that man's—who could have been your brother—now exploding chest, turning you now officially into nothing less than a killer by way of that nationalistic hypnosis that stuns the minds of the youth and turns boys into beasts on every single continent. Don't become the sacrificial arm of another man's irreversible mistakes—you have your own to sort and mend.

The choice of peace is personal, folks—and can only be won a person at a time. A negation at a time, until it predominates. Enough with utopianism and the romantic spirit that has uselessly courted peace halfway in the past, only to abandon her in bed while she sleeps—misled, used, and mocked! We must change and be firm. All of us. We should walk alert and with wide heads, and like domino chips falling in a row, or ripples in a pond that take one common resonant thing to carry it all—like a current, waves that wash and speak of things rightly, we should become part of this futuristic circuit for man unarmed. I know I am trying despite my fear of my own limitations. Which is my way? This—for starters. And as that smooth white stone falls at the center of the black water, the ripples radiate out places unimaginable, my friends. The hairs in your neck will stand on end—like mine have in the past once the wave reached me for the first time—once that ripple reaches you with the sentiment of your very own soul, and the voice in your head affirms that indeed you are not alone, that what you "know" is possible! This all begins by us casting our own stone to the center of the pond. By us not tolerating—by being dissatisfied. Because dissatisfaction is the unquestionable symptom of evil around. And our dissatisfaction beckons our betterment.

Nothing—except nature—should be seen as inevitable. And you are either resolute that things will always be so and savage violence is one more color in the spectrum of the human condition, or else you will heighten your humanity to the fullest in the direction to shake the nations awake into a place beyond our rudimentary and savage design and toward a dynamic that truly earns the title of civilization. You work for either one or the other. "You gotta be a realist" is the stock-phrase of the defeatist, who has been blinded by complacency or a depraved version of personal success to any longer see or care.

You'd be surprised at what your sincerity will achieve and at the power of your word out there. I never waste an opportunity to disagree when the subject comes up, and this is what creates the ripples, this is what makes people stop and question, and like a butterfly effect, hopefully somehow, some mysterious way, it will save lives. To not support means to not stand for it, at all times! Be repulsed, as I am, when you see commercials for the military on television as if they are selling us soap. Open your eyes and absorb the monstrosity behind all that. Think! Think. We are too casual about the truth of it. We look down at some misfortunate, unschooled prostitute, for example—who has had no luck or guidance or choice in this place—trying to make ends meet for her five kids, but we look up at trained killers in this world. Maybe my mind is warped in some way, but I don't think it's me in this case; even Mark Twain once said something to the effect that only once we realize the world is all insane will we come to make any sense of it personally.

The only way to shake the world awake is by changing our leaders—who have for far too long been psychopaths instead of thinkers, and whose replacement is grossly overdue in way too many cases. Where men of learning instead of men of death should be the only ones allowed at the podiums of international forums—men of truth and sense instead of these slithery, tricky, toxic little gun-addled bastards that amuse with their unbelievable perversity, intimidating and terrorizing, or conning their own people into subservience or else managing, with cool (wink, wink) appeal, all that hidden international infernal inside jokes and ulterior and colossal interests where the secret lies behind gold bars and the transactions are finalized through the rapid expenditure of your sons' souls.

Why are these crazy old Viking clowns ruling our nations?—chimpanzees with medals and blood-thirst so repulsive they look like they'll burst into shit-and-acid-doused chunks of bloody meat all over the United Nations at any moment from the froggish overinflation of their evident, insatiably grotesque and indomitable power-addicted egos. It's re-Dick-ulous! Look at what they are prideful of! Look at them with fresh eyes, my fellas! These grand assholes, bosses of vast landscapes, for Christ's sake! Have we gone mad to take this sitting on our hands? Do good men have no balls at all in general anymore? That old saying was true: "All that is necessary for the triumph of evil is that good men do nothing." We should whack all these trolls sharply and mercilessly in the ass with bamboo shoots and then kick them down the fire escape as they roll whimpering; tell them to go back to the drunken old vampire-whores of their mothers.

Watch their words and their manners, my friends, their airs and their venomous gas that stagnantly sits, forming a thick cloud of purplish fog around them. But most important is to look at their handiwork. Look closely at what they've done as best we can . . . with

23

all that air that fills our lungs now, and all that light that trickles in our living, richly enchanted eyes, gracing this page with such ease and gentleness, and with all the luxury that reason and time and leisure will allot us so justly in this beautiful bomb-less moment for that fair approximation we could, with our sense and sensibility, surmise the meaning of all this madness upon the shoulders of all these monsters.

The architects, scientists, writers, philosophers, teachers, artists, and the rest of the others among this ilk of all constructive vocations: those are the people responsible for building what our nations have become. Those people, and no one else, are the ones that have built the physical, artistic, and intellectual patrimonial to our humanity. But these trained robots with the bazookas—what the hell do they do if not blow up and burn to pieces what these true men and women before them have labored so passionately to build? If you have doubt as to how to measure certain things, all you need to ask is, Does this make our life richer? What do they leave behind?

I truly hope they don't come to me stomping with their boot-heels toward my door with inflated speech about freedom and flags, because it's tacky, dumb, and a lie!—all at once. We are too old for that kind of schoolyard nonsense, too tough in the mind for the gross depravity of the philosophy of the killer, and hopefully a bit brighter by now for that military brochure way of thinking that is so unbecoming to any of us—but most especially, unbecoming to all of us as a people by this point in time.

"Defending my way of life"? I will tell this man with the boots, "I am choice-less at your way of death, chosen by you and others like you across the globe. To say that to me is not only arrogant but it's untrue, and false guilt works only for the dumb. This is not my way of life, where I have the opportunity to put into practice what most of the world yearns for in the honesty of each individual's heart, home by home, nor is this your motivation for doing it, either—two wrongs, pal. Do not delude yourself just because these bulldogs whisper these kinds of things in your ear. But let's back-pedal anyways to your warped and sophomoric sense of reality and realize that what you are speaking of is the mechanic of life imposed by way of what I mostly find myself in disagreement with anyhow. I will never participate in the ill-formed—not to mention transient and manipulatively fabricated—sentiments of a government toward another nation simply because I happen to live in a particular geographical soil that at the moment finds itself in obscure and violent disagreements with. This is inane! Your susceptibility to a call to hatred is not—has never been—natural to me. I will not harbor feelings of enmity that are not my own, especially and certainly not for a whole group of people who are likely in the process of being equally misguided by their own governments. So sorry, boot-man; you've been lied to. You have. Sometimes, meaning to do the best things, we do the most horrible ones. Consider that, if you're capable."

A nation who loves her children should not dispose of them like geese in uniform. And nations have been doing this for centuries. This means, a nation doesn't really love its children, a nation loves itself. But even that is weird, for who is a nation, anyhow? Is a nation a true need and a feeling, a feeling generally felt, sensed, and agreed upon by a vast majority of its inhabitants? It would seem so—something like that, at least. Is a nation still a true nation when it acts not as a result of what its citizens want, need, or are compelled to do as an organic impulse, but when the nation's government backwardly prompts the citizens to do and act blindly in the service of some nebulous and occult function? Is this still a nation or something now more sinister? Is this something still "for and by the people"? I will have to say confidently, no! This is some other freakishly deformed mutation of what a nation is—or was, or should be, or whatever it is—it no longer is that. Too many golden ladles in that stew, folks—and they all want the big chunks! An unmanageable colossus of a nation!

How can we expect to uphold and guide and set examples for ourselves on the templates of our forefathers when the country's original identity is now obsolete? It's "grown" beyond it! Our forefathers' "figurines" simply can't play in this weird beast of a nation any longer!—a giant centipede where each leg has a mouth and an independent stomach. And the centipede is blind. And the food is cash! And the spice is blood.

I understand the nobility behind the adherence to a conservative way of thinking, and their stress in strong foundations of all sorts, and so on and so on and blah blah blah—I truly do. I do because most of the old-fashioned SpongeBob SquarePants side of my temperament can understand it. But we must also finally admit to ourselves that the times—unlike heaven and nirvanas—are sadly and frustratingly forever forward marching, and we must accept that earthbound eras are also not immortal. And for that, I've noticed that the liberals have the understanding that if we are to cope with the inevitability of change—whatever this may bring—we must be more flexible in many aspects. And by flexible I mean accepting, without that rage, that time does go on and the next generation will always invariably have new—and often conflicting—ideas (in an array of camps) of that which came before them. But it's truly the only way to go forward. And it is also a fact that yesterday's liberals are but today's conservatives, and so on and so on. Only, a large majority of the conservatives—it's come to my attention—lives with that doomsday, unrealistic fear of the nihilism that will never happen, for even if the pendulum of swaying philosophies will swing left and right, please, never ignore that there's a fulcrum that keeps the pendulum in place, and gravity is always pulling it southward. These will forever keep the bar-and-ball from deviating too far from the center, the center where we—because of our ever-present momentum—cannot stop.

My daughter will think me a fool tomorrow, or even perhaps a conservative, and I'll have to live with the fact that she will probably be right about both by that point. Because it is a fact that not only our joints stiffen, but also our principles—and if this is our nature, I cannot contend with its course. And by then I will no longer be the fire-bearing generation of the world nearly as much as my daughter's will be the one to carry this light, with a much better spirit and optimistic disposition and grace than I. But by then I will hopefully be of a much stronger utility than I am today. And to have any doubt or mistrust in her capacity, when that tomorrow comes, is to have doubted my own beliefs, today! And I surely don't. I will take a fraction of that "soul of yesteryears" when the time comes, and hopefully, by then, I will be as wise and as useful as I hope today to be, tomorrow.

But this will be possible for me only if I'm flexible enough. Then—and only then—will I be saved from rusting away completely in the stagnancy of the water of misunderstandings. I will ride—Alleluia!—along with her ideas, however demented or romantic or impossible they will seem to me! For there's a blue light in the crest of the wave of tomorrow! And it sounds too beautiful to be true, and perhaps I'm working toward the destruction of the pendulum, who knows?—but I will charge forward in the dark and against the wind in the summit of their new wave, and in the back somewhere with the rest of the proud old fools, holding a blade of thoughts in a whitened fist flush at that platinum hilt! I can't fail to realize that by then my worldview might just be slightly oxidized and I will need her fresh eyes to complete the picture and perhaps a whisper or two in my ears of the details of the world that I'm missing along the way. I rest assured today that her generation will lift our kind like a firebird from the ashes we've left behind, and we will both congratulate and apologize. Fear not, and trust. "You are all a lost generation": Gertrude Stein said that, and the phrase is a double-edged sword; it's appeasement for the judged, and a warning for the judge—of what he once was . . . he was the judged himself!

So do not judge the young too harshly, friends; they are only full of life.

We all find our way. But I will say this: Beware! My daughter's coming! Coming through the darkness. Finding her way with her own lantern and her own platinum sword slicing in the fog. She's mean. A mean genius! The kind we've been expecting! And she'll show no mercy!

But at the end of the day, I am neither liberal nor conservative in my totality, since I am both flexible and inflexible (sometimes) given the specific matter, you see. And so I don't necessarily fit truthfully into any of the two partialities (or else I fit into both but fragmentarily: I'm a hybrid composite—much like those new cars they have around now that are the size of a hand grenade and run on anything from corn oil to crushed aspirins—a human reflection of that, you see?—a man for the new millennium, ha ha ho ho hee), so it's not that I can't decide, it's that it is not a matter of deciding for me. I am too . . ."*naturale*" (that's an Italian word—it means "natural") in my day-to-day to pay attention deeply to what surrounds me, and for that I'm often out of touch with everything dealing with the so-called real world. I find my personal fiction difficult enough to handle to be engrossed too fully in things that will bring further aggravation to the wrath-gland! And if I had money, I would purchase a large revolver and about forty television sets so I could release some aggression in the way Elvis Presley used to, by putting bullets into the projections of evil heads. But what am I saying? I'm a pacifist—for lack of a more modern equivalent ("pacifist" sounds like you have a problem with your blood, right?—like an anemia of some kind) and should be speaking not a word about guns and such. But people are indeed notorious paradoxes, aren't they? I mean, shooting television sets would be fun, no? Shooting people, on the other hand—not so much.

I must admit that politics dizzies me to the point of nausea and boredom both at once, and no matter how much I may want to attempt it, it simply isn't organic to my personal thirst. It's one of those fields—unlike art and science—where the newest developments are always horrible, and where nothing is ever—unlike art and science—truly achieved. If music and art are the world's lovemaking, politics is the world's ulcer. And it must be for this reason that I am, for the most part, politically ignorant when it comes to the bits and pieces and specifics of that machine. I do not want to become intricately familiar with something I dislike, and this is my excuse. To me, it's like closely examining shit: I'm sure it's fascinating when you get down to the molecular complexities of it all, but at the end of the day, it's still shit that you're playing with.

But please don't listen to my bias! For it is only from the inside that we can make a real difference. And I don't have that talent, but thankfully other good men in there do! Although it is hard to imagine how it is precisely that good men manage to be able to deal with the rest of those reptilians all around them in there! But trust that it is possible. Look at Jimmy Carter!—a beautiful man!

"Would you die for your country?" This is as absurd as Aztec virgin sacrifices, who incidentally considered their plunge into the abyss of doom a great honor. The only people I would give my life away to if there was no other clinical way out are my daughter and my mother.

Call me narrow-minded but I think it's best to choose to live for a cause than to die for it. Of what utility is nothingness to the human race? Dead meat is only good for barbecues and get-togethers, and I can't see the type of use in this that you couldn't procure at the local market. For so long, we have been brainwashed to make this iconic dead hero part of our patriotic-emotional vocabulary without much personal and individual thought behind it that it's become nearly an infallible truth among the general, if jaded, sentiment in people—all people, across the planet. Why?—because it worked, it worked once, and it worked again. And it's been working since Trojan times and even before, probably! This is—and nothing more complex than that—what at the end of the day is the biggest dirty secret (not-so-well-kept) in that formula that after consuming galvanizes the spirit of young men and women to swell up with this counterfeit, illusory pride all the way to their premature tombs. Pride is a dangerous drug, folks—it's unstable and can be the catalyst responsible for terrible things. A uniform is "instant worth" to kids—of course, the illusion of it. They put it on and they're somebody now. And what better hook for a young man in need of a place in the word, huh? He who searches for the thing that will give meaning to his existence at once. What quicker, faster way to persuade and aggrandize a simple young man's uncertain ego to the status of something tall that people will look up to and admire? Have you pondered on the power of that promise? Have we realized how his innocent susceptibilities are being used to drag him into carnage? Is this rape? Are countries betraying their own citizens' trusts?

Yes! And yes! The worst form of both betrayal and rape. An orgy of blood and meat, and green fabric, metal, and bones—and where the hostess is death and the powerful salivate at the sight of his visceral triumphs!

But the secret is out, folks. It's called mind-control, and you are a damn fool if you fall for it! I might as well call a spade a spade, all right—so don't! This is a warning. A warning out of love—and for your own life! Not mine. I will not go. Don't get in that plane. Or else you'll be killing people, right?—stitching children across the chest with your high-caliber lead right out of the other end of that M-16 in your grip as they fly backward in pieces with not enough time to even scream as their limbs fall to the grass and their blood paints the country road like strawberry syrup á la Jackson Pollock, you fucking psychopath! Or on the other hand, you will wind up with shrapnel all over the side of your head and torso and looking quite ugly and quite dead—and deserving it for being an idiot! I—will—mention!—somewhere very far away from home (where your mom thinks she waits for you) burning to a charred hideousness in a cool damp ditch where the goats piss and where later crows will eat both your eyeballs and a pack of wild dogs will fight over the rest of your medium-rare carcass while a goose picks at your burned scrotum and vultures circle high for the rest of what you used to be—buh-bye.

Wish you were here—huh, Dick Charlie? Well, you're not. It was your choice, your dumbness. My advice to the smart: Fuck wars!

But I mean, please don't get me wrong, if you are a bloodthirsty psychopath, since your mother is a vampire-whore with missing fangs, this is really the line of work you should be looking into—no question. Here you have the opportunity to do what your depraved little monster mind has always dreamt of and, with the approval, support—and congratulations!—of an entire nation and the United States government. Can't get any better than that for you. Go do your thing, American Psycho! Go get yourself blown to as many pieces as that arms dealer's little trinket can rip you to parts.

Oh, Lord (deep sigh . . .).

And that's why once in a while it's healthy to take the time to take a seat, pour yourself some seltzer water, and think a bit about weird stuff like war and vampires and psychopaths and other forms of world leadership. Have that little chat with that devilish little gremlin inside your little skull that is wiser than you give it credit for, and which often will say to you clearly, "Wait a minute! This is bullshit!" Listen to that creature, my man! It's the little voice of reason, can't you see?—the one that stops us from growing wool and forming herds. The voice has no sound and knows a hell of a lot more stuff than you could ever imagine, boy! Some call it God's voice, and I ain't gonna argue with them, cause these old fools are probably right!

I can't even bear the thought of how many great minds have likely been erased in wartime before their due time because of all this nonsense! And because of all these monsters! How many great and illuminating and beautiful ideas of young promising boys and girls, which would have pushed our race a step further, full of virtue for tomorrow, and whose thoughts and spirit never made it to the light of day and whose fate instead was to end up in a pile of rolled-up bloody humanity because of the capriciousness of angry old perverts that decided to rule these kids like finger puppets, holding them to the flames, grinning their demon grins, belting their lofty speeches, their prideful warped deformed putrid nightmares, claiming that podium, closing their eyes, hugging themselves and ejaculating in their raggedy, black-mold rotted pockets in secrecy.

God damn it, what the hell is wrong with us?

The Frank Lloyd Wrights of our time put to waste the Norman Rockwells of our time, the Aaron Coplands of our time, the Emily Dickinsons, the F. Scott Fitzgeralds. Are we sure we want to keep taking such swift and careless chances with minds like these possibly charging chest-first and in our front lines toward a storm of incoming lead?

Look! If someone disagrees quite strongly, he should discuss this with the mother of one of the dead boys—of which there will plenty to accommodate, and I assure you she'll know the truth about wartime consequences better than I could ever want to know. And that someone can start by asking her, "Tell me, dear mother, what did your son's death accomplish?"

I've had enough of this!

When I mentioned courage above, first I was speaking in personal and humanist terms, and not at all meaning to flee out of scale and proportion to the places that bring me grief this way—though it doesn't hurt the soul at all to feel nor is it in vain to get carried away in an instant if what your words want to speak of are worth it! And I know for certain, they—these young men and women who could not complete their lives the way God intended—are worth it more than anything else in the world.

But let's go back to our bluebird, for it is with beauty anyhow that their souls now reside, I'm sure.

Havana: 1980. I disappeared back in that past, and the film and the bird were the only things that existed!—not the theater, not the rest of the kids in it, and not the world. The bluebird, that's where he is, there's happiness! The bluebird in that screen pointed—now as I revise it in retrospect—somehow to that heartbound paralyzing longing that the Portuguese have managed to consolidate into a single—and wonderful—word: *saudade*. There is no explanation—nor will there ever be—of the emotion attached to this word, as its meaning, too, is unattainable. A word for the emotionally unreachable!—few things are as singularly profound. In essence, what you are feeling is also impossible to be understood, by yourself, even. It's like trying to grasp the idea of emotional infinity of some sort that, of course, can never be reached. *Saudade*, as the Portuguese have described it, is a vague longing for something that does not and probably cannot exist, and it's also the love that stays after someone is gone. It's that bittersweet ghost that suddenly happens and, with a mellow rush, forms within you, both at once joyously and with a tinge of melancholy.

And like birds, beauty and art are to be neither possessed nor owned if their essence is to remain unscathed. They should never be understood in their entirety—because it is precisely in their otherness, and not their discovery, where we are to behold them. Instead, these should haunt us, provoking in us that *saudade*, and remaining forever that infinite, unattainable mystery. And this is why, I suppose, the bluebird—like all true beauty—haunts me still.

Regarding Wine, Clowns, Prostitutes, and Other Intoxicants: An Unimportant True Story

Sometimes you just have to pee in the sink.
—Charles Bukowski

He had already made the libidinous phone call, and she was on her way. There was a sausage pizza in the oven, and there were a couple bottles of cheap, vinegarish red wine airing out on the counter. He'd started drinking prematurely to ease his nerves. Samuel Ferdinand Octavius Philippe Ravel, III: *Clunkers the Clown.* Clunkers was from a very long line of clowns. His father and his father before him had been clowns, as had been the father before that! So long his clownish lineage was that it was nearly impossible to trace backward to a generation who hadn't been.

She was making her way up his street as he finished the first bottle of Gato Negro and opened a second one. She was a redhead with wild, curly hair—dyed. She was close to middle aged and hardened—not bad looking if somewhat austere, bordering on the frightening under a certain kind of lighting. She wore hoop earrings and copious amounts of mascara and lipstick. She wore today a white faux fur bolero coat and a solid fuchsia miniskirt with a thick and restricting vinyl belt. Her camisole glittered in sequins, and her shoes were pearly stilettos to match the evidently cheap top.

She rang the doorbell, and he fumbled to the door. He looked through the peephole and could see the distorted fisheye protrusion of her submarine nose. Her fluttering eyeball flickered in the distance. He liked what he saw.

"You're dressed like a clown!" she said to him once he'd opened the door, thinking now she had seen everything.

"And you're dressed like a prostitute."

"I am a prostitute."

"So then, you have something against people meeting in their work clothes?"

"Oh!" She came right in around the clown and stepped into the kitchen. He had a relatively small apartment with an expectedly *cirque* theme of decor—a very loud and complex sensibility.

"Is that you?" She pointed to a framed picture on the wall of a clown holding a large trophy.

"No, that's my father. He passed away." Not that anyone could ever tell the difference. They looked exactly alike; in fact, they looked just like the clown in the small portrait next to that picture, one of his grandfather taken at a fair in Rochester, New York, in 1942 while he was on tour with Le Cirque Fantastique du Montclair.

"What's that smell?" she said, scrunching up her nose and making an unfavorable face, still standing there.

"I'm making sausage pizza. Do you like pizza?

"Do you know anybody who doesn't? But I'm not going to eat it now."

"Why not?"

"Because I'm working."

"You don't eat when you work? Have you had lunch?"

"It's ten o'clock at night."

"Dinner?"

"I'm not here to eat pizza."

"Very well. Do you want some wine?"

"Sure," she said hanging the bolero on the back of the chair and sitting with one leg crossing over the other, swinging the stiletto dangerously close to his shins.

Clunkers went to the cupboard to grab two wine glasses, swishing his polyester pants and shirt. So far, he'd been drinking straight from the bottle. He made his way back and poured two glasses of Gato Negro, and the prostitute's pupils widened with anticipation. She was a drinker, and the telltale sounds so particular to these cases were branded indelibly on her esophagus like an irreversible black keloid on a cow's ass.

"Aahh . . . there." His sour wine breath filled the air, and she grabbed her glass with a delicate plastic clicking of her fingernails. She looked at him and swallowed a large and very audible gulp.

"This is good stuff," she said immediately, putting the glass down and pointing to it with one of the sharper claw appendages. After she had emptied the glass, she motioned for some more, and he poured a second time.

"And there's plenty more where this came from," Clunkers said with a visible amount of self-satisfaction. "I bought several bottles, special for today. No wine in a box for you, missy." He winked playfully with his large clown eyes in an expression that would otherwise send children into fits of inconsolable terror. She started to drink this one slowly, when the ping from the stove announced that the pizza was done. He sat down next to her with a sudden nylon swish.

"So tell me, let's get to know you a little bit here before we start all this," she said, looking at his bulbous red nose and his frizzy, dry, green hair at the sides of his irregularly shaped head.

"Well, let's see. I was born in Michigan, but my parents are French. I came up here then in the late eighties and have been living here ever since," he said and nodded very strangely. Then sneezed.

"Well, that pretty much sums it up," she said, taking yet another monstrous gulp of wine.

"What is your name?" he asked, looking curiously into her strange eyes, those stern lips whose outer edges formed small grooves, tiny crevices with thin, diminutive streaks of lipstick that crawled upward, more markedly when she swallowed.

"Well, I'm Candela," she said while Clunkers took a sip of his wine. A small red drop ran down beside his lips, leaving a small burgundy streak on the white makeup. "So you're a clown, huh?" she said as he sat there, tilting his head to one side, casting an ominous shadow on the wall behind, pondering for moments if there could be any doubt. "So how's that going for you?" she continued.

"Well, it's hard," he said, squinting, nodding—doing something with his eyebrows. "Harder than you'd think. I've been a clown all my life. Ever since I can remember, I've worn floppy shoes and oversized bow ties and this polyurethane nose. I was a clown before I even knew I was a clown. My father was a clown too before he knew he was one."

"Oh, my," she said in real amazement as she poured herself another glass.

"I'm tired of people laughing at me," he said, reflecting, looking downward, and running a thumb against the side of his glass.

"Well, I'm tired of people screwing me, but you gotta do what you gotta do," she said and laughed.

"See? You laughed! Don't do that. Here's your hundred bucks!" He slid the bill across the table in front of her. "I promise not to screw you if you promise not to laugh at me."

"Well, what am I here for?"

"I miss my wife."

"Mmm . . . Okay, then, what's the point if you're not going to screw me?"

"She was a hooker, so I wanted something to remind me of her."

"Well, I guess I kind of understand . . . I mean, I had a husband once and he was kind of a clown. Though I don't really miss him all that much," Candela said, and he got up, took the pizza out of the oven, and placed it on the counter. He cut a slice out and placed it on a plate. He walked back and sat down, taking a stringy, elastic bite out of it.

"You sure you don't want any of this?" His voice was muffled through a wad of dough and steam.

"No, I'm good with just the wine. So what's the deal with your wife? Is she dead?"

"No, she just left me."

"For another clown?"

"No, just left."

"I was joking, man. I mean, think of the odds. You have no sense of humor!" the prostitute said, staring at the clown's teeth sinking into the steamy hot slice of pizza.

"Have you always been a hooker?"

"Well, no. I mean, I don't come from a long line of prostitutes. This is the kind of profession one tends to fall into rather than work your way into."

"What do you think of it?" he asked seriously.

"Well, think of it this way: it's not every day at work you get paid for watching a clown eat pizza," she said, and Clunkers laughed.

"I thought there was no laughing." Candela pointed to Clunkers with her plastic index weapon, holding onto her wineglass so hard she made red waves inside. "Tell me some clown secrets!" she demanded.

"Okay. Thirty-two of us *can't really* fit into a Volkswagen Beetle. It's all a trick! Also, we wear makeup only when we want to blend in with people in the streets."

"I wish I could tell you the same about prostitutes," she said.

"You can fit thirty-two prostitutes into a Volkswagen?" he said, and she chuckled.

"Gimme a slice; I'm starving," she told him after watching him push a doughy fold into his mouth. He walked toward the counter and, with the round pizza knife, cut her a sizable triangle. He flipped a switch, and a long string of colorful Christmas lights came on: the thick kind with the large bulbs.

"I like these lights, don't you?" he said, sliding the pizza onto a plate. As he crossed to the table, the pizza was lit in multiple colors. He sat down and put the plate in front of her.

"Thank you."

"Sure! I'm glad you're having it. Tell me what you think."

She took a bite of the pizza and then took a deep breath through her nose. "Oh, my God, this is terrific!" she said genuinely, her eyes widening inside the Venus flytraps of her mascara-coated lashes.

"I knew you'd like it! And you were passing it up," he said, shaking his head from side to side and pressing his lips together in an "I told you so" kind of expression.

"Where did you find it?" she said with a terrible amount of chewing noise.

"I made it. I made it all! The dough, the sauce. It takes a while. But today is special, so I made it for you. It's not every day I make this," he said. She was so curious, and intrigued—almost—by this clown.

"But you don't know me. I'm no one special. Why go through all the trouble to . . . ?"

"I don't need to know you for you to be special to me. Is anyone any less special because he is a stranger?"

She didn't know what to make of this clown. He crossed his legs and took a sip of his wine while she tore at her pizza. He looked out the window, and she looked at his big floppy shoes. She put one of her hands on his nylon pants and felt the fabric with her fingers.

"Who makes your clothes?"

"We make them ourselves. We are schooled in the art of tailoring! It's a very personal thing, you know. One has to have a very specific sensibility for this. Nobody else can make clothes for us. How could they? They don't know. If anyone else made our clothes, we would look ridiculous."

She took the last bite of her slice and dusted her fingers. She let out a big sigh of satisfaction and sat heavily and gracelessly in her chair. "Thanks, Clunker, that was delicious."

"How do you know my name?"

"It says it on your floor mat. It says 'Welcome to Clunker's House.'"

"Oh."

"It's so nice."

"What?"

"Your doormat . . . It's so nice. It's inviting . . . and happy."

"Oh, yeah, thanks," he said, caught by surprise. Nobody had commented on his doormat before. He was surprised she'd paid attention to it. She was discovering a small thing about Clunkers he probably hadn't discovered for himself yet. Clunkers was not only a very silly man, but also beautiful! He was.

"Clunkers?"

"Yeah?" His attention was diverted back into the room and onto her. He had gazed away outside his window for a moment. The Christmas lights reflected on the panel of glass appeared to be outside, floating in space.

"You should be a little more optimistic."

"You think?"

"Yeah, I do."

"Why is that?"

"Well, because . . . I mean, you make a lot of people happy! You make people laugh. Don't you understand how important that is?"

"Oh . . . ?"

"Yes . . . you should never get tired of making people laugh! Not a lot of people can say that about themselves; it's very important. What you do is very important!" she said, and Clunkers just sat there. Very silent. Looking down. She spoke again. "You help a lot of people! You make so many people happy. That should make you happy," she said, and he sat there just thinking for a little while longer.

"I think it just did," he said with a sentimentality fit for a faded, tacky, flea-market portrait.

"Can I laugh then?" she asked, smiling.

"Okay, go ahead!"

Candela started laughing, and Clunkers was glad about this. He was glad he'd made her laugh. Because she looked happy; she was then and there genuinely happy. And so was he, then and there. Her mascara had run down her face in traces that looked like long skeleton fingers, and she blew Clunkers a kiss that landed somewhere amid his lips and his heart.

"Oh, God, Clunkers! Thank you! I've been holding that for so long," she said as he discovered a small thing about her then. Something she probably hadn't yet. She was not only a hard and bitter woman, but she was also beautiful!

Clunkers looked down at himself and laughed so hard his sides were hurting.

"Can I smoke?" she asked him, pulling out a cigarette.

"Sure thing, do what you want," he said, and she lit up a cigarette and started blowing rings of smoke toward Clunkers. He poked at the rings with his finger.

"If your days are much like today, I'm sure you make a lot of people happy too," he said to Candela, and she laughed, blowing out smoke.

"Oh, Clunkers, Clunkers. What am I gonna do with you?" She placed one of her arms across her belly and rested her other elbow on it; her forearm upright, holding the cigarette, which issued out a ribbon of gray vertical smoke.

"Our time's almost gone," he said with regret. "Do you want to take some leftover pizza?"

"Yes."

"Okay, I'll make you a bag. Thank you for coming; it was so nice having you here," he said, looking back at her as he walked away toward the counter.

"Oh, Clunkers, there's definitely something about you."

She got up and put on her faux-fur bolero. She put a limp hand on his shoulder, reached up, and kissed him on top of his bald head. She then paused, came lower, and kissed him softly on his clownish red lips. She grabbed her pizza bag and left.

Clunkers then sat there on his seat, finishing his red wine while staring at the reflections of his multicolored bulbs hovering in space beyond this room, beyond the glass, beyond the crickets and roads and cars, and beyond the trains and their horns, beyond all sight. Soon enough it was midnight.

*   *   *

"Ladies and gentlemen—welcome to Le Cirque Fantastique du Montclair!" The fanfare came, and an explosion of confetti snowed all over the audience.

After the loud cadence of the band's drum rolls and trumpeting, the curtain opened to a sandy ring and circling spotlights! A Volkswagen Beetle came zooming out through the curtains and raced around the circle once, twice, three times! Then the clowns all started pouring out of it in a string! Two, four, eight, ten clowns! . . . fifteen, twenty, twenty-five, thirty . . . thirty-two clowns came out with a big drum roll and a cymbal's—splash!

The children were going wild, the people laughing in huge waves, the place was alight with fun and craziness! Clunkers was juggling his bowling pins while balancing a unicycle on his red nose when suddenly the whole act froze in place.

Candela was there in the very first row! Part of the tumult, cheering him on—making so much noise. Laughing! Laughing so hard she could barely breathe! She was having so much fun! She was so, so happy! And so was Clunkers; he loved the laughter, he loved all those people laughing at him. It was such a happy day! It could have been even his happiest day, but it probably wasn't. Let's face it, days like this are plenty for clowns.

Zombies of the Enchanted Garden

Beauty is mysterious as well as terrible.
God and Devil are fighting there, and the battlefield is the
heart of man.

—Fyodor Dostoyevsky

It is only in a fictitious town, near a fictitious city, that a story like this can take place, because beauty so rapturous and intoxicating can exist only but by the unconditional acceptance of the imagination. So clean and pristine the city was that it was difficult to believe anyone lived there at all. It was as if the entire collection of buildings had been laid out all at once and were just but waiting for the mass of people to pour in and populate it. But the city was alive indeed—diverse and utopian, almost, if from the fact that there was work to do there as well. Well, not that anyone could ever mind the work in a place such as this. In fact, it would be nothing short of a Midas strike on the luck of anyone who had the fortune to work in this bright and perfect city!

Our town, not at all far from all of this, and where our story takes place, was an adequately complimentary response to this jewel of a metropolis. The architecture was quaint, and though every house was in fact harmonious to the next, there fortunately did not exist the eerie dollhouse repetitiveness so typical of too many suburbs. Here, every house enjoyed its own distinctive identity without disturbing the equilibrium of the town as a whole. The town was a peaceful annex retreated from the city—quiet and agreeable, and a place that was graced by the charms and company of nature: Autumnsville

42

transformed yearly under the slow kaleidoscopic turning of the seasons.

Connecting these two urbanized geographies was a road, one road in two directions—a long road where Fall City was never lost out of sight. As one drove toward the city, swerving on the pavement, its silhouette danced on the horizon—left and right, growing as the road wound like a giant cat's tail. Driving back, the town formed slowly, a boat sailing through mist, a thought taking shape in the imaginings of a waking dreamer.

And driving back into town was where he found himself, and unbeknownst to him, that day, alone, would change everything for him. It was early: three o'clock on a Wednesday. The air was pleasant, and fall crept through a slight and crisp chill. He was the only one on the road, by himself in both directions: a lonesome ladybug crawling along a thin, long, black branch. The speakers blasted a song as he sang along, zooming against the wind:

What a difference a day makes
Twenty-four little hours.

*   *   *

He slammed the door of his Volkswagen Beetle and pushed down the button on his keychain. The garage door lowered—a spooling rumble as the place shaded gradually to a cozy, peaceful, cool gray. Near the top of the garage door, there were small rectangular glass panels that let in a preview of the sky—it was a bright blue with a few sparse, cotton-white clouds. He hopped up the flight of stairs and twisted the doorknob. This was a three-level apartment. The ground level was the garage and storage; the first floor was the kitchen, dining room, and living room; the third level was a bedroom loft with a little corner office and a small side attic.

He walked in as Lynn, his girlfriend, was going through some papers at the dining table—torn pages from a magazine, printouts, and a pad and pen. Above her, there was a stained-glass lampshade her mother had made and given to them as her housewarming present. It was an elaborate piece of stained and blown glass framed in bronze. Her mother confessed it had been one of the more intricate pieces she had made, and she promised that it was not because it was a gift to them that she was saying this. The colors were wild, and it almost seemed as if the piece was meant to be eaten—and that it'd taste like all kinds of candy! She was sought after as a glass artisan but made sure to reserve, secretly, her best work for those close to her. This lamp was a colorful exuberance made of an array of borosilicate glass as well as crystals and metal fibers that formed strands and leaves. The colored glass plates, orbs, and shapes populated the bronze shapes of leaves and branches and flowers that formed the skeleton of the lamp. Further adorning the base were sculpted dragonflies, hummingbirds, and intricate little animals all perched throughout the surface and edges of the lamp. Near the top of the dome, there was a golden crystal cherub made of transparent glass with gold leaflets that gleamed throughout the inside of his body. His hair was golden curls. The cherub stretched his golden love-bow toward a crystal blue nymph who looked, unaware of him, at her reflection on the water of a lagoon, in awe of her own beauty—very much like Narcissus, who fell in love with his own reflection. At night, when the apartment was dark and only this lamp lit the space, the beams of light shot out through the colored panels, projecting outward and in every direction—a galaxy of color transfiguring the space into an enchanted garden.

He walked toward her and kissed her head. She put her arm around him and pulled him closer, pushing his hip against her face.

"What are you doing?" he said, walking around the table and hanging his bag on the back of a chair.

"Recipes . . . for tomorrow. I've got to decide." She handed him two pages. "Which one do you think?"

He looked at both, took a moment, and read them over. They really looked equally good, but he was definitely partial to pecan. "Pecan."

"That's what I was thinking too."

Thanksgiving was the next day, and they were going to make dinner at their apartment—the first Thanksgiving there, the first Thanksgiving at their first shared home. The turkey was in the fridge, already marinated. The sweet potatoes and mint jelly were ready. And the little dilemma of pecan pie versus pumpkin was on account of tradition—guilt?—interfering. Two close friends had been invited: Nicholas and Carmen—another couple who worked in the city and lived in Autumnsville, not two blocks away.

Now that the pie had been decided upon, she ripped up the other papers, tapped on the ingredients list, and looked at Sam with that quirk of a smile. A small but deep dimple formed at the side of her mouth. Her eyes became semicircular just above her apple cheeks. He loved that face—it was crazy looking and way too cute for him to bear, and because of that and a hundred other things, he found her impossibly irresistible! He got up and, breathing deep and audibly though his nose, gave her a tight kiss on that beloved dimple.

"Could you get some red wine as well?" she said in an afterthought. "Sebastiani?"

He folded the recipe and slid it in his back pocket. He grabbed the keys from the dining table just as the cat came dashing through the room, darting one way, then the other.

"What's got into that animal? Felix!" Sam yelped as he jumped, raising his hands, jingling his keys above his head. The cat's eyes peered out from underneath the couch—two small fluorescent disks hovering in the black band of space.

"Jesus!" Lynn said, turning pink with uncontrollable nervous laughter—her palpitations almost pushing through her shirt. "That nearly killed me!" She giggled as her eyes pooled with salt water. "What's wrong with him?"

Felix had come dashing up from the garage below soon after there had been the tremendous rumbling of Mr. Raminoux's Harley Davidson. Mr. Raminoux was an old man who hadn't yet realized it, and who spent most his weekends and holidays polluting the entire town with hours of unbearable noise and massive amounts of carbon monoxide. He was a neighbor. He was married to a plump, grandmamish, pinkish lady who often wore blue and who, aside from tending to her garden with furious devotion, was an avid and talented slanderer and rumor specialist, self-schooled in the loathsome traditions of chronic negativity. Whenever opportunity allowed, Mrs. Raminoux employed much of her efforts in spreading strange, malevolent, and unfounded gossip around the entire town through the utility of slow-moving strings of geriatric conglomerates who served as her personal defamation comity. By taking advantage of their now lackluster activity-less lives, Mrs. Raminoux had coerced and recruited these aged folk into her delusional pseudo-dictatorship-like underworld of contempt and disapproval. To her, they were yet "aged to imperfection." She bore a perennial scowl of derision and looked upon everyone else with marked, evident, lofty disdain and contempt. Everyone was immoral in her eyes, and many—these among others: Sam and Lynn—clearly Satanists!

After Sam and Lynn collected themselves from this ridiculous episode with Felix, Sam made his way through the dining area to the door and down the flight of stairs into the garage. He was just about to raise his keychain toward the remote box when he noticed . . . when he saw. There, not far beyond him, against his car and above the hood on the other side, he could see the top of a woman's head. She was sitting on the ground against the other side of his car! As he stood there, he saw her head moving in tense, circular motions, with an unusual—unnatural—vibration, as if with a faint electric current coursing through it.

"Hey!" he screamed. The bizarre female figure jolted and dropped to the ground with a meaty splat. He stood there for a moment, hesitant, then took his first steps around the car. He made his way around the car and came across a hideous spectacle! Truly horrendous! And he was forced to be a witness. The woman lay there completely nude. She was tense, her legs outstretched, her arms as well, and she stared straight up into the ceiling—her mouth agape in a frozen O. Startled. Her eyes were wide and smoky, and on her upper torso there were stab wounds of different sizes. Dried and crusted blood coagulated and congealed in the wounds. There were partially drying lines of blood streaked down her body. Her right forearm was soaked in burgundy blood, and where there should have been a hand, there were but two sharp bones spearing through ripped skin, fat, and dangling muscle tissue. In her left hand, she gripped the severed right hand, which she had apparently begun to eat. Her toenails and fingernails were painted, and she wore an engagement ring. Her mouth and nose were grotesquely blotched in drying blood, and her eyes had turned a cloudy gray. And it was only then, when he momentarily flashed to register her face, that he noticed. This was Carmen, Nicholas's fiancée!

The enormity of this shock paralyzed him. He scrambled through his brain searching for any plausible reason, any logical explanation that would lead him to a scenario resembling something—if even remotely—like this! She was obviously in need of medical attention, but somehow he could not bring himself to get close to Carmen. His instincts now came in touch with something unrecognizable, something primal, and sheer panic and terror were the only emotions that yielded there naturally: not to come to her aid, to help her or even call out to her, but only to flee. Something in him was telling him to just get as far away from that as possible!

He rushed upstairs in a chilled panic. He shut and bolted the door behind him as Lynn made her way down from the loft bedroom.

"Did you forget something?"

"Lynn, Carmen is dead!—or dying, I don't know," he said, traumatized. Fear had caused dark circles to form under his eyes. Lynn was briefly benumbed by the force of those words. Her senses momentarily lapsed. As shocking news often does, it came too fast for her to take in all at once: she lived this otherwise extremely unsettling moment in a brief limbo. A metallic taste came into her mouth as quick flashing memories . . . recent images of Carmen . . . coursed through her mind. Finally, she began to regain control of her thoughts.

"What do you . . . Sam, what are you talking about?" she said, hoping of course for him to be plotting some kind of strange joke, but realizing, alarmingly, that this would be highly unlikely. His unsettling expression would not yield.

"I don't know, Lynn. I don't know what just happened to her. I can't even begin to imagine what happened to her, but I've just seen her . . . I mean, I just saw her right now! She's downstairs—and she's stabbed but—"

"Oh, my God, Sam! She's stabbed?" she screamed and ran to the door. She unlocked it and scrambled down the steps. Sam came after her.

"Lynn!"

They entered the garage; the garage door to the street was all the way open.

"She's on the other side of the car, but—"

"Carmen?" Lynn said, walking around the back.

"Lynn, just wait—" But before he could finish, Lynn had made her way to the other side of the car. She looked toward the floor and vomited to the side. Sam caught up to her. Carmen was not there! Instead, there was a large streaked area—blood, urine, and smeared feces. The smell was putrid and sour. Lynn was riddled with an irreversible, pulsing dark fear.

Felix was at the bottom of the stairs now, at the entrance to the stairs. His back was arched, and his ears pushed back against his head. He looked at Sam and Lynn intently, and as they hurried back inside, he scurried up the steps right before them.

*   *   *

The voice of Carmen came on the phone: "Hi, you have reached the home of Carmen and Nicholas. We are away from home. Please leave a message, and we'll get back to you as soon as possible. Thanks, and have a good day."

"Try his cell phone," Lynn said. He put the house phone on speaker and dialed Nicholas. "Hi, this is Nick. Leave a message." Sam let out a sigh, pressed the red button, and placed the phone on the table.

"Well, we know she's not dead, Sam, because she walked away and—"

"Yeah, she's surely not dead, but what is . . . I mean, Lynn, I saw her on the floor; she had at least ten stab wounds on her body, and one hand had been torn off—and she had been chewing on it! I mean, this is some—"

"We can't really tell at this point. I mean, God knows—an illness . . . rabies or . . ."

"Lynn, rabies doesn't make you eat yourself or give you the strength to lose pints of blood and walk away! She was responsive . . . at some level. She was startled. She froze and dropped like a possum when I called for her."

Felix was looking uneasy. He was looking at them intently, his feline eyes widened. He looked too as if he had grown in girth—all over—although he also looked very sick. There was a yellowish film coating his eyes, and a thick, gooey string of saliva fell to the floor from a corner of his mouth. Sam started to pick him up when there was a loud bang out in the street and a car alarm started blaring. Felix sprang forward and leaped toward Sam. The cat dug his claws into Sam's thigh and crawled up his body in a painful spiral. Lynn jumped away from the table, knocking the chair to the floor. The cat dug his needle-sharp teeth into the flesh of Sam's hand. Sam finally clenched ahold of the cat by the skin on the back of its neck and flung him across the room onto a grill of hanging pots in the kitchen. Felix bounced onto the counter and then to the floor—landing on his feet—and fled up the stairs to the loft. The kitchen and stairs area formed an acoustic box through which the hollowed resonance of the cat's moaning—too reminiscent of demonic utterances—bellowed through the apartment.

"Oh my friggin' God, that cat nearly killed me! What the fuck!" Sam grimaced in pain, holding his left hand while droplets of blood splattered onto the hardwood floor. "He nearly chewed me into burger meat. What the hell!" A bloody semicircle had been indented in that muscle between the thumb and the index finger; also rings of blood were forming on his pant legs, and his shirt, too, was soaking up small burgundy half moons. Lynn immediately came to Sam and looked at his wounds.

"Oh, Lord," she said. She sounded almost angry, if it wasn't for the fear that was already indisputably shadowed in her words. "There's something not right here." She looked outside the window. The sun was shining, and the white clouds slid calmly, mocking, taunting their anxiety, the fearfulness that brewed in them both. "There's something seriously wrong." She became lightheaded and nearly fainted, but the queasiness soon turned into a piercing ringing in her ear. She walked to the bathroom, slid open the mirrored door above the sink, and took out the first-aid box.

"Sit down." She nodded at a dining room chair and began soaking a Q-tip in iodine. Quickly, she dabbed at the bite on his hand.

"It kills!" he said, pulling his hand away for a moment. "You should feel that and . . . well, no you shouldn't, but . . . that friggin' cat's bite is worse than you could imagine, you know." He laid his hand back on the table, facing up. One side of the bite was not only punctured, the skin had also torn when Sam pulled the cat off.

"See? You can't underestimate these suckers," she said, feigning a smile.

"He's never been this way . . . ever, you—"

"I'm telling you there's something really wrong here; I can feel this . . . you can almost breathe it . . . either that or I—"

"Owww!" The iodine stung him. He had been unprepared and had been staring straight at her eyes when she applied the stinging antiseptic. She continued to dab at each puncture hole individually, and each wound drank from the iodine-sopped swab like a small gaping mouth. She wrapped Sam's hand tightly with gauze, the mixture of medicine and blood immediately flooding the tiny waffle-like squares of the fabric in colors of rust and wine.

"Okay, let me do your leg and your body now," she said, walking around the table, holding the bottle in one hand and the Q-tips box in the other.

"Nah, don't worry about those . . . those are okay."

"Are you sure?"

"Yeah, I'm all right for those."

Felix hadn't quit growling upstairs; he was straining his vocal cords now to the point where voice voice was getting increasingly raspy. Fluid was collecting in the cat's throat, and Sam and Lynn could hear a distinct bubbling through his guttural outbursts. Sam slumped heavily on his seat

"I feel so tired, Lynn."

"Are you all right?" She walked to him, clasping her hands and then putting her palm over his damp, steamy forehead.

"Yeah, I feel all right; I'm just so tired . . . you know, sleepy, all of a sudden."

"You're burning up," she said to him, nervously biting her bottom lip, looking left and right for her purse.

"I'm going to take a nap, Lynn . . . I really just can't . . ." he said, getting up. His posture was hunched and rigid, like that of an old man, as he made his way to the sofa. "May the cat eat me if he wants to," he said, chuckling.

"Not too funny, Sam . . . not at all," Lynn said to him, pulling a bottle of ibuprofen out of her purse. She took out two pills, poured him a glass of water from the faucet, and then walked toward him. "Do you think this is the best time to rest, Sam? I mean, when . . ." By the time she got to the couch, he had already fallen asleep. His mouth was wide open. There were beads of sweat on his face, his neck, even on his eyelids. His coloration had darkened slightly and taken on an olive hue. The carotid artery to the side of his throat pulsed with a steady throb as he breathed shallowly. She looked at him and noticed that the dark circles under his eyes had sunken slightly, where the skin throbbed at the compass of his heartbeat. She was still looking at him when he awoke.

"Here," she said. "Take these two pills."

"Pills?" he said. "That nap served me well."

"You hardly went down for a minute."

"I . . . I feel like I was gone for days."

She walked toward the window again and peered outside. Sam suddenly appeared behind her.

"How's it looking out there?" he said in such a placid voice. She turned around and put a hand on his face. He was cooling. The fever was nearly gone.

"How are you feeling?" she said.

"I'm actually . . . feeling all right!" He wiped his forehead and looked at his fingers, noticing how much he was sweating. "Well, I feel so . . . relaxed, you know—as if I've just taken a long bath."

He swung his arms once and a sort of weightlessness came over him. He walked through the kitchen and felt a rush, a sensation of increasing peacefulness overall. He shook his head from side to side—slowly, and with his eyes closed—and there was a comforting vibration in his muscles throughout . . . tiny tremors that not quite tickled, but shuddered in diminutiveness. He looked at his arms closely and pumped his fists slowly; there was an upward surge of blood through his forearms; he could feel this distinctly—like a murmuring warm caress . . . his blood was alive—nearly conscious! As if each individual cell was an independent and reasoning pod, a knowing, loving entity. He looked at Lynn then, and she looked so lovely. Lovelier than ever, even!

"Have I told you . . . have I said how lovely you look today, my love?" he said in a crushing, beautiful tone—almost as if speaking with someone else's voice. Lynn looked in his direction, noticing the peculiarity of all this.

"Umm . . . thank you," she said with a tilt of the head, the sound of her voice resonating in his ears like a cascade of silver chips swarming inside a thin crystal sphere. As if the voice had rung from a very far distance yet he'd heard it clearly just the same. The last syllable then lingered—resonant, nearly undying—caressing his eardrum as he turned his head and closed his eyes again to relish in her timbres.

"I need to take a walk outside," he said and smiled warmly, blinked slowly, and took a few steps.

"Sam, I don't think it . . ." He walked around her then, unlocked the deadbolt, and headed down the steps toward the garage—slowly, serenely, confidently.

"Samuel!"

Once he'd made his way all the way down, he took the keys out of his pocket and pushed the green button, and the garage door began to lift. Then, he dropped the keys. There was a sudden gust bringing in a small whirlwind of autumn leaves. His eyes closed halfway to block the cloud of dust as he walked outside to be consumed by the fall afternoon. Lynn walked after him. He walked to the sidewalk and stopped. He pushed his chin upward and closed his eyes, breathing deeply, so deeply. What rushed in through his nostrils was no longer just oxygen, he felt, it was pleasure in gaseous form! The generalized sensation that was surely forming in him—his physical and mental states—were that of pure perfection. The wind graced his face and body, and it was as if invisible hands from heaven caressed him. Every gust of wind was a transparent wave of the most marvelous of delights. Out there now, it was neither the slightest bit cold nor the slightest bit warm. It was perfection! His whole body was but a weightless companion. His limbs and body did not go afloat, but neither did they weigh him down. He had no sensation whatsoever of the pull of gravity. To lift his limbs, to carry his body was as effortless as being in water, but without the antagonizing friction of liquid.

He heard what sounded like the rumble of a bass drum. It was such a glorious sound, he knew it would be impossible to parallel—not only was it a sound he'd never heard, but a sound he had never felt. He turned his head toward the direction of the sound and saw what seemed to him blue forms waving in the breeze, pointing upward—illuminated, heavenly dancing crystals making a sound that the most sublime music could never rival. Things began to change. Even contexts began shifting. The former meaning of the world, of things, became askew . . . odd . . . even absurd. The world around him was not only transfiguring, but his nature was as well morphing along with everything else. A universal metamorphosis!

"In changing me, it changes the world!" Sam said out loud.

It was a glorious world indeed, issuing now from within itself! And he turned his eyes toward the sky, and the colors up there too changed: the blue slowly darkened to a wonderful rust color. The clouds were now deep brown, and the sun turned into a blue flame—he found it no longer bothersome to look straight in its direction.

The functioning of his ears became so keen, how his ears processed sound even changed! The sounds themselves all around him had decidedly all transformed now. What he heard everywhere now was not at all what he had once heard or how he had once heard. He looked up to his right in the sky and there came a flock. A beautiful flock of birds that had once been black; they now were glowing and luminous blue. They were lit by an internal radiance as they flew against the rusted sky! Suddenly, there came the splattery-wet rushing sounds of a fat man's feet running down the road. Sam followed him with his eyes, and as the man ran, his shape, his silhouette, morphed into this luminous beautiful figure. Plump and bright. Divine! Like an angel! And from him came the most beautiful of sounds—the sounds one would most certainly expect to come from an angel's mouth.

Sam then heard that voice behind him . . . the one like crystal bells, and he slowly turned around, squinting in the breeze, relishing in this perfection. "Sam! Let's go in! Are you crazy?" Lynn was yelling, pointing frantically at a car not half a block away that had been blown up—flames reaching for the sky, large black plumes of smoke rolling upward. She looked in terror at the bloodied, naked fat man screeching down the street, wailing in horror. Her eyes peeled back as if they'd soon tear at the corners as she implored Sam, one arm stretched toward him, to go inside with her. But to no avail at all. He just stood there, watching her, mesmerized at that celestial apparition that her form had become.

He couldn't understand her any longer. Her voice was purely melodic at this point, as if made of crystal words freely regaling the wind with platinum confetti. Not one utterance of her had even the most remote connection to anything earthly any longer. She was fully illuminated now! Her entire body was radiating light, and her blue eyes were transparent, radiant marbles of a godly magnificence with a source of light of their own. He could not in the least understand her agitation, as he could no longer register fear in others—neither could he understand it, or even sense it himself anymore. This was a condition that had been removed now from him to the remote regions of memory's oblivion. Fearfulness did not exist; nervousness was not even possible. What's the use? As was, too, compassion, meaningless . . . and anger no longer existed for him.

Only three emotions remained for Sam—and these were heightened—hunger was one and a potent one, as well as awe, and decidedly, if perhaps unbelievably, love. A heightened sense and understanding of love.

They stood there now not three feet away, but worlds apart, looking at one another—one in sheer terror, the other in rapturous bliss. Sam suddenly and with outstretched arms beckoned. "Lynn, you really have to come with me!"

She looked at him with a sharp rush of panic as he uttered this unintelligible gargle, his face contorted in some weird configuration impossible to decipher, unacceptable amounts of yellowish liquid collected in his lower jaw and spilled out the sides of his jaw onto his chest. Lynn's eyes widened and filled with terrified tears. Her voice cracked with a single yelp as she tripped on the driveway while running back toward the apartment. She grabbed the keys Sam had dropped, squeezed on the green button, and the garage door began to drop as her figure disappeared up the staircase.

*   *   *

Sam scratched at the garage door, to no avail. No response, and it appeared Lynn would be unyielding. *Women*, he thought, becoming forlorn.

He walked around the building and stood. His flexibility had been impaired. He in fact noticed this but it did not affect him. He tilted his whole body up at an angle toward the apartment. High up in the window, he could see her luminous face glowing, aflame. The blue eyes gleaming and piercing—royal decorations staring straight through him while her voice chimed distantly, glassy and so magically watery—like the song of a crystal nymph and he, her love cherub.

"Oh, my God, his face! What's happening to his face?" she screamed in sheer terror, yet she could not peel her eyes from him. She was glued to that windowpane!

The skin on his face was clinging to his skull like tight leather. It had become coarse and vulgar, blotchy, and there was a purple Y-shaped vein on his forehead swelling up as he uttered those guttural calls. His lips tightened around his mouth, retracting against his teeth like an obscene, fleshy elastic. His eyes were distant, as if the stare of death, which focuses nowhere.

There was a wrenching sensation twisting in his gut. Then came a great suction in his esophagus—like a seal of sorts had broken. Something snapped in there. A windy, audible, hollow gasp resonated then through his vocal cords with a sound that resembled that of a wounded animal. Hunger suddenly overtook him! A hunger of a hundred days! He left the side of the apartment building and began walking straight up the street—searching. His intestines were desperately pleading. Down the block on the opposite side, he saw a glowing angel fleeing quickly past him, its tinkling bells chiming in the wind. He realized for the first time that he'd become helplessly drawn to these now, that they were with a force impossible to avoid, senseless to fight. As he looked at the form passing by him, his intestines gripped and tightened, and he felt a distinct, almost magnetic pull from the running shape. He also noticed that the farther away it got, the fainter the force became—subsiding this way to when, finally, it broke to nothing.

As he walked among the houses, he felt a pull—toward the left, toward the right—like an invisible tug at the very center of his body. When finally he surrendered to one of these, he followed the current and it pulled him in like a warm vacuum. He just leaned back on the tug and followed the pull. As he approached the source, a heightened feeling of well-being poured into him: an incentive—like a sea of feathers rushing through his blood, up and down his legs and arms, his body, and into his neck and head. He saw then a figure, inside a structure much like a giant birdhouse—a glass house . . . a winter garden . . . a greenhouse. As he got closer, the green of the leaves deepened in color, he saw that the red flowers almost seemed to be made of thick velvet, and he ran his fingers through the petals. The glass panels all around the edifice glistened like fine crystal. The figure to which the pull led was directly in front of him now, only yards away; it seemed to be floating! A suspended celestial creature. It looked back at Sam, letting out a string of the most imaginably precious and unlikeliest of musical phrases. An acoustic heavenly flood echoed through the caverns of Sam's senses like a startled flock of glass bluebirds in an ice cave.

"Oh my Lord, Sam, what is going on with you?" Mrs. Raminoux screamed at the top of her lungs as she dropped the elephant-shaped watering can on the ground.

She had been delighting in her compulsive gardening when she first noticed him. He had been crossing the street as she watered those perfect, luscious, red giant hibiscus. He was moving peculiarly, she thought at first—clumsily and as if disoriented, maybe—but then he was finally close enough for her to have a clearer look at his appearance: his sickly greenish skin, the yellow film over his eyes, the unattended salivation, the gaunt, lax jaw. There was a repugnant odor to him of a strange acidity. She recognized him, sure, but immediately realized there was something essential she could no longer sense! He had been altered, that was evident. But how? His humanity had been replaced by this harsh, dry, opaque, unsettling presence—a hollowness that gave her the impression of a terrible, living taxidermy.

Sam took a couple of steps closer, his shoulders broadened as he grabbed her by the mandible, pressing down against the tender flesh under her tongue, gripping the bone like the latch on a fire alarm. She let out a muffled scream as he, with the other hand, clamped down and ripped at the middle of her throat. He dug his dry, hardened, leathery fingers into her flesh, which soon popped in perfect, punctured holes. Spurts of blood shot out as if from small and bloody dolphin blowholes before he ripped the muscles, pulling them out in moist strings. There was one last hollow breath that came from her bloody windpipe as she dropped heavily to the ground in one single, short rumble. He brought the nutritious, bloody handful of tissue and skin and trachea into his mouth. His thick, gooey saliva ate away at this meat like a fast, corrosive acid. He got to his knees and, pulling Mrs. Raminoux's head up, tore another large and forceful bite, pulling now from the rich meat behind her collarbone.

The angel was limp before him. On her neck and back, from where he had been eating, his attention was diverted to the blue fluorescent liquid. His fingers were alight in blue as well, as was his own face—his mouth and nose and cheeks were decorated as if with child's play warpaint. What a feast. The sensation was monumental! *Yes indeed*, he thought. A satisfaction from every mouthful as he had never before derived. His palate was overridden with ecstasy to no end. The taste radiated outward, into his cheeks, conquering now every inch, every cell. And as he swallowed, it was as if his entire body—all of his insides—pulled at the matter, consumed with selfishness and desperation. It was all insurmountable enjoyment; the very absolution of pleasure—palatable, olfactory, sensual.

He ripped and ate at every place of the angel. As he ate more, the splendor and light dimmed away from it, darkening, until it glowed so very faintly that his hunger for it ceased completely. The event cadenced—fading away, and away . . . to nothing.

He then rose to his feet, feeling well satisfied, and he walked out of the greenhouse with a spring in his stiff shuffle. Friendly winds caressed him through his leisurely walk; he felt his hair, his cheeks, his eyeballs tickled and teased by the flirtatious air. His shirt collar rustled, playfully tapping at his blood-encrusted jaw.

As he jaywalked across the street, there came a great blast that filled the town—a giant prehistoric bird squawking, large and threatening, announcing its arrival. Sam came across a house engulfed in blue forms pointing upwards—just like the ones he'd seen moments before, only much larger, more violent, and certainly more beautiful. That blasting sound got closer now, and those vibrations changed inside his ears where the trumpeting of the loud noise sent a hiss through his body, like television static in his blood. A large moving shape pulled up to his side, next to the house wrapped in flames. And then angels began pouring out of the machine. A shower of crystals began invading the dancing blue forms—a thick plume of sprinkles flying up toward infinity. *Wow, wow, enchantment,* he thought.

*   *   *

Lynn ran to the window after hearing the blaring fire truck's siren; she could see the flames from the side window. It was at an angle but a sliver of it was visible. The black tower of smoke stretched upward, and there was the ever-increasing smell of ash in the air. Signs of imminent doom had become desperately clear. She rushed to the kitchen, grabbed the phone, and dialed—something, in hindsight, she knew she should have done from the start! But then again . . .

Emergency picked up but informed her that various calls had already been placed from her area, and that help would be there very shortly! She hung up the phone—fearfully but not at all fully cognizant of the scale of what was developing outside her walls. She threw the phone on the sofa and rushed to the kitchen, turned on the radio, and spun the dial to the local news. She heard the last of the report:

> An alarming number of calls have been placed, authorities inform, from the township of Autumnsville. Earlier today, the first case, a severely distraught, mutilated woman who was found wandering the streets nude and in a state of disorientation . . . she was hostile and violent. Authorities attempted to subdue her, but she resisted, then attacked two paramedics before disappearing. The paramedics have been hospitalized with moderate injuries and high fevers. They have been reported to be very disoriented, and one is showing signs of extreme delirium . . . unintelligible speech . . . won't understand what he's told . . . I've now been informed that a fire is in progress.

Lynn turned the radio off and rushed to the dining room. *I have to leave . . . I have to leave to the city!* She was reaching for the car keys and her purse when Felix leaped from the steps onto her head and started biting wildly on her cheek and neck. As she peeled the cat off her, he tore a piece of her ear off! She slammed the cat on the table and stabbed him several times as hard as she could with the car keys. She held him by the throat while he dug painful—often bloody—streaks down her forearm with his hind claws. She kept stabbing repeatedly, but the cat was unrelenting. He growled and hissed, and yellow phlegm mixed with blood spewed from his mouth. The pain in Lynn's arm was so great she was forced to let him go. He dashed up the staircase, wailing in a voice almost human—like that of an old man talking in the midst of a drunken nightmare.

Lynn sprinted across the dining room, ran down the staircase, and pushed on the garage door remote once again. She got into the car, put it in reverse, and backed down the driveway. Skidding backward, she turned the wheel and, with a thunk, bounced onto the pavement, pointing toward the city. She put the car in drive and floored the gas pedal. As she drove by the first intersection, to her right, in the middle of the block, she saw the fire truck, the jets of water, and the thick tower of smoke rising to the sky . . . and Sam, standing there, arms to his side, looking rather green.

Two police cars zoomed by her in the opposite direction, sirens blasting and lights spinning. Two blocks ahead of this, she saw a large form on the sidewalk. It looked like a dark, dirty mound of meat. But as she drove closer, she slowed down and saw that it was the fat man she'd seen earlier, only now, he was bloodied and partially dismembered. He lay in a lump in the middle of a lake of sticky blood, a naked person—drenched in both crusted as well as fresh, flowing blood—hunched over him, pulling apart his sinewy chest plate. Carmen!—feasting on the fat man's sticky carcass, her eyes clouded gray and an organ stretched from her bite to her pulling fists. A chilled rush went up both sides of Lynn's neck to her head, and she began to lose consciousness. Her muscles were nonresponsive at this point, and the car veered off course and slammed into the side of a house. The airbag deployed, and Lynn bounced a few times between it and the seat. In her numb daze, she leaned forward to leave her seat, but the seatbelt jerked her back into place. She looked from side to side, down, then up to the rear view mirror, through which she saw the morbidly brutal rendition of Carmen's nude, ravaged figure walking toward her. On her face there were grotesque coagulates, and bubbles of blood oozed and foamed out of Carmen's nostrils.

Lynn's ears started ringing; everything became white, and she passed out from terror.

* * *

Sam walked down the wide, semicircular granite steps into a large, dark space. Each individual step sent a rippling pulse of pleasure up his leg as the nourishment he'd taken recently populated every cell of his body. Mrs. Raminoux's blood was nearly dried around his mouth and on his shirt, and he was surprised with the speed and efficiency he was digesting her. He sensed, even, the most minuscule particle of what he'd consumed being utilized to replenish him. He sensed, too, how every one of his old cells was being pushed to the surface and was dying, quickly forming a layer of what seemed like dust on the surface of his entire body—a layer of ash of his former self.

He walked deep into the dark, cavernous interior. It was all black, restful—a void seemingly without time. A permanent hum droned on all around the tank. This was the largest tank in the whole aquarium, underground. Blue-green water light projected on the black walls. It was a circular tank, and the glass stretched upward ten feet: manta rays, sea bass, stingrays, sharks. And today, it was magnificence absolute! By God!—the fish flew around like ghosts in a haunted glass house. Sam's body was so close to the glass it was as if he were in there with them. All alight! All glowing intensities of different sorts. Swimming water saints. He walked along the large circular cave, never once taking his eyes away from the flying carnival—running his rigid fingers against the glass as dust flew off his skin. That fine dust that once was him—puffs of defunct cells—microscopic histories scattered through an indifferent and forgetful breeze. Giant sea beasts glowed in space. Their motion in the water in a ballet with the echoing shuffling of his feet's whispering music. Then, as if he had heard it twice, he heard the damper, restricted sound of a booming roll traveling through the muting of all the liquid. Inside, from above and from the other side, there had quickly dipped a green and long figure, who plunged enwrapped in a tornado of bubbles. The figure glowed like a large emerald phantasm. Once the emerald reached the bottom, and the frivolous bubbles finished their spiral, upward retreat, the shape of a man was revealed, walking along the bottom in a casual gait.

*   *   *

Carmen had heard the thundering cacophony behind her when she stopped feeding from the fat angel. His light was already exhausting anyhow—a fading pulse: white to golden, golden to yellow, yellow to ocher . . . a slow gradient diminishing throb, like a large, dying, luminous heart. When she turned around, she saw inside the car the radiant figure—bright and still. Then it moved: left and right, like a trapped little bird. Carmen got up and began walking toward it when the figure suddenly stopped and fell forward—slumped, still, hung. With every step Carmen took, the figure began to change its color, to transfigure into something . . . something familiar. It sent those radiations through the air, though the cosmos; galvanizing the imperceptible particles of air and matter around it, prompting patterns, frequencies, meaning! Turning nothing into something—signals that were in some form significant to Carmen. The figure had not yet regained movement in the least. But pulsing within it, that became increasingly insistent—like something wanting to live, or coming to life, or to being, fully. The end piece, the last stage of metamorphosis. Slowly, visibly—but not to insensitive eyes—she began growing into a vibrancy. The figure, in her rest, then became electric, and as Carmen approached, her light transmuted. It first glowed golden, but gradually shifted into a beautiful green glow! Carmen was now only inches away from the car when the figure inside straightened her head. She came by the window and there formed that spontaneous yet unexplainable but unmistakable bond: adoration and love! The figure turned its head, her eyes now alight in a glorious red. The radiant rubies of both meeting—recognizing!

Carmen!

Lynn!

They both thought at once, and they both heard at once. As they stared into each other's scalding, flaming red eyes, they noticed the bonding current fusing them.

Isn't it wonderful? Carmen thought to Lynn.

Lord, it's marvelous. This is marvelous! Lynn thought back.

*   *   *

Sam was filled with curiosity, but he was also filled with a more powerful sensation—a more powerful emotion. It was as if he and this shape had something in common; as in a dream where things are not explained but one just somehow understands them! A strange and strong fellowship—a commonality. He pushed his face against the glass and, through the murk, followed the movement inside the tank. The long, green figure got ahold of one of the white glowing ghosts with a swift, violent swipe and began tearing at it with its mouth. The light of the prey then beginning to dim, and dim until all the luster was then completely gone. He released the opaquing little saint, and it sunk to the bottom of the tank, lifeless and black by the time it reached the bottom.

The figure then took notice of Sam and began walking toward him, like a man walking on the surface of the moon. He got within a distance where only the thickness of the glass was nearly the space between them: water on one side, air on Sam's, but an invisible cocoon of faint electricity encapsulated them both.

Nicholas! Sam thought in his direction.

Nicholas smiled at Sam as a small, thick cloud of yellow phlegm rushed out of his lungs and out his mouth. *This is freedom, Sammie!* he then thought to Sam.

They walked twice around the circular tank, each on his own side of the glass, their green hue lighting the walls as the two emerald people strolled around in the blackness of the aquarium.

*   *   *

The sun had gone down, and the stars were out. The night was glassy and beautiful, people were running for their lives, and the screams of terror echoed throughout town. Cars were set on fire. On a recently manicured, richly green lawn, a policeman—missing both eyes—feasted on the body of a slightly obese woman in a retro flower nightgown. A gay undead paramedic and a gang of now-ghastly firemen ambushed a house full of horrified senior citizens—Mrs. Raminoux's slander comity, no doubt.

Lynn and Carmen staggered back home, delighting in the transfiguration of the world, imbibed with a joy unparalleled and enveloped by a beauty never before seen by anyone.

Carmen, everything is so . . . wonderful! I can see so clearly. Carmen, I love you, Lynn thought.

Everything is so clear now. I understand it all. How could we have been so blind, so lost? Carmen said, kissing Lynn on her lips.

The sky was so velvety, and the blue moon seemed made of snow. Angels rushed by with their hopeless, musical cries as emerald bodies chased after them. The road to the city was filled like a string of green seasonal lights. The city! In the distance the city rose, aglow in white light.

The city! It will be filled.

The city! The entire world!

They'd reached the driveway when the force came in their direction—a force that brought euphoria . . . happiness. The women turned their heads as the town spun 180 degrees while Sam and Nicholas glowed green through the night. Nick's hair was plastered to his face, his whole body soaked in salt water; Sam walked alongside him, wearing a police hat, three gunshot wounds glistened burgundy on his chest. Lynn walked toward them as an unlikely, clumsy contortion formed on her face. Gargling sounds and a groan came across toward them.

I can see, Sam, she thought to him. *I can finally see!*

As Sam's scabbed, coarse mouth stretched sideways into a grotesquely tender attempt of a smile, coagulated blood cracked and flaked off his face onto his shirt. Carmen lost her balance and fell on the ground, snapping one of the two splintered bones of her arm. She raised the forked limb to her face with disappointment and something nearly sad conjured up on her face. But she immediately suggested that, since it was probably past midnight, they should have an early Thanksgiving.

The group staggered toward Sam and Lynn's home and up the stairs. Lynn took the turkey out of the fridge. Mr. Raminoux's gas tank exploded outside as he violently ran his motorcycle into a telephone pole at 104 miles per hour while attempting to escape; seven zombies immediately pounced and devoured him in a savage frenzy! Felix came down from the loft—a small, green ball of fluorescence, his eyes glowing red with love.

Lynn turned the overhead stained-glass lamp on. The colors began to resonate, bouncing throughout the rooms. The light shot outward in all directions; the entire apartment became aglow with a multitude of colors sizzling around them—permeating through them and inside them and with a beauty too unbearable for any living mortal. A beauty so profound it would kill a man.

Their thoughts were now identical: *Oh my God, we are one! I can see you! I can see it all! I can see your heart! I thought I saw you . . . before. I thought I saw you. But not like this! Never like this! I'm so sorry! I've been so foolish. I love you . . . so much. I love you all so much!*

They were four but became then one. They glowed among each other, their bodies magnified in the vibrations of the colored lights. The colored lights that were the spectrum of God. Their eyes! Their eyes were alight with an infinite number of colors—all the splendor of love was set free and metamorphosed into the mysterious material of light—colors impossible for us to see and beyond our capacity to understand them as of yet. On this magical Thanksgiving night, terrible and beautiful, four zombies ascended to the zenith of all possible joy.

They gazed, enthralled, at their hearts, a gift from no giver, seeing each other as God intended, understanding it all finally, and drowning in a precious and invaluably fortunate moment of absolute enchantment.

A Demon Wants Your Shadow: A Nocturne

Tag! You're it!

This is how the story ended, and I felt so . . . silly? Because I had just finished reading when the strange nervousness came over me. It was at around 3:00 AM, and I never went back to sleep. Because I couldn't. So I just lay there, still, frightened by nothing. There was a hollow breath in the room all around, and a warm, faint, black pulse oppressing me—almost imperceptible but definitely present. It had suddenly manifested in this space, and the thickness of the atmosphere was like black cotton that shied away from my face soon after I felt its fibers against my cheeks—like wind . . . almost . . . like a solid, static wind. I lay on my bed facing up. A shard of light—headlights—came slicing across the ceiling, briefly casting angular, running triangles of light around the bedroom's walls.

I sat up, got out of bed, and went to the kitchen. The sounds of the passing train echoed metallically beyond the apartment. I looked through the glass toward the station. That was where I saw the man for the first time: standing on the platform—distant, undefined, and looking in my direction, motionless with his hands at his sides, mouth agape, a hollow, dark oval like a black egg. It was all darkness in this room except for a faint violet blackness that was almost nonexistent . . . a darkness that cast objects into suggestions, hazy premonitions of shapes.

I opened the fridge, and its yellow light attacked me, lighting me up, drawing a long and unfair shadow. A grotesque version of my black silhouette dragged across the floor and crawled up the wall behind me. I looked back at it, and I must confess it gave me the sensation of awful company. As my head was turned, I looked at the smoky residue from my imposition against the light. My eyes then wandered toward what was beyond and noticed the man—his gaze still fixed on me. The shadow behind mimicked my every nuance; it was true to the impossibility of absolution when it comes to human immobility—unless in death. It moved with me, elongated, unnatural. The impossible anatomy that it suggested flatly climbed the wall and the cabinets as it betrayed the perfect imitation of my movements. And even though I was in charge to dictate all its routes, I was suddenly overtaken with the feeling that it had been studying me; as if my shadow were only there as a perfect facade! A perfect instrument, a vehicle—an opportunity: the preposterous scenarios that can creep into the mind when in solitude.

I poured myself a tall glass of milk and closed the fridge door, rendering the room back into its former blue blackness. And with the dark came the humming stillness that heightened the self-awareness that was there in darkness. I didn't turn the kitchen light on right away, and I did this purposely; I was not going to let myself be chased by childish fears. But as I was finishing the last bit of milk, I reached for the switch and swiftly flicked it. My glass was still up to my face as I looked down, and there was a significant time before my arm's shadow appeared on the counter. I put the glass down quickly. A brief moment later, the small streak of milk on my upper lip cooled to a harsh chill. A wind—a cold wind—had rushed through the front of me. And this was a wind for which there was no possible source. The apartment was sealed and locked; all the windows were shut. I was . . . concerned. And then it came—the sensation. There's always an inevitable trepidation whenever one is alone but has as well the certainty that one is not. I wrestled against this unfounded fear and turned the lamp back off, in an effort to force myself to face my inexcusable fear. I then went to my computer to shake off this uneasiness—I wanted to divert my attention, divert it to something mundane and compensate for the raw anxiety I was feeling. The screen came on, filling the area with a local fluorescence that was comfortable enough.

I had started working on a story around two days prior, and so I opened it and began typing again:

> It was when he opened his eyes that he realized he'd been hovering around the house—horizontally, in the same position he'd been in when he was in bed. The sheets were still on him; and by his side—as if escorting him, or worse yet, carrying him (in a casket?)—there was a woman. She was walking along as he floated all through the spaces not far from the floor. He spoke to her, but she would never respond or would never even hear. He could not lift his head. In fact, neither could he move any part of his body—his movements were so restricted he could only circle his eyes. He could not see her face, but soon enough the woman turned, and he recognized her at once. Aurora! His daughter—only grown up! But he recognized her nonetheless! It was her, without a doubt, and she cried, and only cried as he tried to speak to her, but he, himself, could still not make a sound. And she could not see him trying. Was this part of his future? He thought. Was he—from the confines of slumber—visiting his own future funeral? Aurora . . .

I kept typing this way for a while, and the fear was beginning to leave me. I was gaining momentum with the writing and even came to a point where I forgot completely about the nonsense of the past twenty minutes. But not too long after, as I was typing the conclusion of the chapter, there was something so definite, something so present, I could not dismiss it. I dropped my hands on my lap and sat there facing the keys when, from the last set of kitchen cabinets, I located some indistinct sounds. At first it sounded similar to the faint sound of a teakettle just about to boil. I stayed very still so I could make it out better. I turned my head slightly toward the sound and could discern it now without question. It was the sound of two children whispering to one another! One whispered . . . then a brief silence . . . then the next took over—almost like they were deciding or planning something. A boy and a girl, clearly! And only as I turned around did the whispers cease! I wheeled myself back a bit in my chair on the plastic mat underneath and very slowly twisted myself around on it. I stood up, carefully, and walked slowly toward the wide open black nothing where the cabinets were. My sideburns were chilled, and the hairs on my arms all stood up on end. The hardwood floor creaked once, and I held myself in place. A garbage truck beeped outside. Then came the banging of the bins and the dumping and some more beeping.

The light of the monitor went off, and I momentarily went blind. There were a few short moments before my eyes got adjusted to the dark. Then, right in front of me—in the space not two feet away—I saw a bubbling, distorted vision in midair! I thought at first it might be my eyes growing accustomed to the darkness, but no; it was clear now as then that very space condensed visibly into a static black shadow, standing in front of me. The shadow was the shape of a person—a figure with its arms at its side. As car lights came flashing through the window, the shadow became a sharp, flat standing cutout that suddenly fell flush on the floor, where it attached itself quickly to my feet next to my own shadow! As the car drove away and the lights searched through the inside of my apartment, the two shadows—one chasing the next—ran a semicircle around me until there was no more light and they both disappeared into the blackness of the kitchen. As the headlights flashed off, I went blind a second time. Then, a loud banging from the cupboard, and a crouched fumbling—like someone quickly but clumsily crawling under me—dropped me to the ground!

This was definitely not imagination!

My instincts had been right from the start, and this was unrelentingly real. The shadow, which had stood before me moments before, was eyeless, yet I could distinctly feel its close, dull stare. The banging went silent when a very loud "Shhhhhhhh!" came hissing from the lightless kitchen. The monitor light came back on behind me, and the glow cast a feeble blur of my form into the hollow black murk in front of me as the fuzz of my shadow moved forward into that pitch-black abyss. As it came on, I was just about to yell, "Oh, my God!" But instead, words were forced into my mouth, and I screamed, "Just play the fucking game, you retard!" in a girl's voice. Shortly after that, out of the cupboard, came a boy's voice, angry and strained: "Who are you calling a retard, Yvonne?"

Then—all went quiet. Not a sound. I was still on the floor and wouldn't dare move. I looked all around me and held my breath for a few moments—the buzz of the fridge and all that silence. Nothing. Stress related; this is unreal! Stress . . . I kept lying to myself! Because the alternatives were too horrid and weird or impossible to even consider. I got up on my feet and went to the living room to turn the standing lamp on. The living room was a large, square room with a hardwood floor on a level a little higher than the other rooms. Two long steps led up to it. At the far end of the living room, there was a floor-to-ceiling sliding glass door leading to a small terrace. I stood in the middle of the room in the yellowed brightness, surrounded by still objects—sofa, coffee table, chair, bookshelf, television. There was nothing odd in that space, but my nerves remained raw and unsettled. There was something askew. Something was definitely not right! I panned the entire room, but I couldn't figure out what it was. What, what? It was then, when I looked closer, that it rushed into me at once, and then it was undeniable. It was suddenly as conspicuous as trying to tell you it wants to be noticed! In terror, I was unwilling to accept this—mainly since it was evident that what I looked at was an impossibility. I looked to my right, and all the shadows were slanting in that direction—as they should be . . . from that lamp, yes. All the shadows . . . except my own. My shadow lay in the opposite direction from all the rest. It elongated and cascaded down the steps, losing itself into the penumbra of the shady black breath leading to the void of the kitchen.

I stayed looking, as in a trance, at my shadow—a bodyless shade that buzzed at the ridges in an unjustified blur. I stood there, made of stone, as it stood there with me, still and silent, and eerily observant of me. Then, and with no action whatsoever from my part, it swerved to one side and then snapped back into place again—as if it had lost its balance for a moment. I was then very frightened—the worst kind of terror! Because there's no guessing. And the worst guessing is communication. Communication with that is something no one should want to experience. To know you! To know that you know you are well aware of it! The intention alone, and the uncertainty of this, was not something anyone would participate in willingly! Not anyone who was sane anyhow. The meaning and all possible results of the horror of its world are too far removed from the capacity of guessing, and the approximation is the ultimate of human terror . . . I'd think.

There's a hidden knowledge among us all that the horrors that linger where that dwells—and that certainly is not here—brings a terror beyond any that any torture imaginable could bring. You can never wash away from your sight the terror you experience in the face of the demonic. No. Once it gets you, you will seemingly experience an eternity before it does what it will. It'll show you things that will challenge your capacity to tolerate the worst thing you could imagine ever witnessing. Because the terror will not only be yours, it will also be the additional terror that comes with the original terror. This first terror is itself an eternal prisoner that lives in perpetual horror—the entity that chases you brings with it, too, the demon that plagues it. What terrorizes you is a tortured slave!

I trembled violently, but the shadow was now unmoving—frozen in place as I shivered uncontrollably, disobedient of my shaking. A silent preview of its world. The shadows of the objects around me still remained in their place when my shadow began slowly to shrink forward . . . to come toward me, dragging on the floor. I tried to move. I could not. My shadow came all the way, all the way under me, forming a perfect black circle—a puddle of black shadow; of course, there was no overhead light. I braced myself and looked downward. Two grotesquely thin shadows like malnourished brittle arms began emanating, elongating from beneath me to awkward malformations. The light went off in the apartment as if a large, black hand had snatched it away. I began to run as I heard a fire truck's alarm blast outside, jolting me momentarily out of my frightful paralysis. I tripped on the steps, and I rolled on the floor, as my eyes were not yet adjusted to the dark. As I fell, I gashed my right eyebrow, which began to bleed substantially, but I ignored it. I made it to the door, unlocked it, and rushed onto the streets.

Outside was completely deserted. The pavement was wet, and I was barefoot. I heard a lone car in the next block, swishing its tires against the pavement. In my pajamas, I walked at a fast pace and looked behind me and around me as I walked. The air fogged in front of me. I walked and walked for what felt like kilometers—in that and this direction, in any direction. I didn't know where I was going or where I wanted to go. Away, that's all I knew—I wanted to get away! All I was certain about was that I wanted to be as far as possible from my own apartment. I was getting very cold, and my feet were growing numb. The clouds of breath in front of my face became larger. I had walked in so many random, desperate directions, I ended up in a neighborhood that did not look even remotely familiar. It was a ghetto, and desolate. The only sound around me was the buzzing of a streetlamp. There was a big empty lot that looked as if it might have been the former site of a building complex. There was a concrete structure—like a foundation—and a little girl was sitting there, her legs dropping into the rectangular well of the foundation. She wasn't moving, and her head was hung. The place felt still and frozen, but now the temperature seemed to be growing less unkind. It was so late! Was she lost? Had she been abandoned? She didn't appear frightened or distressed. As I approached her, I saw she was tearing something with her fingers—a book. When I got close enough to see, I realized it was my book! The book I had just been reading in bed: *In Search of the Bluebird*. She noticed me as I got closer and turned around quickly; she looked straight at me. Her gaze was sharp. She then threw the book on the ground as if she were upset. I flinched slightly, and then I asked her, "Are you lost?"

"No," she said. She got up and faced away from me.

"What are you doing out here? It's so late . . . aren't your parents—?"

"Just play the game, you retard!" she said, and I froze. In front of my eyes, as I stood there, she seemed to be changing form under her clothes. She grew slightly shorter, and her head shrank proportionately. Something—like pieces of metal—fell out of one of her pockets; I could not see what they were . . . and then a small dead bird—blue. On a faraway building, in the direction she faced, a light came on—the only one light in the whole complex.

A voice yelled out of that window, the sound echoing through the buildings walls, "Who are you calling a retard, Yvonne?"

An airplane with no lights flew above without any sound, not two hundred meters from the ground—a black shark against the navy, starless sky. The light of the building began flickering until it went off. The girl in front of me let out a horrid yelp, took off her clothes, spat on the ground, and started running, beating on her own body with her hands! As she ran away, on her back, the skin began to crack like arid clay!

At the base of the ruins stood a square stone with a bronze memorial plaque:

In Loving Memory
Cedric and Yvonne Johnson
1993–2000

"You don't know who you're messin' with—" The soft voice came from behind me. I turned around carefully, my bare feet shuffling against the moist ground. There was an old black man with a white beard. He wore a checkered red-and-black flannel jacket and fingerless gloves, and he was crossing the street toward the lot. Then a very skinny black woman with bulging eyes walked from another direction toward me. She looked African—deep black. I made my way over under the streetlamp.

"Where am I?" I asked them. "I must be turned around."

The lady started laughing, and the old man grinned.

"Well, if you don't know where you are," said the man, "it's already too late for you, my boy."

This was completely senseless to me. "I'm sorry, I don't understand—I've been having a really . . . bizarre night, and somehow I ended up here. I don't know this place. I need to get back somewhere around Darwin Avenue—around Sixty-Second Street?"

As I asked this question, a sudden terror came over me. They were standing so close. I could feel their weight—or at least that's what I thought—but I realized as I stood there that they had no shadows of their own. My shadow stretched forward and split into two parts that ended below them both—side by side. As I moved to one side to shift my weight, my shadow gravitated toward them like a compass. Their eyes were fixed on me. They followed me as if their pupils were connected to mine by an invisible string.

Then the skinny woman said to me, without erasing that white grin off her face, "Sam, you can't escape the game—we didn't."

As she said these words, I tried to wake up from this nightmare. Who were these people? They were speaking to me with a tone of familiarity that caused in me nothing but sheer terror. I had the sensation that their former existence had been replaced by something else. My gaze pierced deep into their eyes, and I sensed that there was, behind the calm facade, something tortured, imprisoned in there—something that was screaming out things no one could ever and would never hear! Their former persons were trapped in the bowels of their own bodies. They were looking outward as this vessel moved. They saw through the murk of their former eyes, walking and screaming in silence as something now piloted their agonizing bodies, their entities. Imagine watching yourself—from the inside out—watching yourself do things you are not commanding. I thought of possessions and decided to stop thinking.

The old man shrugged and the woman said, "It's your turn, Sam—so enjoy it."

I asked her how she knew my name, and she said everyone there knew my name. That, once you got there, your name was already known.

Where is "here," and who is everyone?

I looked back. Now there were two kids sitting on the foundation—a boy and the girl exactly as I'd first seen her. I walked slowly toward them and saw that they were leafing though the book . . . occasionally reading. The book was back to how it had been—no longer torn. They turned around and looked old for one moment—or burnt—but once she began speaking, their faces flashed back into pristine youth.

Without a word from me, the girl first spoke. "We'll teach you how . . . you just have to do it and you'll be fine . . . that's all." She got up and pulled the boy to his feet. "Let's go to the train, and we'll take you where you need to go."

I was the captive of this uncertain and ghastly dementia. My fear compelled me to acquiesce . . . obey. The sight now didn't seem unusual, yet I knew I was in the waiting hall of something horrible . . . something eternal. I was in a place where things to come would certainly be unpleasant and vulgar . . . unsettling and contradictory. Beneath the things that are most innocuous in appearance, a bitter strange essence can linger; it will bear with it the infusion of an unjust, mind-boggling, and puzzling horror. Everyone was a prisoner here, and it was a dark, bleak, unpredictable circus. Everyone there would be selfish and terrible, and their routines would be maddeningly terrifying and alien to outsiders, but normal—even necessary—to them. Rituals would be performed, acts beyond your worst possible nightmares, and these acts were the very things that place could not go on without. This is how everything remains in balance . . . how the sanity of the grotesque and demonic lives and enjoys itself—the pleasure in the putrid and the suffering. To relive nightmares is the only way to reiterate the purpose of this tense, entrapping place. The dreams exist in confusion in which every day is rearranged and you know nothing new. In perfect unpredictable terror, the mind will sometimes suffer as much as the body. Everyone here was terrified as well as a horrible perpetrator. No peace—only fear. The friends you make would surprise you and horrify you eventually—make you witness a terror from which they'll feed. And what I grew to know for certain was that I would never leave. If I tried to go somewhere, there would be nowhere else I could go—there was no somewhere else now. This would follow me. It would be ever present.

The children tugged at my hand, and I walked behind them. We walked out of the lot and began walking down the road. My feet wrinkled from the moisture and the cold as I walked along the rough pavement, slapping painfully as I hurried. I noticed the children made no sound at all on the ground. And in the puddles by the curbside, they cast no reflection. As far as the world was concerned, they did not exist! They began walking faster, then faster, and I kept chasing after them, following them all the way. At least this was a constant—some repetition to keep the terror at bay.

We reached the train station and began climbing the iron stairs toward the platform when I heard a sound—a sound of distant moaning. "What is that?" I said.

"It'll be here soon. You'll see," the girl said. "Come!" We walked up the platform, and the moaning was getting closer.

"We are almost there," she said, and there was the sound of an approaching train in the distance.

"This is it, Sam, it's coming. But don't worry; we're coming with you. We always come along!" she said as I looked around. I froze. I recognized where I was! Open-mouthed, I stood in place looking across at this sight! "Lord," I said, my arms dropped languidly to my sides, and I saw a figure walk into the kitchen. The light of the fridge went on and lit up the shape in front of it. It was my apartment!—there, but way in the distance! Oh, my God, it's me! I could see myself . . . clearly. I . . . I remember this! I remember the man on the platform! The man on the platform was always me? Me . . . now! I couldn't take my eyes off this image. From the kitchen, I looked in my direction as I stood at the platform and saw! We noticed each other. We did! And then . . . there she was, right behind me . . . standing—the skinny black lady was standing there right behind me all that time? I looked back and—Why can't I see her? Why can't I see her from my kitchen? She's right there standing so close behind! Can't you see?

Once we got to the end of the platform, I looked down and there it was, an indiscernible figure on the rail below—the source of all that moaning.

"Oh, my God, what is that?" I yelped.

The girl laughed and then knelt closer. "That's you, Sam!" she then said to me, looking down, not peeling her eyes off my body down there.

"What do you mean? What do you mean, me? How long have I been there? What am I doing there?"

"You've been there for a while, Sam . . . for a bit now," she said, checking her nails.

"If that's me, then what am I?"

"You don't know?" She looked back at me, her mouth agape. "You're only his shadow," she said as my head filled with an increasing electric buzz. Suddenly, I became weightless. Once I looked down at myself, I realized I had no body! I was a substance-less black cloud in the shape of a man and immediately hallucinated that I was staring right into my own living eyes and flashed inside my apartment, where I stood in front of myself, who could not distinguish me! I sensed light . . . then I was pulled downward . . . toward the figure below at the rails, about to be crushed by the train. I was completely powerless against it as the train's lights approached. I went down all the way behind and underneath the body that was mine—or I was his. And the train was now coming fast. A fraction before it would have collided with the body, for whom I was its shadow, the flash of headlights flung me backward in a black beam of blackness before everything at once disappeared.

*   *   *

so much hollow noise . . . soft hollow noise . . .
so much hollow noise . . . soft hollow noise
all this soft hollow noise in here . . .
all that space . . . that black hollow space . . .
warm, and nowhere . . .

tired . . . and blind . . . hollow air . . . starts . . . starts
here . . .

Now. Right now . . . and everything is black in here. And I'm
warm. And it's . . . now! I can hear sounds . . . hear sounds now. I
see a shape . . . watery shapes far off . . . bubbling.

I hear the faint sound of paper. And of breathing.
Breathing . . . Oh, Lord . . . I know . . . I think . . . my God. I
understand! I can see them forming. I can see everything forming!
All around me . . . here in this place. I can see now . . . It is your
breathing I sense. I can see through your eyes reading my own
words!

I'm here. I am here. With you. I can see your body. I can see
through your eyes. I now understand how it works and what I need
to do . . . trust me, this story will change once you start.

Tag! You're it!

A Savior's Prophecy

8:33 AM Tuesday. Sam Salvatore walked into the elevator, as that almost predictable morning group did with him. Saw most of those familiar faces—stale, pale, wan, and weird. Powdery eye bags rested underneath the tired gaze of women like little *Bonsai*-sized saddlebags. The purple cadaver-like coloring of the women was hidden beneath layers of aromatic plaster foundation, colonizing an entire surface of what would otherwise be made up of living tissue, paying homage to the ancient Japanese art of *Kabuki*.

Most of them rushing into that communal crate were acquainted only by the quotidian vertical traffic they shared on mornings, lunchtimes, and ends of the day, where there surfaced, on occasion, something resembling—especially on Fridays—a thing like joy. Some, Sam had noticed, had a method of greeting that came across as a dismissive, condescending grimace—almost like they were doing you a favor. What did it mean? That face, he often wondered. He felt it was useless to contort one's features in such a way, that if one were going to go as far as making the effort, one must at least conjure something up that was remotely pleasant. And that's exactly why he didn't. Not because he was unfriendly—God no!—but because he had gotten up not an hour before this and his facial muscles' responses were faulty at best. And so, for the mornings, he did not risk it; instead he left his face at its natural state of rest, unencumbered with the outside development relating to the neurotic. He employed only his neck instead—since it was too a part of the body that seldom earned any judgment—yes. He contracted his neck muscles so that his head tilted forward in a nod.

That was enough. After all, facial expressions are so often subjected to unexpressed, and often unwarranted, internal bashing—disdain, dislike, even repulsion!—among so many things directed at this particular body part.

The face, in fact, is a precarious and dangerous instrument. Depending on the sort you wear, it certainly can be either your best friend or your worst nemesis! It's a thing of luck, really—or lack thereof. The gut, also, keep in mind, is another part of the anatomy that compels immediate judgment from strangers oftentimes, dependent too, of course, on its physical specifics subjected to the taste of third parties—as is also very much the case with the ass, you see. These parts may sometimes propel people into unspeakable wars in the mind. The emotions these body parts are capable of galvanizing in human beings can cover a wide gamut and can range anywhere from utter disgust to excruciating sexual excitement! Believe it. It is true.

Heels—just to illustrate by contrast—reside not only at the literal bottom but as well at the figurative lowest point on that totem pole, at the opposite side of the anatomico-emotional spectrum of the ass, which places quite high on the anatomico-emotional totem pole. Heels could easily be considered the antithesis of the ass, say, to an everyday pedestrian of average proclivities and for whom this would compel much of nothing at all. Heels are like the Switzerland of the body—in the sense that it's a neutral area that interferes with none of the rest of the senses. They don't provoke or stir things around, you understand. Heels are body parts of no extracurricular utility; they are strictly functional. They are conservative as far as anatomy is concerned, and if they could vote, they would probably vote Republican—since they are all about established structure and a bland but stern constitution. As opposed to breasts, who are clearly liberal body parts, more lenient and cooperating and lots more fun and who would vote Democrat. The ear, hmm . . . well, you see, that is a treacherous thing—one would think since it's responsible for such an important function that it would have nothing but function, but no, this fleshy shell of cartilage, if slightly altered in shape or size, can absolutely obliterate an otherwise perfectly good head. Never mind that it is through this weird conch-like, rubbery apparatus that you may get to a woman's heart—were you foolish enough, of course, to go seeking for your own demise this way. Love is a cup three parts honey, one part cyanide—and it's always worth the drink. Because your death is worth the honey.

Eyebrows. Well, very thick eyebrows on a woman can act as a potent deterrent for those strange men who are fearful of complex and heavily populated areas. It is a disorder for those who fear them—equivalent to a type of follicle agoraphobia or something close enough. Heavy, bushy eyebrows on women are often telltale signs of a much deeper concern—especially to said "follicophobes" who are very mindful of these otherwise passable traits. Come on—get retro! Embrace your forefathers. Frida Kahlo, even!

Earlobes . . . well, earlobes are a cherished arena for the connoisseurs, but certainly not a body part topic that should be reduced to the clumsy amateurishness of the layman and thus should be left alone, since the sensibility to appreciate this topic is of such refined and precise scaling that it would be a disservice to cover it in a general casual venue as this is.

Lastly—but not least, in fact, the first to most, except to some in the clergy and all the Castrati—we come to the private body part. The private body part—male or female—is an odd, ugly, small, and powerful monster—who has the tendency (in fact the faculty!) to turn otherwise ordinary, well-meaning, law-abiding pedestrians into loon-crazed, frenzied, troublesome, unnatural beasts! These body parts are one of God's best little jokes and riddles—the catnip of the human mind. They are strange, undecipherable traps! Which in the event of their absence, or come the event of the sudden absence of our inexplicable interest for them, the entire race of people would be wiped from the face of the planet like a Kleenex doing its thing in a college dorm.

Tenth floor. The bell pinged and the doors opened with a breathy swipe, letting the broader silence into that tense, temporary heat of the crowded elevator ride. *Ciao!* he thought to himself as a ricocheting conglomerate of high-grade elevator tension closed behind him. *What is in the ceiling of this elevator? Please, Lord, allow me to see it, too, one day,* he thought to himself with what he may have thought was irony painted in his face. He walked toward the robotic eye of infrared that hinted at an aspiration, a laughable pretension of future, and showed it his card. Beep.

This baffling contraption of modern technology made the door open by forces inconceivable to all who worked there. And yet they made it part of their daily routine as naturally as they understood blunt and evident things. He was in awe every day of this thing, but of course . . . in secrecy! The world evolves beyond us! This pseudo-philosophical thought lodged somewhere in his brain for the moment, and since there wasn't anything otherwise around to complicate things for him this early, he allowed this idle neurosis to linger: In spite of us, technology has its own brain, you know. We have made things that make things that make things. But the result is that no one can understand how the last thing made got there! Nobody can understand how it's . . . possible, how it really works! Not like the hammer. I'm not talking about knowing how to use it. I'm talking about knowing how it works! How it moves . . . technology is an evolution that is upward moving on the inertia of the first idea, damn it!

He pulled the large glass door open. The place was still fairly empty—only partly lit. He liked this. The office gray and empty—not yet fully populated. It was precisely because he was not a morning person at all that he liked it this way early in the morning. Slow.

Sam worked in this place as a temp. The money was good, and things had worked out this way for him. He was, however, in spirit, and truth, a composer—of music: symphonic and chamber. He had studied at Juilliard, but his talents in politics, business, and public relations had all been compromised into his talents in composing. How does that saying go? God gave beards to those with short chins? I don't know. The job in the city paid his bills, but precisely because his political talents left much to be desired, and because of all that comes with having a political mind, debt was for him—as it is for most others—a constant! The people who find their way to become exempt from taxes and debts are criminal conmen and politicians. That's how he thought, because the alternative of blaming himself was unnatural to him. Though they are supposed natural enemies of one another—politicians and criminals—their modus operandi are indistinguishable in many respects. They exist in mutual envy—or perhaps fear . . . or competition? They aspire for the same—dominion. Only criminals are slightly more, um, honest about what they're doing . . . of their intentions at least. You know at least to stay away from a criminal.

There's something about the sociopath that is very attractive and effective out there. We say it's bad but somehow—you go figure—they end up being our leaders. Most of our big-wigs are sociopaths. They have to be! Look at them. Extremist, crazy, hyped up, maniacal, loony personalities rile up people—convince them. Seriously. Extremes win your vote! Pornography. Murder. Deep throat. Die hard! Keeps them stunned and armless—subservient, obedient, paralyzed, shocked, seduced, belittled, infatuated. Sex and death make the world work. Because they are such strong persuaders and subjugators. They are indirect forms of oppression. A country where you have unabashed whores and proud soldiers is a powerful country, because one can fuck you in cold blood and not feel a thing and the other can kill you in cold blood and not feel a thing. This is an intimidating thing. Think about it. Not just anyone can do either of these two. And we got a countryful of these maniacs?

A whorehouse in Cambodia is a very poetic essence of all that. Absolute perversion—double violation, double penetration; sex in the muck; cum and napalm; mud and blood. Somewhere across the globe, I assure you there's an American hand gripping a Desert Eagle .50 caliber semiautomatic pointing at an underage blow-job forehead dripping tears and saliva onto the sand-crusted boots of this man who will be received with shivering flags and confetti and medals upon his chest and a dead twelve-year-old prostitute barely making a dent in his memory. BANG! Birth of a hero!

He who can fuck well and kill well is on top of the food chain up here, folks! Goddess-whores and lauded assassins—they too exist close enough. Come out to your balconies! Bravo to our pornstars and soldierboys. Or else . . .

You'd best eat them or they'll eat you. Who's they? They is you, too. There's no they; only us. The cannibals. The frantic little beasts. Food and the hungry: both the same thing! Who the heck's that gnawing on your back?

Sam didn't start feeling human in the morning until several minutes after his first coffee, and so he went over to the machine to pour himself a mug of hazelnut before heading to his cubicle. Oh, for *cripes* sake, why can't people dump their used filters in the trash once they're done with their thing?

Back at his desk, he put his bag down by his chair and put the mug on his desk. He took off his coat and hung it on his chair. He turned on his computer tower below his desk and sat down. There was a Post-it on his monitor.

> Sam—
> Unless you pay attention to
> this you will be dead before
> the end of the day.
> Please believe—
> It's now 8:38 AM

What the hell is this? He looked at his watch, and it was exactly 8:38 AM. He quickly panned around. All the computers were turned off. No one around his area was in yet—they usually started pouring in around nine o'clock. He got up and looked around. Shana's computer, at the corner, was off. Molly then walked by.

"Hey, Sam."

"Oh, hey, Molly. You're here early today," he said to her—the Post-it glued to his fingers.

"I stayed in the city yesterday."

"Oh." He looked at his finger again and the back of Molly as she walked away. He looked at her for anything—a clue . . . a slip. She betrayed no sign.

This was a weird joke—he thought—but a good one because it had worked! Only it had worked too well; the precise time on the note? That made it a bit too perfect. He walked to the graphics department to look for Dave. He was one to pull something like this, but he wasn't there, and his computer was off. Barbara, the graphic department director, was the only one there—and she was just getting in, turning the lights on.

"Oh hey, Sam. Early bird. What are you doing here?" she asked him. He stood there, looking bewildered, staring at Dave's empty chair.

"I was looking for Dave. But—"

"Yeah, and of course you were going to find him here at this time," she said to him, flinging her gym bag on the table.

"Yeah, I know. I didn't realize. See ya." He crumpled the piece of paper and threw it into Dave's wastebasket.

This was becoming somewhat—if not very—unsettling. He hurried back to his cubicle, looking over his shoulder, and sat back down, turning on his e-mail program and the news. His boss walked in.

"Morning, Sam!" he said, clicking his office light on.

"Oh, hey, morning, Rich."

Unemployment on the rise, the war in the Middle East, another suicide bombing in England. Oh lord. Again. He forced himself into his routine. Tried to ease back into normalcy. Tried to ignore this terribly good joke! E-mail booted up. The most recent message in his in box was entitled "ME." It was from his own work address. The message was dated "Today, March 28, 8:45 AM"! This sent a quick chill up his body. The light all around the office seemed to amplify—everything became more real. He grew cold and vulnerable—like a target. Something he could not see, but something that could definitely see him! This is not possible! I've been here all this time! He looked at his watch, and it marked 8:46. This was no longer a joke; it was growing into something disconcerting. He sprang away from his desk; he didn't dare open that e-mail. He ran to Dave's cubicle. Dave still was not there! He stood there once again looking down at the empty space. Barbara leaned back in her chair. He grabbed the note from his wastebasket, unfurled it, and walked toward Barbara. She wheeled her chair back as he made his way over and spun it around.

"Barbara, I found this note on my desk this morning—some kind of a prank, I guess, though I'm not finding it in the least bit amusing. Do you know anything about it? Do you know if Dave had anything to do with it?" She creased her eyebrow, took the note from him, and grew relaxed again.

"Come on, Sam. Who do you think you're messing with?" she pushed the note against his chest. He grabbed it. "That's your handwriting."

She was absolutely right! My God, how can I not noti—But! A pallor came to his face as the room darkened around him. His sight became muted for a moment, and he walked out of the room without a word. The note clung to his fingers for a few seconds before it dropped to the ground as he walked to his cubicle.

"My own handwriting," he muttered to himself. He hunched onto his seat, looked to his feet, and knitted his brow. He remembered then the ink on the note. The purple ink. One of his own pens. Only his purple pen wasn't in his pen cup. Oh God! He reached into his knapsack and scrabbled among cables, iPod, book, cell phone. Suddenly, he felt it with his fingers. He grabbed it and pulled it out—his purple pen. Impossible. He grew agitated and dizzy—then . . . a small epiphany: I.T. The guys in I.T.! This resonated in his head like the sound of a rock thrown into an empty metal can. This would explain the prank—somewhat. This gave him a small measure of peace, or at least some hope that this thing could, would, stop. The e-mail. I.T. has access to all of this—to everyone's e-mails. They sent the e-mail to me from my own account. He went to a nearby empty cubicle. He didn't want to call from his phone in case they avoided him, kept this thing going. "Hi, this is Dan at I.T. I'm not currently available. Please leave your name, extension, and a brief description of your problem, and I'll get back to you as soon as I can. Thank you." He waited a few minutes and tried once again, and again from a different phone—same thing. Dan hadn't yet arrived, and he was the only one from that department who knew Sam well enough to pull a prank like that.

Sam hung up that phone and walked back to his desk. With trepidation, he moved the mouse; the screensaver blinked off, and the e-mail list flashed on the screen. He raised the arrow to the message—"ME"—and double clicked. What he read sent a brief convulsion through his body and his ears began to ring:

> Now that you see this not a joke, you have to pay attention to everything I say.
> This may very well save your life. At least I'll try. But you must listen . . .

Sam had to get away from there! The note continued, but he couldn't bring himself to read on! He felt exposed, vulnerable. And in imminent peril. What is this? Who is sending these things? How? He had no enemies; he could think of no one who would want to harm him. What was this? He shut his computer off. He jumped out of his chair and flung his knapsack across his shoulder. He needed free open space to get away. He needed somewhere he could think—hide, erase, eliminate somehow what had just happened—whatever that was. Tomorrow! Tomorrow it will be all clear. His instinct against this was powerful, stronger even than what his intellect was telling him—which was that it had to be a very elaborate prank. But even so . . . even if he thought this was what it had to be, he was, regardless, petrified. He framed himself in his boss's doorway.

"Richard, I'm sorry but I gotta go. I have an emergency that—just came up! If anyone has any questions, please have them talk to Rachel. She can help. She knows all my stuff. I'll be here tomorrow, but I really need to go."

"Sure, no problem. I hope—everything's okay?"

"Oh yeah, yeah, yeah, everything is fine. Don't worry. I got it," he said as he started walking. He turned right at the corridor just as Dave was walking in. Sam mechanically looked at his watch. It was 9:07.

"Hey what's up, Sam? Taking an early lunch?" It was obvious he was just getting in—eyes swollen from a hangover.

"Oh, hey, Dave!" Sam said, clenching back on the uneasiness that was brewing in him.

He palmed the exit button and pulled the great glass door open, pushed the red down elevator arrow . . . turned around and waited. There came the ping, and the doors gasped open behind him. He spun quickly on his heel and lunged inside to the back of the elevator where he stood, rigid and nervous. The elevator stopped on a floor below and let in a small group of people. Sam looked at everyone with mistrust. The hiss of loud music came from the headset of a bicycle messenger. Two corporate humanoids talked in a cacophony of counterfeit, empty, and soulless rumbled ranting. If minotaurs could speak, he thought, this is how they'd probably sound. There was that ping once again, and the doors opened to the wide sounds of the lobby. The sounds of people and cars from outside were thrown inside, wafting on the gusts of the revolving doors. He walked passed the security guard and pushed through the doors and onto the city sidewalk. He looked all around as Manhattan spun 360 degrees, and he stood at the center of this gigantic gray carousel.

Sam walked down the block alertly—carefully and fearfully. He cut right and went into the deli at the corner—to Duke's. Duke's was where most of the people he worked with went for lunch. They all agreed that the prices were remarkably high, but the convenience and the quality were good persuaders. There was a Korean woman who worked there; and she wore her hair in a fashion that did not adhere at all to the current rules of contemporary society—some would go as far as to say of the planet! As a matter of fact, it showed a total disregard for order or established structures of fashions or even all sense, even. They call her Coif, or *Le Coiffeur*—but of course not to her face, because that is not polite, or something of the sort. It is not customary to cause a stir in people in our country. Anyhow—the hair itself was a kind of heliotropic headpiece resembling a perfectly groomed helmet that seemed to hover a fraction of an inch just above the skull by forces unknown, but surely similar to magnetism and other influences probably involving the sun and energy panels, one wouldn't doubt.

There was a hint of a partition toward the back of the hairdo that didn't quite manifest, where two small tufts of hair overlapped demurely, precariously hanging on by nothing more than a prayer—and a feeble prayer at that . . . a prayer of a child who is not practiced and who does not yet understand the concept of faith. There was something strange or even stoic about this lady but, at the same time, ridiculous. It was a laughable stoicism—like having a great pride in something silly, pride in inconsequential things. Probably a crystal elephant collection; who knows?

The stiffness of her neck indicated right away that the source of her present pomp was directly related to what resided atop her head. This was obvious and was also the cause of much irritation around the place. She behaved in a way that communicated immediately a fervent belief on her part that the strange hairdo alone bespoke an inherent presence of the sort that signifies a sort of superiority over others. That this is but a mere indicator of the respect she deserves and demands—just as a crown on a king is his symbol of authority and omnipotence, a regal license for granted whims or unchallenged cruelty. She could very well have been delusional, clearly, but to a very fair extent—and giving credit where credit is due—one must agree that to have the courage (or obliviousness) to sport a head manner of that caliber was a thing that surely had to earn several degrees of respect.

She worked the main cash register. A series of stickers, knickknacks, and attachments (such as an array of writing utensils, paperclips attached to rubber bands, erasers, and a stapler) demarcated her space—and her body language and affected movements suggested too a close relationship with someone of relative power around that business—perhaps the owner of the establishment? Though it was clearly not a formal relationship, her secrecy and mystery alone gave her some kind of privileged status well above the rest of the girls at the surrounding cashier stations. Whatever it was, something was up with that one.

Sam made it all the way to the heart of Duke's but was uncertain of what he was to do next! Remaining stealthy and unnoticed was key. But even this would not guarantee he would not be found! This thing had known where he would be—and when. He went to the back, took a right, and opened a door to the refrigerated section. Grabbed a Red Bull. Everyone around him was suspect. He panned his gaze around, wide-eyed. Like a radar scan, he registered every particle of information that made its way into his brain. He processed with raw sensitivity every nuance, every move, every look of everyone. He walked toward the front. At the counter, he fumbled through the display of protein bars. He grabbed a Cliff bar and slammed that and the Red Bull on the counter.

"Seven fifty," *Le Coiffeur* said to Sam in a voice that denoted duty and boredom, and a look that portrayed something beyond the reach of guessing—only that one knows, withholds detailed knowledge of something interesting, something juicy, something unpredictable and bizarre.

He pulled out a ten from his new leather wallet and this time did not protest in his mind about the price. He zipped open a corner of his knapsack and dumped his Cliff bar in there. Duke's was on a corner—with a main entrance facing Broadway, and another, smaller side entrance, on Forty-First Street. He went backward toward the small side door and exited through Forty-First, walking east toward Sixth Avenue. He'd made it to the corner of Sixth when he cracked open the Red Bull and skipped across the street to Bryant Park; he found a shaded, hidden bench where he felt he could shelter himself, have a place to gather his thoughts.

The old carousel that graced the park every year was already set up, but it was not yet in service. It was just stuck there, resting—the lacquered horses and dead light bulbs frozen in eerie silence that unsettled Sam in a gray and strange way. There was something clearly demonic about carousels today. Bad vibes. Something just not quite right about how they go around, and around, and around all the while the horses, frozen in that painful and grotesque grimace—pretending, but imprisoned in synthetic paints and shellac or whatever the heck . . . forced to go around and around and around at the compass of those happy tunes ad nauseam—trapped and tortured behind a hellish grin—of joy? Oh, the glee . . . the children! The souls of the creatures trapped in a cast of wood, seeing the world spinning from within the confinement and arthritic rigidity of their own body/casts; their screams subdued by that steel gag and the ringing of the music, the shrill of the children's piping. Locked-in syndrome! Jean-Dominique Bauby immediately came to mind, and he pictured the French author in his wheelchair, children on his lap, going around and around the thing into perpetuity to his death. How satanic. He grew fearful, and dim.

Now, in that foggy afternoon, accompanied only by the sounds of their own breath in the vacancy of their own horse heads, they wondered—too weak to insist or plea—why nobody noticed. Tomorrow he'd spin around and look at the yellow horse in front of him, contorted into that eternal and rheumatic neigh—a pried-open smile exposing their lacquered teeth and tongues gleaming in the sun. Crimson velvet royal reins attached to the bit for the little kiddies to pull on. The metal fittings made hollow moaning, echoing, and rumbling noises inside the horses. Kick the cast ribs with your boot heels! It was a young boy's world; time to ride that plastic horse in circles until you're too old for it. Look ahead and not outside or you'll throw up! Tons of pocket change slipping, falling on the planks of wood, slipping through the cracks and away from beggars' hands. A waste. A ride. A little moment. Spin in circles till the end of time, when the Apocalypse chips away at the paint, once that all-consuming orb has swept all life into a history none will witness. Four thousand years after that, in an arid flatland of what was, in a bygone era, New York City, the horses will finally crumble to a windblown dust to be set free into a deserted, radioactive, and barren earth.

Sam peeled his eyes off the carousel and shuddered. He looked upward at the leaves of the trees, the peaceful rustling and the sounds of the cars around him, the pigeons, the clouds, the wind, the voices, his solitude, his place in the world, his disappointment that he had so carelessly imposed on himself, his good nature, his loving character, his compassionate personality, his humor, his sense of grief for what is not his, yet it is if by the kinship of a whole humanity as his sister. He finished his Red Bull and sank deeper into this urban sanctuary away from it all—at least far enough. A patch of dirt surrounded by miles of concrete and moving metal and pulsing flesh. He was safe. He crushed the can of his soft drink and for no reason at all lamented war now. Because it was in him to lament such things. Men after the destruction of other men? He thought and hung his thought with the clarity and acuteness of innocence. What is that? What is that?

He decided then to go straight home, spend the rest of the day there—hidden away. Let today just—slip away . . . fade; by tomorrow, this would all be over. The notion of his own death lingered above him though, now—an infernal mistletoe and the grim reaper, his girlfriend. This was no small reason for unrest; it was a strange and dark and perturbing thought. Because it was certain! Death is certain! He obsessed on the matter for a brief length and thought again on the certainty of it. And, to the deeply religious, he thought, uncertain at best. Unfortunately for him, he didn't believe in heaven; this was because he was one of those who believed that one must be completely honest with oneself if with no one else. A sign of true belief was to adhere to the principle of your beliefs 100 percent. And, if one's beliefs were, in fact, that there is a heaven, then one should be more than excited about dying; it's only common sense—yet nobody he'd ever known had ever been excited about this, and he wondered why. If everyone truly believed in eternal bliss, then everyone would be in a hurry to get there. Funerals would be celebrations and not at all what they are today. But that is not the case, and so he deduced that there must be no true believers, only those who, like the rest, are terrified—who would like to believe.

He was reaching inside his knapsack, fumbling through his things, rummaging around for his Cliff bar, when something stuck to his fingers. He pulled his hand out and there was a Post-it note glued to him—written in purple ink. In his handwriting.

His eyes widened in terror. The city around him swelled outward three times its natural size. The Post-it flapped in the wind as he placed it closer to his eyes to read the words in dread:

You can't go home!

9:23 AM

He raised his forearm and pushed his sleeve-cuff aside; his wristwatch showed precisely 9:23 AM! He gasped and sprang to his feet, startling a group of pigeons into sudden flight. He shook the paper off his finger and watched it fall in the wind, sweeping across the dirt, the concrete pavement, and into the bushes.

He grabbed his cell phone and immediately called his friend Adam. "Adam! You have to do me a favor. I'm having a real . . . weird, messed-up day. I can't explain now, but all I can say is I can't go home, man. I need to go to your house—just for today . . . for the rest of the day. I'll explain later," he said, agitated.

"Okay, okay, man. Calm down. Just come here; you know there's no problem here. What the hell is going on?"

"I'll tell you all about it when I get there. I'm coming right over, just don't go anywhere until I get there—please." He hung up and started to make his way to the Port Authority—Forty-Second Street. He didn't want to waste one second. He walked briskly; his breath made fast clouds in front of him. *Why can't I go home? What is waiting for me in my home? Who's been writing these notes for me—and how?* He went through the automatic glass doors at the station and, looking all around him, walked toward the magazine stand. He bought a *New York Times* to use as a shield to conceal himself through the trip. He ran up the escalators to the left, made another left into his gate: Bus 166 via Boulevard East. There was a relatively long line of people, surprising for a workday, he thought, but then it was not often that he made his way into Jersey during the workweek in the morning. He was going to open the paper to block his face when a family pushed against him as the bus made its way to the gate. The people began pouring into the vehicle, pushing all around him. He paid and walked all the way to the end of the bus. When everyone was inside, the bus pulled out of the gate and onto the overpass that led into the Lincoln Tunnel, shade, then the light rushed into the bus, flickering—cool and warm—as the sun hid and peeked behind and beside the buildings as the bus lurched forward. He sat by the window and opened the *Times* wide to block his face from everyone. He was not going to take any chances—so he'd sit this way, all the way to Adam's.

He opened the paper to the Arts and Leisure section and his face chilled frozen as pins and needles rushed through his hands up his arms onto his chest!

There, stuck to the page, on a Post-it, was another note.

Please do not get onto that bus!
9:28 AM

With clenched fists and white knuckles, he scrunched the newspaper up abruptly against his lap. His hands shook, his jaw and arms trembled as he—almost reluctantly—looked into his watch. It marked 9:35! Oh, my God. Too late? I'm already here! Now wh—

There was a commotion in the front of the bus. In a scuffle, he saw a man push two other men back. The bus was, at that point, at the mouth of the Lincoln Tunnel. The one man stood there in the middle of the aisle, holding something in his hand—up high. It looked like a small flashlight attached to his jacket by wires. And the man yelled, "Allah Akbar!"

*   *   *

It was all white—blinding for some moments and without a sound. Then, the omnipresent, overpowering light drew back, revealing everything. Sam unscrewed his squint, looked forward into the space, to see, in front of him or otherwise to find himself nearly at the center of the Port Authority Bus Terminal! He was in the Port Authority Building. But it was empty. There was no one around, not a single person in the whole station. Kiosks, booths, shops . . . all forms of business, vacant—even the sanitation bins, with their brooms and rags and mops attached, lingered statically unaccompanied now. His steps could be heard from every place, echoing throughout the hard hollow amplitude of the large station.

He walked toward the street, past the magazine shop, past the electric double doors, and onto the sidewalk. It was a wide open splay of sky and concrete and iron . . . and this, too, deserted. There was the expected traffic out there—all of it—only, it was all frozen still, and there were no people in any of the cars. Neither were there any people—not one—to be seen anywhere on the sidewalks. The entire city was empty—frozen, fossilized. The traffic light changed from green back to red. The neon signs on the businesses and the LCD billboards kept going, unfazed by the apparent and sudden annihilation of a whole race.

While he crossed the street, he heard the radios inside the cars tuned to different stations and wondered, Whose voices are speaking through the sound waves? Ghosts? There were no birds either, no pigeons, no life at all—except for him.

He looked at his watch. It was 8:22 AM. He passed a newsstand and looked at the newspaper: February 28. Looked at the headlines:

Unemployment Soars

War in the Middle East: War of Necessity or War of
Choice?

Another Suicide Bomber in England

He walked east up Forty-First Street, crossed Seventh Avenue, Broadway, and stood in front of his office building. He walked through the revolving doors—of course, no security. Deserted. He came out as the elevator pinged on the tenth floor and walked in, past the coffee machine, past Dave's station, and into his cubicle. He sat down. The air was crisp in there, and there was total silence. He looked at his watch: 8:37 AM.

The revelation came to Sam all at once . . . a prophecy in this godly instant where there is no time. Existing in the immaterial spaces between moment and moment, where life is not allowed to transit or discover or even know, but only God—and thus only through his allowance that it was so.

Almost in disbelief, he went along with what he now knew he must do. God had pointed the way, and time as such exists only to mortals. He reached into his knapsack and pulled out his purple pen, grabbed a Post-it, and started writing:

Sam—
Unless you pay attention to this you will be dead
before the end of the day.
Please believe—
It's now 8:38 AM

*   *   *

The alarm blared in Sam's ear. He hammered it with his fist, and it was just at this point in his odd dream that the clock on his night table struck 6:30 AM.

He dragged himself out of bed. The sun was strident through the vertical blinds as he brushed his teeth and shaved. He jumped into the shower, then got dressed in the usual hurry . . . put on his watch and flung his knapsack across his shoulder. He stepped out of his apartment and sprang down the flight of stairs. Outside, where he drank the air, fine and chill, there was not a cloud in the sky. He walked toward Boulevard East to the 166 bus stop and looked at his watch: 7:30 AM. He'd beat the rush hour and get there a little earlier.

The bus came out of the Lincoln Tunnel's cavernous gape into the light of the city—like a giant birth, where the bus then roared onto the ramp and into the cool darkness of the gates. He walked out to the escalators and to the din below. He scurried among the mob and the noise, past the magazine shop and the sanitation men, past the ticket kiosks littered with rubble, through the automatic doors, and into the loudness and the moving mass of steel and people that slithered through and out and in all four directions. He crossed the street and got himself the *Times*. February 28—headlines:

Unemployment Soars

War in the Middle East: War of Necessity or War of
Choice?

Another Suicide Bomber in England

He walked into the building and waved to security. There was already a small group of people waiting at the elevator. He nodded to one of the girls who worked on his floor, though he didn't know her name. They all rushed in and were trapped in one of those preciously awkward elevator moments where everyone looks in every direction and tries not to breathe on one another. One passenger looked straight at the ceiling. Sam looked up there but, as usual, found nothing.

The elevator arrived at the tenth floor, and he walked out carrying his ID, ready to flash it in front of the robotic eye. He opened the heavy glass door and let the petite girl pass in front of him. He was certain she would not be able to tug open the large glass doors herself without a cruel, sad effort. He stopped for his morning coffee and dispensed of the refill someone had left inside the coffee maker. He walked to his cubicle, put his bag on the floor by his chair, and turned the computer on. He suddenly saw it!

"Oh my God!" he said audibly.

In front of him in purple ink, in his hand writing, there it was! As he pushed his cuff aside, looked at his watch and read the Post-it note.

He now knew!

Sam—
Unless you pay attention to
this you will be dead before
the end of the day.
Please believe—
It's now 8:38 AM

*   *   *

Sam did not go home then, although he did ask for the day off once his boss arrived around ten minutes later.

Hours after that, he sat at a nearby cafe looking at the television news, seeing himself on the screen, interviewed here looking shaken, and stunned, and somewhat agitated, on how he had saved everyone on his bus . . . how he'd stopped this disaster—one carnage less. "Where is our *savior*? Where is the promised love?" Sam muttered into the microphone.

*   *   *

The next morning, he bought the *Times*—February 29—Headline:

Samuel Salvatore: Savior in Attempted Suicide
Bombing

Two Girls from Ipanema: An Old American Journalist's Prayer and Plea for a Desperate Young Woman at the Edge of Suicide

She'd been standing right at the edge when I first saw her—her name was Simone, I later found out. She stood there looking down to the crowd that had already formed once I made it to the balcony of the *Sol Ipanema Hotel*, where I'd been staying on assignment.

I'm a journalist but I knew at once the *assignment* would take a backseat to things more important than sports. She stood right at the edge of it, and all I could see at first was her black silhouette plastered against gray rolling clouds and those triangular flags lining the crown of the building flapping, as if desperately beckoning. My chest sunk—immediately. And in a moment, I lost all hope in goodness and could think of nothing more than to question to a void how there could be so much cruelty in the world. She could have been no more than seventeen year old, from what I could tell—and already at the edge of death? One—single—step away from it. From the end of everything. I dropped to my knees and began to pray, to pray like I haven't prayed in many years. Many. I heard the firetrucks blasting their sirens from blocks away. Below, many people pulled on the arms of a woman on the sidewalk, who was now collapsing in agony—despair. The most terrible of despairs. Her mother.

I looked up at Simone, her palms pressed against her eyes, then pulling down against her face. Her fingers over her eyelids. Her eyes, crying at the thoughts of her own demolished spirit.

Her body was alive—full! And at the verge of such ultimate tragedy that it provoked in me nothing but hopeless fatality. Powerlessness. Terror. And a sense of horrible . . . simply horrible premonition to a bitter and irreversible and enormous grief. Then what washed over me was confusion: anger! Anger at myself for not having anything to direct it toward.

I beat my own chest. And love surfaced. "Please God, let me be there!" I pleaded. "I can help. I can help. Let me do something. Don't take this girl away. Don't waste this girl away. She's seen too much but she has still so much to see! Tell her of the good things—tell her now of your good things for her! She needs to see these things. She deserves them. And please tell her well. Tell her so she knows, and so she believes." She stood there. So vertical. So still. Strong gusty winds blew in the height! Her chest rose and she breathed deeply. Her body quivered sharply and turned around! Her head . . . and her body. She spoke to someone. I couldn't see. Someone who had made it up there! Simone swung her arms and leaned forward! The crowd screamed in a wave. She touched the ledge with the tips of her fingers, pushed up, and got straight again. She again turned her head. She raised her arm and held it back! She was telling the person to *stay back*! The person slowly moved forward and formed fully. It was a girl! Her name was Silvia, I later found out. She was her friend—her good friend since early youth. She was still a youth! *Oh my Lord!* Silvia got closer and the mother below got to her knees; she locked her fingers. The mother then raised her hand to her daughter, who looked down and pushed her fists against her eyes. Simone trembled.

"Lord, have pity on this child!" I began praying once again. "Look how she trembles! Look at her, Lord; I implore you! Take pity on this suffering girl!" I was screaming now. My fingers had turned white as I clenched them together toward Jesus in heaven. "For all that is good and right and sacred in this world, dear Lord!"

Silvia, her friend, came closer now—her arms outstretched and wide open, her fingers stretched out, tense . . . with all the power her heart could summon!

Simone's arms fell by her side—languid, limp, and lifeless. The finale! She looked up at the clouds! And her chest began to pulsate with fast breathing.

Silvia dropped to the ground unconscious then, and I began screaming across the distance: "*Menina! Menina! Deus sta cá! Deus sta cá!*" (Girl! Girl! God is here!). I screamed this pointing to the ground, pointing to this world and with one hand on my chest so she understood I was telling her the absolute truth!

Simone looked across and saw me. She saw me! "*Please garota!*" (girl), I called into the air, leagues between us, hoping the wind would carry my old and pleading words and convince her—restore this poor and desperate soul. "Step down; step down."

She swayed her arms, side-to-side, and crying, side-to-side, side-to-side. "No, no," I whispered now across the distance. Softly, all the time. All the time. "Take your friend's hand. Your sweet friend; take her hand; take her hand. Go ahead. Take her hand. You see? Now you will be all right."

Silvia now stood practically next to Simone but from the safety of the rooftop below the ledge. Looking up, looking up at Simone: a saint in distress. "Take her hand," I said again. Silvia then put her head against the ledge and began to cry, her shoulders jerking. But Simone bent down—her legs and body trembling—and she stroked her friend's poor little head. Her dear old Silvia, who wept in a sadness with no bottom. Silvia raised her head from the cement ledge, and her eyes welled, drenched in holy water from the depths of her soul. "See how she loves you?" I said. "She loves you. We love you. We all love you. Remember—remember those things worth remembering. They are so many! So many, right? You see? See? You are young, *menina*. You are so young. You can be a fool and silly and all that again. You have to."

But Simone pulled her body straight up again and said a few words to Silvia. Silvia shook her head and put two fists against her chest. Simone began sobbing again. Deeply! Her body jerking. She looked down as Silvia, a few feet behind her, grabbed her head with both hands and then tightened her fists on tufts of her hair. Paced side-to-side, side-to-side, with her hand on her head this way—speaking through her cries. Simone was taking to herself—quickly, then made the sign of the cross very fast across her body. Then she crossed herself again—and again in rapid succession as she raised her chin up toward the sky.

A scream!

And I went blind. My eyes closed on their own.

Below.

Below the mother tore at the shirt of a man. Above. I looked above.

Simone was there! She was still there! This guy seemed to have just gotten there, and the mother beat him now in his face and his body. Two men pulled her away, and the man stood there. Like a lump. He was breathing heavy now, his shirt ripped and in tatters. He was barefoot. The mother leapt at him, and the two men pulled her back again. She shook side-to-side like a chained beast in a rage, both arms outstretched, but they would not let her go until she collapsed from exhaustion on the ground, weeping. Then she threw herself flat on the ground face-down to weep some more as the daughter looked down from the edge. The man was in his sixties—stout and short and something immediately slimy about him to the instinct. Simone looked down and squatted on the ledge.

A black ribbon came flying off her head and her hair blew freely and violently in the wind. Silvia was a statue. Only feet away from her, the palms of her hands pressed against her face. Her eyes, clinging to Simone—to her friend and to her friend's salvation. Below, a skinny man came running from the opposite side—from the left toward the crowd—when the fat stout guy tried to run away. But the skinny man caught up to him at once. He kicked the fat one in the gut and punched him twice in the face when the fat one came down to his knees as if pleading—shaking his locked fingers in a prayer, to have mercy. The skinny man, now wiping tears from his own face, kicked the fat man in the head, and he went down immediately like a pig that had just been shot from a great distance. Simone's mother got up and ran toward the scene and kicked the man in his body and his head. The fat man sat up when everyone dispersed around him! His face was bloodied and his eyes swollen from that beating. But he got up, raising a large revolver and spinning around. He waved it at the crowd and then warned the mother, warned the skinny man. The crowd moved back; some ran away, others dropped to the ground, ducked behind cars. He looked now at Simone, who looked away from him and straight at her friend. "Silvia!" I heard her. I heard Simone yelp! I heard her voice echo through Ipanema as she stretched her hand toward Silvia. "*Salvame* Silvia! *Salvame!*" (Save me!).

Below, the fat man raised the revolver to his mouth. Loud bang!—sputtered echo through the buildings. He shot himself into his skull and dropped to the ground like a sack of grapefruits. Simone's mother rushed to the lifeless body of the man to kick him. To kick and spit on his wretched corpse!

"*Durante nove anos!*" the mother yelled at the lifeless beast. For nine years! For nine years, young Simone had to endure cruel and dispiriting abuse, cruelty and threats in silence from a man, with no regard for her soul, and thus God dispensed his justice here today. "*Porco! Animal! Bestia!*" Her mother beat him to no possible consolation, which only time and the reblooming and healing of her daughter's spirit will bring to all of them.

Simone then sat on the ledge—twenty-seven floors up in the sky—and Silvia came closer. She flung both arms around Simone and pulled her tight, dropping backward to the safety of the rooftop. She would not let her go for many minutes. She stayed there—lying on her back, holding on to her best of friends with all the strength that she borrowed from God. Not moving. Not letting go. She was not to let her go—ever again!

I ran below, and the ambulance and the fire engines and police lights were spinning around this scene. There was a white sheet thrown on the body of the fat man, where blood soaked at the top and ran into the gutters.

The two girls came out of the barren construction site, and the paramedics jumped on them at once, throwing a thick blanket over them for comfort and cocooning them to isolate the shock. Simone was paralyzed. Silvia was drenched in tears and shook violently. Her mother ran up to them as well as the skinny man who followed after—knuckles bloodied: Simone's brother Paolo.

Just before she was pulled into the ambulance, I had a chance to look deeply into those gelatin eyes. I heard their names. Her mother and the medics helped him into the cabin of the ambulance. The medics gave them both fresh oxygen, and just as the doors closed before they pulled away, I was glad I could tell her, "You did good, Simone. You did good. You're all right now. You're safe and everything is going to be all right. Everything is all right now." The doors shut and the ambulance left, blasting lights and sirens. "Today is a good day," I said to God. "Thank you, Lord. Today is a good day!"

I went to fetch the story that was my assignment after this, since it was, after all, the whole reason I found myself in Brazil . . . and let me tell you that it was the best game I've been to—ever, probably!—even though the States lost to Brazil, ten to four.

I'm loving life. Truly.

Ghost of Carmen's Past

She runs her fingers along the nape of his neck. The silver moonlight casts bronze hills on his back. Her weight on the mattress is substantial, broad, warm, and generous. She would have done the same for the past few nights. He could love tonight more just only if she was there.

It happened in November and it is still that November. She could never come back. She would never leave him. Silver and heavy. "Carmen, stay a while—beyond the light and beyond the coming of dawn. Stay here and I won't open my eyes—I promise." The sky is a general birth every morning, erasing the blackness and, with it, Carmen.

Why won't you yield to my plea? The sun is coming—you're gone once again, and again I remain to hope that you'll stay. You disappear. Your weight lifts, and your body dissipates—permeates the walls.

*　　*　　*

The wet wheels on the pavement. The tick of the turn signal inside the cabin of the car. Faint orange light against his hand, and the windshield wipers insist like a metronome. Drops of water collect on the glass. Defunct maple leaves on the curb wash away to the gutters of the town in the scurrying translucent currents.

A cemetery to the left—so long. So many stones. Is it possible? The rain is barely audible inside the car. Three pigeons take off, flying at the light. A woman in black opens her umbrella and steps out of the church. It's Wednesday.

Where am I driving to? That horizon—not far enough. Drives around the block and heads back. Cobblestones and a gray sky. Gets out, shuts the door, and walks inside.

*   *   *

His coffee steams the windowpane. The day is static and colorless. The home is a hollow olive waiting room to a strange, new future. Carmen stands in the hall. She'll walk in any minute.

He doesn't move. Sun brightens slightly and erases her.

He walks, and the rocking chair moves for a while—wishing? Another window . . . and every window just the same.

The sky fades darkly, and the day leaves. He stands in an indifferent obscurity.

*   *   *

We lost Carmen, Sam.

November.

He lies down and pulls the sheet around the bulk of his body. Moonlight floods the room like spilt mercury. The empty spaces of the house condense and form her body. Her weight sinks into a space beside him. Her heat radiates against his back. Her fingers grace his neck again. "It's time, Sam," she whispers in his ear. The heat of her words warms his face and lingers briefly. He sits up in bed before she becomes immaterial.

*   *   *

"She made it, Sam!"

"Have you decided?" The voice on the telephone.

"Yes. Carmen. We'll call her Carmen, like her mother was."

The Loop of String

Matthew was splitting logs out by the cottage when he saw it! He couldn't have imagined it, could he? It was there for way too long.

"Mom!" he screamed across the damp, as he dropped the ax on the moist, leafy earth. His breathing formed quickly in agitated little clouds. His arms hung limp at his sides—fear paralyzed him. "Mom!" he yelled again—louder. When Rachel came in running to the deck, she found Matt standing, wobbling slightly.

"What's the matter, Matt?" she yelped, looking at him and around him. "What's going on?" Rushing, she gripped the wooden railing, swinging her body around and down the steps to find him motionless—his gaze fixed in space, his mouth in an open, silent O! She grabbed him by the shoulder and looked at him deeply—then she looked at that empty space in front of him, at the block of air that seemed to transfix him.

"Matthew, what's going on? What happened? You scared me half to death! I thought—" She took his head in her hands, brought it to her chest, and pressed her lips against the top of his head—relieved, upset!

"What happened, Matt?" she asked again, and he wouldn't look away. He didn't want to lose the precise point, the exact spot where it had been. He lifted his hand and pointed straight ahead.

"Right there. Right here—right there it was."

"Right there what was?" She tucked his hair behind his ear.

"Just right there! At first it just looked like the trees and the leaves were shaking—side to side—like a tornado. A small tornado or—really quickly! But then it all went pink, and a blur! Everything behind that spot—everything beyond that spot was a blur. And then just like that—I saw it! A piece of a house appeared. Right there in front of me—a window. A perfect window. No doubt about it! Only pink, and see-through. It stood there for three seconds—about three seconds."

"Oh, my God, Matthew, you scared the crap out of me," Rachel said. She rolled her eyes and sighed, relieved.

"No! But listen . . ." Matt pushed her away. "You're not listening to me. I actually saw this thing! I was—"

"Matt, you—"

"Jesus! This thing happened right in front of me," he cried in frustration. "I couldn't have imagined it—it was as clear as I see you. I saw the window to this house, and when I looked through the window, I could see a window at the other end of the house too. I saw through the house!" Matt's eyes were wide. He needed her to believe him—after all, he was telling the truth. He had seen what he was describing. Now, whether what he saw was real or not, that was altogether another story.

"Matt—it's okay, honey. Don't be afraid. It's cold out here; you've been swinging that ax, splitting those logs all morning. You're exhausted—got lightheaded. You lifted your head too fast, Matt—you got a rush and saw stars. Come on, I'll make you lunch." She put her arm around his neck, locked it, grabbing her wrist with the other hand, and spun him toward the cottage.

"I didn't see stars, Mom—I saw a house. I've seen stars before. I know what you're talking about! That's not it. When I sneeze, when I get out of bed too fast—that's when I see stars. This was different!" They started to climb up the steps toward the deck into the kitchen. "Oh, my God, totally different."

Rachel was separated from her husband—very recently. It was still fresh, and the fate of the marriage was still undecided. She'd never been one to rush into decisions; she didn't want to do anything she couldn't later take back, especially since she was angry still, and hurt by the whole situation. No matter how one tries to convince the other otherwise, infidelity is not a problem of one. She felt deeply. Infidelity has repercussions! Everyone takes it personally.

And it's one of those things for which the only remedy is to lie to oneself—both parties. She didn't know.

Matthew had just turned twelve. William and Rachel had been married now for fifteen years. William had been unfaithful. Rachel had been nothing but exemplary. When she'd confirmed her suspicions after she discovered a number of tacky and indiscreet clues, she'd confronted him and he had no choice but to confess. Betrayal damages the guilty more than the other way around. Their image is close to irreparable. The significance of this person now becomes warped in every context—past and present—reevaluated to the detriment of the cheater. Doesn't look good. Betrayal in the background was too bitter a thing for Rachel. It was like a looming smoke cloud, now, that followed them everywhere. She was not angry for what he had done to her. She was angry . . . saddened, at what he had done to himself. He had tarnished his own self. What a pity. He isolated the love—and respect—that was only for him, reserved and exclusive. Gone, in one instant. And for what? Sex? Love is such a fragile little thing sometimes. And carelessness will wilt it away, many times beyond resuscitation. Since this separation was not final, there was no need to stress Matt, so he was told his father was away on business—for "a while."

She washed the lettuce and tomatoes in the metal sink, putting them into the strainer that sat on top of the black granite counter. And it was not because she'd believed Matt that she looked at the spot occasionally. She looked because of that strange, childish curiosity that grips us, even when we are in complete disbelief. She flung the water drops off her hands before drying them on the green puffy towel that was folded over the handle on the oven door. From the large metal fridge at the opposite side of the sink, she gathered sliced ham, mayonnaise, and Dijon mustard. Matt pulled off his fingerless gloves and threw them on the counter before walking over to the sink to wash his hands. Matt was an "old soul"—always way too grown up for his age, even when he was still small—at least in his rituals. In his interests and mannerisms, too, he was a young old man. Even Rachel's friends, when asking about Matt, called him her "little old man." Rachel never needed to tell him to brush his teeth before bed, never needed to tell him to wash his hands before dinner, never needed to tell him to go to bed! Everyone knew he got this from Rachel, who was by no means a square, but knew what to do and when and where to do it. Well . . . maybe a bit of a square—why not?

Rachel finished preparing the sandwich for Matt and slid the plate in front of him. He took a first bite, and she poured him a glass of apple juice. He made a face at the juice but didn't complain any further. She thought she'd been unfair. She thought that, at least to humor him, she should give some importance to what had happened—or what he thought had happened, anyhow. Even if she believed—and understood—that overexcitement and exertion had provoked this hallucination, it didn't make it any less important to Matthew; she should make the effort to share his side, show some interest, since it was a fact that it had been a strong enough experience to make a deep impression on him! Speaking about it would be constructive, she thought, and in a way, it'd help Matt let the episode pass and fade . . . forget about it.

"So, Matt?"

"Mmm," he said, chewing. He licked a dot of mustard from the corner of his mouth. He seemed in a daze, and he swung his legs from the stool. He seemed in a trance, deep inside that wilderness that is a youthful mind.

"What was it exactly you saw out there?"

"I told you already." His pupils widened as he returned to the room. "I thought you were paying attention. I would have expected you to be paying attention." He frowned, looked down at his sandwich, and then took a gulp of juice. "It nearly gave me a heart attack!"

"Well, no need to be overly dramatic, Matt." She laughed and pulled a stool close to him. "Just tell me in detail what you saw."

"Okay—but listen this time!" He placed the half-eaten sandwich back on the plate. "Okay, so I was cutting wood out there—you know—then the air . . . the space right in front of me . . . started vibrating! Like . . . a space a lot wider than I can stretch my arms out. About one more arm's length, right? Then, that shady pink thing started forming! After that, the shape . . . the image of the window appeared. Right there! Right in front of me. I looked through the window and I could see through the house! Like I saw through the window—at the window on the far end of the house and through that window as well, to the other side!" he said.

She stayed quiet, looking at him for a little while. Thinking. "And so what was on the other side?" she asked.

"Trees! There were trees on the other side!"

"Well, you see, Matt?" She leaned back on the stool and smacked the granite counter. She twisted her mouth and snapped her fingers.

"See what?"

"You saw a funny shape when you got lightheaded, and the trees you saw were the trees out back! We have trees all around here, Matt. We are in the middle of a forest." She cupped his face. Her hands we cold.

"The trees were spring trees!" he said with a bit of impatience in his tone.

"What do you mean?"

"We are in winter, Ma! These trees all had leaves. They were full."

Rachel stayed quiet again for a while, concerned. Not at all that she would ever think or believe such a thing, but could something be wrong? Could something be happening to Matt?

"What else can you tell me? How did these windows look? What else . . . did you see anything else?"

"Inside, in between . . . I didn't have enough time. Like I said, it must've been about three seconds—or less. So I didn't have time to scope the room. But I could get a general idea—furniture inside. There was definitely furniture there."

"Furniture?" Her jaw dropped.

"Yeah—like a couch. It was dark inside—a couch, maybe some big armoire off to one side. I don't know. But there was definitely stuff in there." He lifted the sandwich, nodding, raising his eyebrows.

"Mmm . . ."

*   *   *

"Well, there doesn't seem to be anything wrong with the boy's eyes, Mrs. Dudda," Dr. Collins said after examining Matthew with his small flashlight. "His pupils are responding normally, and also his blood pressure is normal, and his other vitals. He's twelve, Mrs. Dudda. I understand, as a mom, you should be looking after your son's health—well-being—but trust me, he's strong as an ox! You don't need to be worrying about him this much." He put his hand on Matt's head, winking at the boy, who shook his head at his mother's overprotectiveness. "Put your shirt on, son. You're done."

Matt lifted his shirt back up over his shoulders and buttoned it. He leapt off the examining table—his sneakers squeaking on the floor.

"Wait for me out there, Matt. I'm coming right out," Rachel called after him as she grabbed her purse and flung the strap over her shoulder.

"Doctor?"

"Don't worry, Mrs. Dudda," the doctor said, swinging his chair around, taking his wire-frame glasses off and holding them on his lap. "It is not uncommon for young kids to have these kinds of episodes. Especially when they are overly excited—stimulated. Like you said, he was in the yard, doing heavy exercise—with an ax! Short, momentary hallucinations—or misinterpretations—are far from rare at his age, okay? And these are certainly not from any physical anomalies or other problems. He is fine, Mrs. Dudda." The doctor got up, placed his hand on her arm, and led her out of his office.

*   *   *

"Well, I had to take you, Matt. I was worried. Maybe there was something wrong with your eyes. I'm sorry for being concerned, but . . ."

They were driving back home. Rachel's hands firmly grabbed the wheel to the SUV. The road was winding and buried deep in the midst of woods. Matthew looked out the window quietly. He wasn't at all upset, although by his silence and unresponsiveness one might think he was. He stared out the window at the passing trees—most of them already barren. The road, unusually hypnotic today . . . numbing . . . a moving trance. The repetition of the wooded scenery, the lines on the road passing beneath the vehicle, the steady vibration rolling under them . . . a visual metronome.

They arrived, and Rachel turned slowly into the pebbled driveway, pulling up to the side of the cottage. The air was thin and smelled of snow. A milky smeared mist was suspended just above the water of the lake that was some distance off. There was a small dock where two rowboats were tied up. Matt looked toward the lake, and his mother—after a flawed hesitation—asked him, "Do you want to go fishing or something, Matt?" She tried to compensate for her guilt, clearly. She sensed that maybe Matt felt his feelings had been dismissed—that he had not been taken seriously.

He had gone fishing alone already several times before, so she trusted him—and besides, he was a good swimmer; there was nothing to fear. Though she would always keep an eye on him.

"Sure, why not?" he said, his face brightening up. She motioned to him with her head, and he immediately sprung toward the back of the house and into the shed, where he grabbed his fishing rod from behind the door. There were several others rods, older ones, on the wall, but this one had been a gift from last year's holiday—this one was expressly his, and from Dad. He also grabbed an orange life-vest, a metal can, and a small shovel. The shovel and can were for the bait. His father had taught him how to dig up earthworms. His mother was making her way up the steps of the deck when he came running out with all his gear.

"Don't go too far, Matt."

He knew where to go for the bait. The previous year, his dad had shown him one spot by the roots of a big mossy elm tree when they'd gone fishing together. Matthew missed his father markedly—and expectedly—since it had been a couple of weeks since he'd seen him last, and although they spoke regularly on the phone, it wasn't at all the same.

When he'd dug about ten or twelve earthworms, Matt walked to the small pier and put the rod and the can on the bottom of one of the boats. He got in, causing the boat to rock from side to side. He sat and grabbed hold of the oars. Looking back, he dunked them both into the water—a soft, boomy, watery sound swelled up and filled the entire radius of the lake. He began paddling toward the middle, cutting through the immobile, thick mist like a finger through a cake's icing. His view of the house and the lake, like a scene not wholly real because of its perfection, orbited around him. The water was a flat plate—the boat slid through the surface, digging a smooth streak that followed closely behind. The cool air chilled the back of Matt's neck, causing bumps through his arms; he shivered. All around him was a gray, pasty, dull green—vast—as if he were the last person on the face of the earth. He could see the indistinctive silhouette of his mother walk by the large window at the side of the cottage like a ghost that takes form and then withdraws. A choir of trees stood as a silent army surrounding the lake, and not far through the distance, there was an island on the other side, deeper in the true middle of the lake. The island was not inhabited; it wasn't sturdy enough to build on it. The ground was swampy, and he planned to one day go explore it.

This is far enough, he thought and pulled the oars inside the boat, placed them down along the length of the embarkation. He grabbed the rod and pinned it between his thighs. He picked up the bait can, but before he pulled an earthworm out, his attention diverted to the spot. He was visited by a brief fear that sent a shudder through him. There it was—still, vacant, ominous but undisturbed now. A brief space—air, trees, dirt, dead leaves, and some rocks—nothing more, nothing less. He pulled out the worm and held it in his fingers as he lowered his eyes toward it, wriggling it between his fingers. He grabbed the hook and, with his thumb, removed the cork from its tip. Then, he pierced the worm, sheathing the hook into it—the body of the worm revealing the metal as it traveled up its pinkish translucency. The worm, impaled on rusty iron, began to die, and Matt pondered the pain of the animal—if it was equivalent to ours, since it's not a concern we are ever taught to entertain when it comes to things such as these. To ponder the pain of those who are dissimilar to ourselves is an esoteric, useless fancy. As a matter of fact, the consensus universally seems to be—at least by what our behavior confesses—that those who are dissimilar deserve to suffer.

He dropped the hook-and-bait into the water below and waited. He waited, but not without thinking and fixing his mind on what he had seen . . . what he knew! The sky shifted above him slightly as he waited a while longer, and his mood flattened into a stagnant hazy lapse.

As he slumped and anticipated sadly for that bite, he looked at the spot often and for long periods at a time. Then, too, he grew sure of what he wanted to do. He knew he would see it again. He was going to see it again because he was going to wait for it as long as he could. He wasn't imagining things. No, and he knew that much. He looked at his legs; his pant legs had ridden up, revealing a fragment of his shins. He grinned with pride: puberty was striking, and his legs were starting to get hairy.

Something then tugged at the line.

*   *   *

"What did you get?" asked Rachel as Matt trudged into the house.

"I got this!" Matthew lifted the catch of the day by the gills. One fish—one miserable, small, gray fish. "Can I eat it?" He jutted his chin forward with a grin.

"Sure, but you have to clean it and gut it yourself," she told him, repulsed at the sight of this poor animal.

"No problem!" He dropped it in the sink, and a clammy, moist splat rang on the metal; he went through the drawers for a knife and found the one with the yellow handle and serrated top ridge that was just for scaling and gutting misfortunate fish just like this one. He knew this from last time. His father had taught him how to do it—how to hold the fish so that he didn't poke himself with those spiny fins, and how to scrape against the grain, how to scale before gutting so as not to get any of the scales inside the fish.

He liked scaling, he thought, as he began the process; he liked the sound of it too—like a small toy machine gun. He daydreamed as the scales shot in all directions like slimy plastic confetti, sticking to the sides of the sink . . . to his hands—one or two flipped to his lip! He grabbed one of the larger scales with his thumb and index finger and looked closely at it, turning it against the sunlight, seeing the rainbows that formed on it . . . a tiny flake, like a prism.

The fish was scaled clean. Not a single scale left on it. He rinsed it and ran his hand down its limp, wet, rubbery body—placed it on a paper towel. He washed all the scales off the sink and swept them into the compost. He placed a hand on top of the fish and held it firmly while he made a fine and careful slit along the bottom of it. Then, with his fingers, he gutted it under the pressurized jet of warm water.

His mother was sitting at one of the stools just staring at Matt; she could hardly believe how he had grown; he was almost a young man already. Where had the time gone? She looked at Matt with a surge of melancholy. She thought about past years and about William. Her son was a lot like William too.

Matt worked on that sad fish so seriously, so purposefully. Rachel almost knew what Matt thought about—he looked as if he felt almost prideful of the fact that he now could do things. He had a knife, and the catch of the day! This was certainly not a duty of children, he probably thought. Yes, he was likely proud; he looked that way.

"I'm going to wait for it," he said to her, grabbing a dish from the cabinet above and placing the cleaned fish on it.

"What?" She was pulled from her trance.

"I'm going to wait for it. Tonight! I know I can see it again."

"Oh, Matt. Can we let this go?" she said, dropping her arms to her sides. "Do we really need to dwell on this, honey?"

"Ma," he said, waving the wet knife in the air, "you're not taking me seriously! I told you I saw what I saw. I'm telling you. I'm going to see it again."

She sighed. "Matt, it's not that I'm not taking you seriously, honey, it's that we went over this already. I don't want you to start . . . obsessing over this now." She stood and crossed her arms—shook her head. She was about to speak again when—

"I'm not obsessing. Clearly you don't understand. I just want to make sure—for me." Nodding, he washed the knife with soap and water and put it in the strainer. "It's for me, okay?"

"Fine, Matt! Do what you want. But I don't want any part in it. I told you already how I feel about this. I'm over it." She backed away.

"Fine. I never asked you to be part of . . . anyhow, that's fine. I was just telling you. Do we have any limes?" he asked, taking the knife back out of the strainer.

"Huh?"

"Limes. I want to marinate this."

"Oh, yeah . . ." She went to the fridge. "One—two?"

"One's okay, I think—it's small so . . ."

"Here." She handed him the lime; they avoided eye contact.

*   *   *

There was a flickering green glow coming through the window, but he could not hear the sounds of the television. He had grabbed a striped canvas folding chair, a bag of Twizzlers, and a thermos full of apple juice. His mother was adamantly opposed to junk food, something Matt could never understand, but the guilt she had felt earlier that day had persuaded her to buy him a pack of Twizzlers—and she almost bought a bottle of Coke, but he had to settle for apple juice.

The fish had been surprisingly good for being so pathetically small and ugly; Rachel had suggested adding white pepper and sage to the marinade, which had really made it that much better. She had a bite of it after much insistence from Matt, and she was surprised, in fact, that the little monster could yield—unbeknownst, and in fried death—such pleasures to the human senses.

He waited and waited there—and it seemed to be the theme for Matt this day: to wait. Waiting at the doctor's office, waiting for his meal to bite, waiting for the fish to fry . . . and now, waiting for this. Whatever this was. He was growing impatient and was running out of things to keep himself busy, so he started throwing pebbles at the spot—in an attempt to maybe provoke a reaction of some sort. He didn't know, but he wanted something to happen. He wanted to prove—even if only to himself—that he certainly was not crazy! But then, as he was fading surely through boredom and into slumber, and as twilight had come to transfigure the sky into a violet mysticism, it happened. He dropped the thermos as he was picking it up for a sip when it appeared, and in a matter of seconds, it happened again! Only this time, it was longer—and something else happened!

He sat there frozen and open-mouthed when the pink vibrations began. There was a faint ringing in his ears from nerves when the window came into view not three feet away from him. He had been right about what he'd seen beyond it. A couch! And from it—clearly and without question—a girl began to rise! As she stood, their eyes locked. Her eyes grew wide and her face looked frightened! She thrust her face forward in disbelief, her eyes piercing straight and inarguably at him. She moved her mouth, saying something, only there was no sound at all to be heard. She then pointed straight at him right before turning abruptly, tripping on the floor, and running then in the opposite direction—away from him!

It had all happened in a matter of seconds. He was petrified! There was no question. There was a girl sitting in that room, looking straight at him! Not only did he see her, but she seemed to have seen him! She knew—saw—he was there also. She looked scared by what she had seen. Horrified, even. And she was moving her lips—talking, telling . . . telling somebody.

"Mom!" Matthew ran into the house, his voice trembling under his thumping heartbeats—apple juice all over his shirt and pants. His mother jumped and turned around. "Okay, you can't! You have to believe me here! You just have to!" He was extremely agitated. He was hyperventilating, and his temples were beaded with sweat.

"Okay, okay, okay." Rachel raised her voice, got up, and grabbed him by both shoulders, trying to calm him. "Okay," nearly whispering now to subdue him. "Tell me!"

Matt went around and plopped himself on the armchair, unwound his scarf, and threw it on the ground. "I saw it!" he said and sighed. "I saw it again. Only this time it was worse!"

"What do you mean worse, Matt—what did you see? What happened?" she asked him, sitting at the edge of the couch.

"Oh, my God, it was bad! It was—it was longer this time, and I saw someone. I saw someone behind the window, inside the place." He pointed in front of him, palm open, fingers forward like a blade, his eyes wild and red. "She was sitting. As soon as I looked in the window, she was already there. She looked at me! I was petrified! But when she looked at me, she looked scared. She looked straight at me and looked scared of me," he said, scrunching his fist against his chest. "She pointed straight at me! Straight at me and she said something—but there was no sound. Then she ran away from the window and everything went away."

"Matt . . ."

"Mom, I'm telling you the truth. I'm telling you the truth! There's some spooky shit happening here!"

Rachel was worried; she was concerned—what could be happening to Matt? If this was a new phase, she had no idea how to cope with it. What could she do? How do you go with the flow with something like this? How would William deal with this? Was this in some way a response to Matt's father being away? Did Matt have a hunch, maybe, about the separation? All these questions raced through her mind as she tried to figure a way to deal with her son's emotional misdirections. She knew well that children's responses, their emotions, tend to misfire. She couldn't know for certain what was happening with Matt.

She slapped both her legs audibly with the palms of her hands and got up. "Okay, Matt, tell you what!" she said, feigning belief. "Tomorrow, I'll sit with you out there—for as long as it takes—and wait for it with you." There was a pause before he spoke; he tilted his head to one side, suspiciously—but then was convinced.

"Thank you," he said to her plainly His hysteria had certainly subsided, and he seemed relieved that at least she was willing to take him seriously—as far as he knew, anyhow. "Thank you, thank you!

And I have another idea," he said, tapping on his temple manically. "I will make a sign!" A grin crept across his face.

"A sign?" she said as she walked around the couch. She didn't understand, and things kept getting . . . weirder for her.

"Yes. A sign. I couldn't hear what the ghost said, so I'm guessing she can't hear me either."

"Ghost? These are ghosts now?"

"What else?" he said to her, running upstairs.

After a short while, he came back with his whiteboard and markers. He popped the cap and wrote on two lines across the board:

Are you dead?
What year?

He snapped the cap back on the marker and shoved it in his pocket. "You can't make it so long that they can't read it. It lasts for only a few seconds, so . . ." He showed the sign to his mother.

Rachel grabbed her boy and held him close, kissing him on the head. She then walked into the kitchen and grabbed a glass from the cupboard and filled it at the faucet, all the while looking outside. It was all black and hollow—and to the right, the lake lay inky and still, and lights from a house on the other side made their way crisply through the glassy night like yellow earthbound stars, twinkling bits of fragmentized purity.

She came back into the living room. Matt was flipping channels. "Nothing good is on," he said, flipping too quickly for her to make out anything in particular. They flipped channels for the rest of the night, and Matt talked for several minutes to an unconscious Rachel before nudging her to a sudden and disoriented semiconsciousness—like a jump-cut in a movie where the brain scurries and gathers all the scrambled pieces of one's confirmable reality at once and in a fumbling hurry—where in less than a second you need to assess place and context . . . and of course identity, hopefully.

Reality: where the mind lives incarcerated, confined by dictums of physics and the approximations thereby dictated by five senses into a composite of gathered incoming stimuli. The price to pay for living . . . truth, but God knows we all keep trying to escape even that by the vicissitudes of our imagination, who so frantically wants to flutter away from itself when in oppression and confinement—or even stagnancy. He (God) is himself witness and manifestation of this. Since creation itself is the part of God that confesses a need, thus a dissatisfaction with what was available to him. Our need to create is but the mirror dissatisfaction of God's primordial universal angst . . . that inexplicable artistic necessity to fill with his whim what mute need was begging to be brought about. There's gotta be more than the present truth, God thought, and he created the cosmos. Because nothing was not enough existence. Something is an improvement upon nothing—and thus so on and so on goes on, creation. It goes on forever, improving upon its former.

And so we stretch and continue this tradition, only in our scale, but our form, like the cosmos and its laws, will be inseparable from God's way. Not just man, but all is in his form, because all is him. Of course, this is only one way to read the all. We read with our eyes, the blind with their digits, and at the end, there might be only one book, but a billion ways to read it. And they will all be right ways. Right is like, what makes sense, or what looks good; it always depends on who you ask.

God doesn't necessarily have to exist. If you don't wish. But if he does, he's something like this: He feels for you when he doesn't even have to. A feeling soul without a practical necessity to have this feeling . . . is perfect. Because in the emotion, without reason itself, lies absolute sincerity, absolute love.

God as creator but as artist and as an entity with the capacity to be dissatisfied, and even in his largess, capable of this we call weakness. A being omnipresent but as well with a need for love and for our comfort. He needs us not to serve him, but more to help him understand himself. He's perfect in every way, in the way we even disappoint ourselves. In giving us freedom, he gave himself grief.

Rachel woke up fully as she and God suddenly separated their communion. Matthew got up. And they both went up to bed.

*   *   *

Rachel was already making breakfast when Matthew came down in his flannel pajamas, his hair awry, but his teeth already brushed.

"Morning."

"Morning."

"So today's ghost buster day, huh!" he said to her as he took a seat on the stool by the granite slab island in the middle of the kitchen, the heel of his hand squeaked on the surface as he drew it across and rested his chin on his forearm.

"Yes, it is, my friend. Yes, it is. I'm ready to be, umm, spooked out of my socks!" she said, sliding a plate of scrambled eggs and ham across the counter. Matt stretched his arm out, pulled it toward him. She slid him a fork.

"Okay, so," she started, "I'm going to make twenty sandwiches to last us, bring a bucketful of water, and if we have to go to the bathroom, well, I guess it's the trees' unlucky day." She scooped some scrambled eggs with the spatula onto her plate, grabbed a stool across from Matt, and started her breakfast.

"The earlier we start, the better," he said, his voice muffled through a mouthful of egg. "That way we won't miss it!"

"Okie dokie." She opened her eyes wide, nodding.

*   *   *

They dressed in many layers. It was cold that day, so they wore plenty of wool. They wore hats, hoodies, and mittens. Rachel had made sandwiches and brought a Gatorade cooler full of water. They brought two folding chairs and the phone.

"Is there anything in particular we should be doing to call them?" she asked.

123

"Mom! It's not a séance. I don't know how this stuff works." He propped the whiteboard sign on his chair facing the spot. He put the marker in his chest pocket.

He looked critically at the board. "There, I think it's dark enough," he said, looking at it—he had gone over the letters once again that morning.

They sat from ten to noon. Nothing happened, and Rachel was beginning to get tired of it. Only she couldn't break the silence, break the promise, break character . . . her pretending. So she endured the wait—grabbed a sandwich and fixed her sight on the Canada geese circling the lake. Slumping on her seat, she wondered tiresomely when this would all end—when Matt would finally give up. She hoped to God he wouldn't make her stay there the entire afternoon!

Then it happened! It hit her all at once like a ton of bricks and a knife of ice through her spine! The air began vibrating and shaking right in front of her eyes! She was frozen, and a billion impossible thoughts ran through her brain. She could not believe this. It was just as Matt had said. He hadn't lied! The air—at almost touching distance in front of her—was vibrating, and there was a pink glow forming. Matthew adjusted the angle of the sign in the direction of the disturbance.

Are you dead?
What year?

The shaking pink haze then came into sharp formation, and there it was, standing in front of them. The window was translucent and pink but clear and real. Clearly standing behind the window, they saw a girl and a man. The apparitions appeared frightened, and they were staring straight at Matthew and Rachel, who then noticed the girl had a paper in her hand. The man and girl stood, mouths agape. The girl flashed her paper and pressed it on the glass of the window:

Are you ghosts?

They stared stone solid, and there was no question. They were all aware of each other's presence. In a matter of seconds, the entire scene dissipated and everything returned to its former normality. Rachel sank into her chair unable to move. Her jaw dropped as her stare fixed on an empty spot midair.

*   *   *

"Well, Matt, there obviously has to be a logical explanation to all of this stuff," she said to him, biting the skin on the knuckle of her ring finger. The curtains were drawn. She'd rushed them both up to the cottage immediately after the vision had dissipated.

"I told you I wasn't bullshitting you, Rachel," he said. He was sitting on a kitchen stool.

"Mom. Mom! I hate it when you call me Rachel."

"Mom."

"I see that. I see that, Matt. What the heck is going on? Is this place is haunted or . . . ? What the hell am I saying?" she said, pressing on her temples, holding the phone in one hand. "I don't believe in ghosts. Do you believe in ghosts, Matt? You don't believe in ghosts."

"Well, I don't believe—I mean I didn't believe, but this thing . . . what the heck is this thing if not . . . ?" He couldn't finish.

"This is just bizarre—too bizarre. I'm—"

"Yeah but—I mean ghosts, but—but they had a sign too, Ma. They were asking us if we were ghosts—and they looked scared . . . petrified! So if they're not haunting this place and they're not ghosts, what the fuck are they?"

"Matt, language, please! But, yeah . . . this is just . . . I mean, I saw them, Matt. They were standing right there in front of us. They were looking straight at us. They knew we were there looking at them. I mean they knew!"

"I know. It's real. But what the fuck is it?"

*   *   *

The next morning, Matt woke up early. He was the one to make breakfast this time—scrambled eggs, buttered toast, ham, apple juice.

Rachel walked into the kitchen; her son looked up from the pan. "Hey!" he barked lowly.

"Hey, Matt," she rasped in a morning voice and sat on a stool. "What's the deal, what are you doing?"

"Ah . . . I woke up early, couldn't sleep anymore. How'd you sleep?" he said, looking at her, studying her, then laughing. She didn't seem to find it very amusing. "I was thinking—"

"Oh—what were you thinking?" she said, grabbing a piece of toast from the plate.

"Well, I think we gotta go wait for it again today," he said as she sunk her teeth into the toast, chewed, and swallowed.

"You have to be kidding me. We are leaving! And we are leaving soon. Today!"

"No, no—wait! Just hear me out. We have to wait for it again. It's obvious this stuff—or they—don't mean to hurt us anymore than we want to hurt them. Right? I mean, they are just as surprised about us as we are about them! Did you see their faces? They haven't got a clue either! I think they want to know what's happening as much as we do. You saw their sign. They think we are haunting the spot! They read our sign. We'll answer theirs and see if they come back with anything." He slapped some scrambled eggs onto a plate and slid it over to her. She sighed and looked beyond Matt, and beyond the window behind him, into the trees and the dirt beyond them.

*   *   *

It was around 4:30 PM, and they had been taking turns out there—in and out. And sometimes the two would stand out there together. Matt held the marker. He had written a new sign:

Not ghosts
Where are you?
What's happening over there?

This was not particularly clever, he thought, but as he was a novice at communicating with the beyond, he figured these questions would be as good as any. If they were ghosts from the past, he would certainly find out more about them. Now that it was almost certain he and his mother ran no risk of harm, they were more at ease. The terror was now replaced, however, by sort of anxious curiosity. As Rachel came down the stairs from the deck, the area became disturbed again. Matt stood in front of it, holding the sign.

"Come here! Run, Ma!"

She ran quickly and made her way next to Matthew just as the scene came into focus. Those on the other side had the look of anticipation—and of heightened alertness. But they too no longer looked fearful.

They stood there side by side. The girl held the man's arm closely, almost shielding herself with it. The man stood tall and lean. The girl was very pale, and with fine lips and very a fine, birdlike nose, and large, feline eyes that tapered at the corners, slanting slightly upward. She had dark hair with an unusually strident gleam. The man had a full white head of hair although he didn't look very old at all—around forty, if that. His beard was also all white and trimmed very short around the contour of his jawline. Their clothing was very odd and not at all familiar . . . impossible to describe. It was only after reading the ghost's sign that the full impact of this spectral scene hit Matt and Rachel:

Not dead—year 2500. You?

The scene, as it had before, faded to nothing, leaving Matt and Rachel in the lonesome dusk with only the trees and crickets as their scenery.

Ghosts! Ghosts? They had not even been born yet. *Their grandparents' grandparents had not been born yet*, Rachel was thinking as she stood in place. This was 2010! To the man and girl in the window, Matt and she had been dead for hundreds of years now. A living ghost! Is that what I am—is that what Matt is here—everyone? This is nuts! She was at a breaking point, nearly, and suddenly she turned and ran up the deck stairs into the house.

She grabbed the pone and dialed her friend Clarise in Boston.

"Clarise!"

"Yeah?"

"Hi, honey, it's Rachel."

"Hey, Rachel, sweetie, what's going on—"

"So I'm not dead, right?"

"Huh?"

"I'm not dead! You're talking to me on this phone, right?"

"Rachel—" Clarise started laughing at the other end. Matt walked into the kitchen, holding his sign. "What the heck is this, babe?"

"Okay, you see—so I'm alive and not a ghost. 'Cause ghosts don't talk on the phone or eat sandwiches, do they?"

"Um—not that I know of. As far as I know, they scare the living shit out of people in Victorian attire."

"Okay. What do you know about time travel then?"

"Huh?"

"Time travel!"

"What the—well, I can get you a nice . . . umm . . . used time machine—it's got a few million light-years on it, but it's in good condition—but you gotta give me about a week." Clarise started laughing.

"No, Clair, seriously! Didn't Joseph tell us something about 'bout time travel one—?" Clarise's husband Joseph was a physicist. And Clarise was a casual student of the paranormal.

"Not time travel—but a fold in time. There's this idea that time can be . . . depressed—it can be affected by an event."

"What do you mean, an event?"

"Well, from what I understand . . . Okay so, just as black holes bend and absorb light, they also affect time! I can't really understand all that too well. It makes no sense to me, really, but Joseph explained it to me like this: Think of time like a string—a long, long string stretching in both directions to infinity, right? Now let's say you take that string and place two fingers—one of each hand—at two points in the string. These are two different points in time. Follow? Now let's say you start bending this string by bringing these two points together until you make a loop in the string. And you then touch your fingers and make the two points in the string meet. This, then, causes a depression or a distortion of time—two different points in time meet! So, theoretically, when this happens, one can see things and people from those two points in time. I mean—the people from point A can see people from point B . . . and vice versa."

"Oh, my God! But what makes this happen? I mean what could make this happen? This fold in time."

"Well, supposedly something powerful enough to bend it. I don't know—an event that's so cataclysmic and large it can affect time. Which, I mean, has to be pretty heavy stuff. You certainly can't do it with a time machine, if that's what you're thinking." She laughed. "Why? Are you trying to go to the past and stop that bastard husband of yours from sleeping around? Sorry, I couldn't stop myself!" She laughed again.

"Oh, screw you, Clarise!" said Rebecca, a bit hurt, but chuckling a bit, finding the humor in her friend's comment. "Listen, I'll call you later, I gotta take care of something here with Matt, okay?"

"Okay, honey-cakes. You know I'm here if you need any more info on time travel and the paranormal—or anything else supernatural. M-kay?"

"Mmmmm . . . Bye!" She hung up the phone and looked straight at Matt, but it was as if she was looking through him. He turned, went into the kitchen, and closed the door behind him. Rachel followed him into the kitchen. Looking to keep busy, she made some pasta while explaining to him, as best she could, what Clarise had said about the bending of time.

"Matt, they're not ghosts, just as we are not ghosts. They are alive, just as we are, only we are not there yet. But where they are, we are already long gone. Does that make any sense?"

"Actually no. It makes no sense. But whatever it is, I think it's pretty, ahmm . . . pretty fucking cool is what it is, how it all happens actually, how they can see us like that!"

"Yeah, I guess it's pretty cool," she said, putting some oil in the pasta water, looking straight outside, now trying to wrap her brain around what she had seen and could almost comprehend, though hardly believe. "We need to go back there tomorrow."

"Oh, for sure! What did you think?"

"And stop cursing like your father."

"Well, someone's gotta do it!"

She laughed.

*   *   *

2010—New York State
Matthew and Rachel (Mom)

Matt carried the sign outside. They had left the chairs out there. Once again, Rachel had brought the Gatorade thermos and sandwiches in a cooler. It had rained during the night, and the wind, still moist, smelled of earth and wet bark. Their wait was to be expected, of course, but even boredom couldn't erase the apprehension—that small seed of unexplainable fear that lingered despite their new—and less frightening—understanding of this odd phenomenon.

This time, it came at once. After they had been waiting for just a short while, it began. The distortion started and seemed more erratic than usual. The space in front of them shook in all directions, violently and with a snapping sound now. A muted crackling was also now coming through—like the sound of coal emptying into a grill, or firecrackers inside a barrel in the distance. That's when it appeared. The father and daughter stood up from the couch and ran toward the window. They were frightened once again, though not frightened at them this time—something else . . . something horrible . . . imminent! The girl held her paper against the windowpane.

Second York
Armageddon
Soon

The image was fully formed but kept vibrating, shaking, convulsing! They looked at Matt's sign. The girl read it. She looked into Matt's eyes with the semblance of terror and despair—she looked into Matt and Rachel's space, around the cottage, the forest, beyond the trees. To the girl, it was an impenetrable window into an unreachable safe heaven! Salvation was so close yet so impossibly far. Matt dropped his sign, and Rachel grabbed him and held him close to her as he was making a run toward the impalpable window. More than ten seconds had already gone by, and the image still remained, though shaking violently as the color intensified. The girl let out a yelp, though there was no sound except for the continued crackling. The man and the girl spun their heads around and looked behind them!—and through the window, far beyond it, they saw. The great flash! A dome . . . like a massive, giant egg yoke—a great dome of light that blackened the sky behind and above them, the sky that had been bright and blue only seconds ago. The dome began expanding, growing in diameter and swallowing everything as it grew. The girl dropped her papers. Before the dome reached them, they turned once again to face Matt and Rachel. Their faces trembled, and they had no choice but to close their eyes, bracing each other, father and daughter, hunching forward, they caught fire! They did not move. And there, aflame, their clothes ripped from their bodies; then along with it, all their skin tore from their bones upward with the ease of disrobing. A tornado of fire swallowed all things.

The entire image before Matt and Rachel then turned into a large block of intense light—a bright square glow and nothing else. The square hovered there for a short while, where it then quickly tightened to the size of a pinhole—incredibly small, impossibly bright! The crackling turned into a singular steady ring, and the pinhole disappeared—like the last insignificant and singular vestige of a fire, that suddenly extinguishes to nothing.

Rachel gripped her son tightly in front of her. They stood motionless for several moments, their gazes transfixed in midair. Matthew released himself from Rachel's hold. He took two steps forward. His ragged breathing seemed to be the only sound in the whole broad space.

"Oh, Lord, Matt," she said through a breath. Matt turned.

"What just happened, Ma? What just happened?"

"The End, Matt. The End just happened," she said, her gaze fixed on the vacant, lifeless space.

"The End of what?"

"The End of everything."

*   *   *

Epilogue

Through a fold in time, an event so powerful had changed the very fabric of all history—and the loop of string met there. Only then, only there—and only them: Matthew and Rachel came to bear witness to the end of all time . . . the end of our time and of the world as we conceive it.

Armageddon had brought about this event as we had brought Armageddon upon ourselves. In a few otherwise insignificant instances, a boy and his mother had seen, in front of their eyes, by a cottage near a lake, an entire humanity disappear into a flash of light the width of a pin. But what was the use? What could be their use? Who in their right minds would ever believe them? Who would believe something like this? And, even if someone did, what could possibly be done about it?

Hence the third era of the blue planet will begin anew from the dust to which we all at once returned by our own hands. Perhaps, after the new beginnings brought about by some billion loops around the sun again, this earth will be given a new kind of man—revised and tender, strange and merciful. Superior in that he's willing to be wrong. Perhaps this planet will be a world where the new God will set all rules for continuation, abstracting the evident mistake he made when viciousness and vengeful rancor was an implement of utility for both good and evil . . . a world perfect enough for our God too to also be willing to absolve himself for his only godly imperfections. For only when he's willing to forgive himself for creating us thusly, will he then be truly divine.

Dedication

To all the victims of wartime nuclear holocausts.
To the tens of thousands wiped out of the face of life in seconds: Hiroshima, Nagasaki.

A vote for disarmament

The Two Deaths of Tanqueray

When I find myself in times of trouble,
Mother Mary comes to me, Speaking words of wisdom, Let
it be.

—The Beatles

Red. For the most part, red. And the strobe light snares against her body that hasn't yet broken the first bead of sweat. Her torso is what looks the best: fine titties! Like some kind of elongated reptile designed for sex. Squirming, provoking juices in you—in your mind, in your pants, taunting you from the second ring of hell! Oh, sweet damnation. That's how she moves. Oof! That's what it looks like here, as if she can't get enough of it. What a slut, man. For sure. And it's true for the most part. I will let you in on that. Her body is calling it all the time, and becomes alight! Her whole face lights up whenever any look, any suggestive preamble is pointed in that direction—sex, I mean. Any scenario that would soon after manifest into that—oh yes. It is where peace is, somehow. Sexy wacko! How does that happen? Makes you angry with lust? Ha-ha. A good sort of anger and you are a fool. Angry at yourself? Because you can't compete? Ha-ha. Anything obscene is her turf, and it really can't be any other way considering where she came from. Well, not so much where, but how. How she came to be—to be this. But that's not half as important to the story, though it's a fact that it's precisely because of it that she has such a . . . tolerance? Yes, tolerance for lack of a better term, simply because, in all honesty, I lack the total understanding to consolidate what this is into a singular, accurate, fair word. She is invincible, that much I know.

If you were a prude, you would call it tragic at best—her way, I'm referring to, her lax, even barren view of it all, you know—of herself, her "actions" . . . the meaning, the effect these could have . . . the potency of them and so on. Her detachment is a puzzle to you, her resolved approach toward the world and the fact, too, that she's willing to be a commodity?—an object of use?— a performer?—and with no qualms or weird deals about it, mind you, or else even a thought that requires much time. At least if she hated it, her story would be somewhat different, but this is not a different story, this is the story of Tanqueray Princeton, and this is how it goes . . . for her. It really is. This is how she deals, even if she's oblivious to the fact that she's dealing with anything at all. Because the reality of the matter is that, if you are a prude, your feelings toward her are so much more disapproving—even hateful, perhaps. By the same token, your cowardly mask caked under the false layer of politeness will not allow you to bear your feelings completely, nor adhere at all to your true convictions in the truest sense of the word!—and by true I mean outward signs, sincerity and so on. Because your goodness (or whatever it's called) trumps all, and there are two emotions in such a damned individual (which I hope is neither you nor I . . . God help us!): the prude has the actual opinion, and that little twisted pseudo-benevolent squeaky fabrication equivalent to a . . . to a verbal doily? I don't know, it doesn't sound right. A sugar-coated bullshit judgment now caramelized in mint and sucrose or something, for the sake and service of politeness. But at the core . . . ooh, at the core there's certainly potent cyanide. Fuck them! Because they're lost in a stunned and weird land of fluff and hypocrisy and something low fat!

No point in going into a profound psychological deconstruction of this nineteen-year-old at this point, but we must know that one of her claims to fame is that she likes trumping any of your most lascivious extremes. And she does this with ease and also enjoys being called a whore, among other common pejoratives, which she regards as empowering somehow. And she's not making that up either, nor is she doing that to amuse you in some way. You can call it twisted if you wish, but she would call it her perspective . . . that's if she called it anything at all, which I doubt. She's as wrong as you are, and most likely you are both wrong—and probably so am I, who knows?

People are like a meal served at a fine restaurant: the kitchen is the past, and the plate that makes it to your table is today. You sure know what the dish looks like and what it tastes like—but how it became to be what it is . . . the secrets, the spices . . . those are all hidden in the kitchen. Why you're jumpy, why you're funny, why you're quiet, why you're wild, why you're deeply religious, why you're a prostitute. All these are more symptoms than conditions. Symptoms of your past's illness. Just as your body fights bacteria, your character fights your past; grapples with it, denies it—embraces its virtues and tries to become only them! Only that part that has been celebrated, that has been useful, acknowledged, recognized, and that which has impressed upon others greatly—that we focus on. In other words, the thing you do best, you seek so that it defines you. Times change, and a philosopher was a viable answer many thousands of years ago to the question, what are you? Not anymore, though I believe "a man" was a viable answer in no era.

If it's about having the times up in arms about how a lady should behave and so on, well, she has certainly gotten the attention of the times—and more. She's beat it, twisted it, stood it on its head, fucked it, and not cared about it one bit because her concerns are well beyond anything she could think of right now—but it certainly isn't your shock either that she's after, or anyone else's, for to her there's nothing shocking about what she's doing, though there's certainly something curious about your reactions—your simplicity, your bizarre incomprehension, your easily impressionable spirit. These stir some intrigue in her. She exists in a place where your taboos are her breakfast.

Sunsets, sunrises . . . these happen but don't punctuate anything in particular to her. Day and night are both the same—sleep is when you can, when it fits, and so is eat. Somehow she has conquered an area most don't get to tame, and she's a virtuoso at playing the sex game. She plays it with ease as others—the virtuous, the pure and flawless, and righteous and good and upstanding and moral—weep for her soul while she keeps fucking unencumbered through your smothered and appalled disbelief. She probably likes it—what she does, I mean. One would think. You would think. Would you? One would judge. Let's do that—though. To "like" is so qualitative applicable to the rest of the society she's so evidently outside of, that to capture the essence of how she truly approaches, or feels about, it all is beyond anyone's real understanding, or even guesswork—understanding of the range of those vibrations within her that can approximate the askew feelings that are her emotions in the face of such things—how these would translate in some form to ours . . . emotionally. Likes, loves, needs, can't escape—who knows?

She's a different animal from what I am—stronger, I suspect.

But most members of modern civilized society would agree that she was in fact brutally raped at the age of seven. Penetrated violently, repeatedly, and anachronistically—in every conceivable, unripe, unwilling, undeveloped, unready, and fruitlessly repelling orifice of her person. This is an undeniable constant in Tanqueray's total equation. She calls this experience, however—flatly, shrugging but perhaps, even in the midst of her confession, disassociated. Though she does not know of such things, such terms or even their meaning. Such defenses of the mind, their existence, their possibility. The day when she lost her virginity, she says, was the day she caught a head-start to becoming a woman. Thus became the beginning of her definition of a woman: someone who could withstand invasion and survive. Someone who was there for invasion and survived.

"You lead the life of a star!"—the shadow had told her that, and she laughed, gripping the hot member as that milky goo fell on her, then the ground. "And a performer!" What did she know? How could she know? Exploitation? Violation. What—is—that?

Mornings and days and evenings were a haze of strangeness and costumes and flashes and tripods sometimes, and sex and sex and more sex. What is sex? Feathers and masks, and trips to where?—and confusion and years adding up bit by bit, but sex became a thing like any other then. A series of awkward intrusive sensations to beheld with no degree of doubt any longer, but the transformation was sure under way. The metamorphosis into the incongruous breed she'd become later on. She didn't know she was being broken apart nor did she know that her picture would never again come back together completely unblemished.

Raped, then forced, then tenderized, then made subservient, then willing, then addicted . . .

But ironically, Tanqueray did not develop physically after that. It was as if the violation of her small body, itself, had sent some biological mechanics into shock. Into a sort of stagnancy—it's hard to say—but her breasts remained barely buds—girly, and close to her body, as if to be kept away from the reach of intruders, as if her body, in conscious rebellion, refused to bear fruit, or was reluctant to give men the satisfaction ever again of taking complete, lascivious pleasure in her flesh.

But in spirit, however, it was another thing, for she was more than strangely willing if not completely pursuing of—and too unfazed by—the invasions of sex. Malignant pleasures she indulged in. Pleasures that to the prude (and easily impressionable souls) hold malice in such extreme and decadent ways!—and that's about the only way we too could prescribe it or see it, I'd suppose, if for no other reason than because we can't understand it. Everyone wants to be a savior to those who mutilate themselves; it's an instinct. And it seems, in some form, excessive promiscuity is an act of self-mutilation. It's the erroneous affirmation that one's soul is worth nothing—at least that's what it speaks to my intuition. Or else my spirit is turning prudish.

If you were to see it, see her, qualify her, you would too probably shun it—see it as some kind of propagation of rape of sorts . . . a variation of it, yeah. Certainly you would see it as a wrongdoing, unacceptable, improper behavior, something unethical, strange, or done for reasons you can't rationalize. But she's become the perpetrator and the raped here. She's her own victimizer now. That changes things. That cancels all possible outside effort in making her the victim. She comes out a victor!

One can easily say or see she made sex her weapon, then. The very same wound that had been inflicted when she was seven years old, she turned around. She turned herself into a strange breed of aggressor, so that at least through that persona she could not be hurt again. Quite the contrary; she could not even be reached through it. It became her shield and source of power. Was she misled? Perhaps, if she is measured by our biased psychology, but let us assume that as she sees things—her stance—that if she derives more pleasure than these others through it, she will be getting back!—somehow. Perhaps even getting back some of herself. No damage is possible this way—her willingness defuses the aggression. In every penetration she modifies the other's intent—offsets the man's predictions, every time. She dominates it all. This, of course, would not be, or rather no longer is, a conscious choice at all but, instead, a mechanism of the mind, an assertor, a compensator. "Fuck my ass with all you've got, you fat, dumb trick!" she'd scream at whoever it was who would be thrusting into her at any given time—so harsh that it would shut them down, put her in control of everything. The power would be funneled out of them, completely, their rhythms made nervous and unpredictably weak. She was impenetrable now. She was the violator and the humiliator, even if the fat, dumb tricks didn't know it, even if the fat, dumb trick was in fifth heaven and enjoying every minute of it. But she lived in her world—not theirs—and deep in the sepultures of her rageful mind, she raped every . . . single . . . one of them. She was getting her revenge, daily!

The lights lashed on her body, repeatedly. The chrome squeaked against her back now—burned!—growing steamy, fogged up with her salty vapors. And the glitter on her tits that pointed up toward the disco ball grew more visible with her sweat. She glistened—a terrible, urban nymph. A libidinous jewel, she gripped the chrome like a robot's cock, and her hand, still chubby with youth and the semblance of schooling, seemed out of place in this scene, dimpled and spongy, masturbating this cylinder of metal. Indeed, her whole body was insulated by a cozy layer of fatty, unfinished skin—an allure most welcome to the beastly and horny. Her optimal physicality added to her anachronistic deviant proclivities . . . it is stunning to the mind. She provoked a riddle, a challenge—disbelief, grief, and undoubtedly, in so many cases, extreme lust.

She spun around. Spritz of sweat solidified in the strobe as her ass bounced in place, fortuitously biting down at the edge of her polyester bikini bottom. She slid in a split down onto the hardwood stage, and a sliver of chicken skin . . . the edge of her pussy . . . was revealed in the reddish light, a wedge of her outer lip—her labia majora—about to be strummed like a bass string by the elastic. This crevice, now hot and breathing, fogged the polished hardwood. Her eyes rolled back into her skull, and an invisible molasses formed all around her as the methamphetamines took over the majority of the functional—sensual—chemistry of her brain, sending her into a spiral of artificial spiritual comfort—well-being and maybe forgetfulness, but never forgetting the pursuit of pleasure! Oh no—oh yes. But is it pleasure or is it that she's terrified? To lose control, to forget, to lose the grip of the familiar—the intrusive member close by, assuring her that things are steady, constant, reliable. She needs to test so that she can affirm again and again that she can handle anything and not feel naked ever again. Vulnerable. She needs that reassurance—or else she could be in the open, alone and ignorant to some looming threat. Her neurosis is nothing like yours. She keeps her terror close by. Some say: face your fears, fight them. Others say: become them, and you'll destroy 'em.

She got up. Her ribs pushed against the layer of skin, and her skeleton kneaded blindly underneath her living flesh. Her back arched, her nipples tightened to a pink defiance, but her lips relaxed, they were supple and gleaming, hanging red in the intermittent violence that hints at a desperate, frantic, and impersonal fucking. This was precisely what was racing now through her anarchist head. She's happy. She's now beyond that certain point and was suddenly very happy. Her mind went blank; she dropped to her knees, dropped her body forward, and pushed her ass up, high up with her face flush now on the ground. Beneath the synthetic fiber, her pussy pushed against the material and slightly opened, unseen. She loosened the ribbons at the sides of her bikini, ripped that piece of clothing off her crotch, and stuffed it in her mouth—it started to taste like sex. She crawled ass-up as the lights still beat on her as if she's a slave from some strange and perverse galaxy.

Mikhail stared at her ass from across the room, grinning. He sat in a booth talking to some fat black guy in a leather coat and counting an amount of money; she winked at him with a smirk as bills—ones and fives—from some old man's fist—flew toward the stage like flakes in a snow globe. Looking straight into her eyes now, Mikhail motioned with his head to the fat black dude, who looked back at her in some kind of dumfounded trance. She shrugged and smiled and nodded.

"Okay, so twenty minutes. You can fuck her in the mouth, but you can't fuck her in the ass. That will cost you more—a lot more, and please don't get smart in there," Mikhail warned in his Russian inflection that sounded more laughable than threatening, but in fact, he very much meant it. He tried, too—with his body, and awkwardly—to affect some kind of polite professionalism to glaze the tone of these words, but that attempt clashed with his Puma tracksuit. Nothing made sense; in fact, it all promoted something quite venomous and seriously frightening in this odd little man.

"I wouldn't think of anything like that, don't you worry, man," the fat dude said to Tanqueray's pimp boyfriend.

"She's real cool and enjoys what she does, okay? You are nice, and the rewards are great, believe me," he said through his ridiculous, high-pitched accent as he sipped a cosmopolitan. The black guy thought it was too feminine drink, but he didn't say anything at all. He just looked over at Tanqueray, who was on stage fingering herself and licking her lips, staring straight back into his eyes.

"Okie dokie; you are the boss," the fat man said without looking back from the stage.

"You are God damn right, I'm the boss!" Mikhail punched the booth table and the fat guy jumped back. Mikhail's eyes pierced through this guy with a strange, foreign, and imprecise look. There's a meaning behind the eyes, the fat guy's sure of this, but it's simply culturally disparate and ineffectual under any American standards of body language. "Don't patronize me with any of you bullshit. I know your kind, Heavy—"

"Okay, man; cool it . . . I'm not—"

"Another word from your fat, blubbery mouth and you go home to spread peanut butter on you balls and have you dog suck your dick for you instead—okay?"

"We're cool, Mikhail, man, come on—"

"We're not on first names basis!" Mikhail took a sip of the cosmopolitan through a straw. He winked at Tanqueray again with a mouthful of liquor. He swallowed and then cast his eyes toward the fat man again in a threatening squint. "You come with reputable references," he said through clenched teeth. "But I wipe my ass with references! You hear me, Tubby? Tanqueray's pussy is gold at the end of a pair of legs, you understand this, Buddy Love?" Then, a little quieter, he said, "Seriously! I don't need your black ass or your attitude making noise in any of this shit. This is my turf, Heavy-D. My deal, my shit. We gotta start on good footing, man." Mikhail's casual tone stretched out the last syllable. "Come on, don't be a nigger about it," he whispered, with a sweet honesty filled to the brim with a racist sort of paranoia. "Do this right." He squinted, sniffled, took out a baggie of coke, opened it, and snorted a bit.

"I agree," the big guy said, chuckling and shaking his head from side to side. Mikhail nodded and rubbed his nose.

"Good!" Mikhail yelled just as the music softened. "I'm glad about this, Heavy. Coke?"

"No thanks, it . . . makes my dick limp."

"Good thinking, fatso—" He put the drug away and arched his eyebrows. He tapped his pocket. "And, listen, this could be the start of something . . . good, you dig?" He leaned forward with a grin. "If you like Tanqueray—as I'm sure you will—we could make arrangements should you choose to . . . you know . . . make more frequent visits."

"Sounds fair," the fat guy said, nursing a warm Sam Adams Lager, peeling off the label nervously. His fingers looked like charred sausages.

"I mean this bitch will blow your mind." Mikhail laughed. His foreheads began to bead with sweat from the coke. He unzipped the tracksuit slightly. "Nobody has asked for their money back.

They've maybe asked for their souls back . . ." He laughed some more, looked at the crucifix hanging around the black guy's chest, and then called across the bar for another cosmo. "And yes," he said whispering—but loudly—pushing his torso across the table, "she will take it in the behind. But it will cost you a lot more, and she needs to get to know you a little better—*capiche?*" He made a gesture like sizing a penis and pointed to him, suggesting at the reputation that preceded his . . . blackness. He arched his eyebrows again and then leaned back again on his seat.

Across the room, Tanqueray rounded up all the bills from the stage. The strobe had stopped for the time being, replaced in the intermission by a steady yellow light that made her look like a humanoid in some kind of surrealist scene: a scavenger picking things up from the ground . . . some kind of creature picking berries, the things that guarantee her continuation, her survival. She is a gatherer. She is in the flesh, natural, not a thread of clothing on her. Beautiful, unaware . . . lingering and going about her task unannounced, uninhibited, matter-of-factly, obviously, and without a hint of self-consciousness. The world in some other form, and as it comes to be . . . takes a strange liquid shape.

Tanqueray finished her set and stuffed all the money into her purse at the corner of the stage. The music started again as she leaped into the stripper's restroom like a gazelle. Another creature stepped on the stage . . . defined and alive. A seed in our galaxy of questions.

* * *

Mikhail grabbed Tanqueray's face—which grinned back at him—somewhat forcefully with one hand and turned it to the right. "Tell him something!" he said, nodding at the black man and grabbing his cosmo with his free hand, taking a sip.

"I'm a very filthy whore, and I'm going to give you a very good ride. But remember, you're paying me and not the other way around. That means the product—that's me—behaves how the product behaves. You don't know your way around the product—the product does not respond according to previous arrangements. Understood?"

She had walked out of the strippers' lounge clad in some kind of luminescent top . . . some sort of netting—real cheap looking in the lighting of the club. Her skin was milky white with freckles that didn't show up when she was on the stage—not many, just a few across her shoulders and her nose—and not in a million years would anyone in their right mind guess that already, at seven in the evening, her belly was filled with two other men's semen—one just procured on an independent operation in the interim between the last performance and now. Her lips were extra glossy from some of that cherry-flavored application she had put on in there for effect—not that she really needed any of that. After all, she was only nineteen and so ridiculously supple.

Tanqueray was half Croatian and half English; the Croatian side—her mother's—gave her those tulip, meaty pink lips and that rounded face, as well as those slightly downwardly slanting eyes that can give one the false impression of harmlessness. From her mother, too, she must have inherited that extra layer of spongy flesh all through her body and ass, which lifted up firmly and outward still—of course. From her father she inherited nothing except her viciousness, and this, it can be argued, was more an imposition than a genetic contribution. She had a kind of arching of her torso more prevalent in blacks than whites, where her pelvis tucked under in a way that made her ass push back and up and appear suggestive, promoting sexual thoughts despite the real context. She was aware of this attribute, but she was not skilled enough to hide the fact that she is mindful of this. Like I said, it was as if she was built for sex alone. She wanted to promote this, and she did, well beyond the imaginable, almost as if there was no thinking brain in there. But sadly, strangely, mind-bogglingly, there was! Doesn't she care?—the rest of us dart our gaze, avoiding direct eye contact. What do people think? The easy route!—how many times has that been said, thought, about such things? Such—people. What does she think of herself? Doesn't she care what her father thinks? What would he say about all this? What do they think?

The truth is simple, folks. Simpler and crueler than you may want to think. You may want to bypass the reality of certain things and pretend they have no kinetic culpability, but the dry fact is that, when you have been raped, screwed, violated, fucked!—at seven!—you have been forcefully, and at once, thrown far out of society! You . . . are . . . outcast! At seven—here—you are already out and don't even know it yet. You won't realize until later . . . much later, years down the line. Though not many, not many years at all. You learn this. There's no going around it! There is no world, no society in the world for a screwed seven-year-old. No society for her can/will/could exist!

Society is a conglomerate of like-minded, semi-equal peers, right? Relatively, at least. Or clumps of such people if with slight differences—stress on "slight." But can you imagine this society—her imaginary society—the society of screwed and raped seven-year-olds? No. It will never materialize or embrace who she has been made to become. There's a very powerful emotional restructuring that occurs when a person's insides are gripped, twisted, violated, and tormented by being put in a position of abysmally disadvantageous carnal utility and exploitation—a different animal will emerge from this. It's an unavoidable . . . do you feel comfortable with the term "experience"? The word here is both accurate and troubling. Once something like this has finally occurred, it puts very strangely colored glasses between the creature and the world. This new animal grows up too. This new animal is intelligent; it sees, it learns, as well senses her own differences uncomfortably and compensating; the indisputable fact is that she is of an uncategorizable askewness with the rest of what surrounds her!—that something she can't quite put her finger on at first. But she certainly knows—she knows she's different. This animal is, finally, Tanqueray—a snow leopard in the Sahara.

Let's continue for the sake of the heaviness of this topic—and redundancy. Okay—once this has happened, there is no going back. There just isn't. And sometimes, things are as simple as that. Anything she would attempt after this would be a hollow mimicry. Think about it. Child's play? Give me a fucking break! A strange, meaningless puppetry. Where is her society? Who are her peers at this point—who shares her little-big sorrows now . . . her perspectives? Where's the rest of her kind? How does she grow? How does she form? How does she see everything else around her? Who shares her concerns, the same ones? Where does she belong? Who is she? What? Is there anything left of her? Hopefully, there always is. And this is our wish—always. But always from that lofty cradle of the untouched and pure that we are? Or else I'm just angry for her? Resentful? Resentful at double-edged judgments?

But thankfully as well, it is the hope that lingers below the immense cruelty that has evolved—this new and impatient, forward-plowing civilization that is so intent on incomprehension! But not totally soulless, though truly doubly moral. You can't have it all, I suppose, unless you are two-faced. We have no compassion for whores, yet no one ever stops to find out how it was exactly that she became one. Hating a whore is as tasteless as hating a severed leg; you are hating a large wound.

Ah—but thank God we have our coconspirators, our affirmed views, our polished, clean, and sane concerns. Our society! We have so many to spare telling us how we belong, throwing their approving arms around our shoulders. We are good. We are right. We have our whole world to back us up—and God on our side! We are the winners. Fuck that—we are the world! Alleluia! So good it feels to have all the concurrence and support of the millions, folks—the good, the moral, the well-structured, the sane, the virtuous, the vicious, the greedy, the false, the egoists, the powerful, the ones who have found the loophole escapes and the pathway to happiness in all of this. Also we must be especially thankful to the prudish and the delusional. Ah, but enough; this is all but resentful speech, for I fail to mention the ones who had the good sense to bring up those among us who are made of a high ethical fabric and compassionate characters!—those few and rare animals that often make it into our lives in the form of surprise and offer hope, and who put us to shame. Thank heaven for them—truly.

Hard to see here, hard to find it in Tanqueray—the humanity we are used to. Sure. The humanity that throws itself in our faces like cotton clouds and the like, which makes children smile widely. That self-evident and unblemished grace so particular to a life of silk.

Impossible. She is sharp like a knife. She's so beautiful and looks so deadly—you'd love and fear her, I assure you that.

Even the prude would lust after her in secrecy, and were he to be snatched in half by lightning at that very moment, he would go join in his best Sunday clothes the rest of the cock suckers in the second ring of hell!

She had been transplanted, yanked from the roots and set on the hot pavement by herself! No earth to be found for miles. No soil—the blaring sun upon her. And eyes . . . all the eyes of us looking down at this scene, now, looking down at her, hating her so very, very much for being such a sinner. Spitting at her grotesque, self-deprecating ways—condemning her easy choices. Easy harlot—no virtue. We relish in our righteousness and take in with some aberrant pride at our numbers, our peers, our like-minded confirmations, allies, our beloved conglomerates! Affirming once again that she really . . . really doesn't belong! Cast off, she goes, once again!—we second that transplant, emphatically, and rape her once again, strip her of all she is with our lofty disdain and repulsion. We all fuck her deep in that old wound that we somehow have managed to find and which is no longer—and for ages hasn't been—between her legs.

*　　*　　*

"That was easy."

"Was it?"

"It's because he's fat and hideous. It's the contrast that kills them!" she said, lighting a cigarette. "They see themselves so fat and blubbery and grotesque; then I come in, my skin like satin, my pussy like pink cotton candy, wrap my legs around their big fat guts—they die!" Her wrist went limp; she laughed and blew smoke out the window.

Nearly ten at night now, and they were cruising down the street in a classic, red Chevrolet Impala convertible.

"You're in a terrible state," Mikhail said, chuckling, but actually meaning to say something more like, "You're terrible."

"And you can forget the mystical myths with this one."

"What do you mean?" he asked densely.

She rolled her eyes above a grin. "His dick was like a thumb! Or a toe! A black chubby toe! I had to concentrate not to burst out laughing at the guy. He just sat there at the edge of the mattress . . . a mongoloid, looking down at me like a retarded child at the doctor's office while I blew his ridiculous thing."

"Disgusting—nigger dicks infuriate me!" He gripped the steering wheel and slightly rolled his knuckles forward.

"Listen—so I'm looking at the clock and kind of reminding him with my eyes, you know, humming there, as his gut rested on my forehead like a meat sombrero. His lips hanging, and he's groaning, and I look up at this crispy, charred Buddha, and he says, 'Okay . . . okay . . . ' in between . . . between gasps. I was like—in my head—'Okay, okay what? What the fuck do you mean by this, you imbecile?' I was so pissed off, kind of. But he just kept saying this shit and pressing his eyes like I was tearing out a limb! Then he goes: 'Okay, stop!' So I take the toe out of my mouth and tell him to just relax and lie back. I say he's making a fool of himself—right? So he lies back and the bed goes in, like, ten inches, and I promise you that as soon as I wedged my pussy onto this little knob, all I did was get comfortable on his twig of meat when he groans like some kind of animal and goes lax . . . completely and at once! He just looked at me like he was looking into the very eyeballs of God, for Christ's sake. He had this ridiculous, grateful look on his face. By God, I wanted to slap him!" She took a puff and exhaled into the rushing wind. "Like I loved him! He looked at me like I loved this crazy, fat bastard . . . back!" She started laughing again and flicked the cigarette onto the pavement. "'That was great, thank you,' this animal says, hyperventilating, after I go up and down like I'm riding on the back of some tired bull. I tell him, 'Well, now you know, Heavy . . . cotton-candy heaven pussy? That's what it feels like.' 'Yes,' he just says with a nondescript unintelligence dashing across his gaze, man. I tapped him on his wet chest and told him, very confidently, 'And next time, you can fuck my ass; I don't think there will be a problem.' I felt bad about laughing when I said it, but I don't think he got it. I don't think he got much of anything. I don't know if he's sure he knows what just happened back there. Why don't you put the top down?"

"I'm telling you; you are like a Jedi."

"I am a Jedi. Put the top down."

Mikhail slowed down the car and put the white top down. Then he pressed forward again like some kind of subaquatic predator-demon cut loose to wander the urbanization by permission of Poseidon. The breeze came in, and the balm of the summer heat lapped at their cheeks, sticking to their bodies. Vapors mixed with the fabrics, the underarm responded, the neck went clammy and reactivated the colognes. They rode low, and the hubcaps set everything in motion, a spinning disk that made the city quiver like gelatin, distorted like some strange and idealized dream; life here was a chant with a liquid and electric choir, music from an older rendition of the universe as it had aged and was close to collapsing, an existence erased by God many times over already, but resonant in the souls of all that lives today.

The night and neon, and the smell of crispy money, chrome, and sex was in the air—fine grins, and youth, and palm trees lined up along the pavement, and a gun, and drugs, and brand-new polyester clothing of leisure. A whore by your side who's a beautiful terror with a pussy so sweet it'd make a grown man weep and pray to it. She'll laugh at your dick, take your cash, and blow you a kiss at the exit . . . roll out without a trail of smoke, if a faint trail of a rare perfume should linger for far too short a time, that faint memory of her brief robbery will leave a flaky milky hint on the highest ring of your now-withered manhood. You'll be four hundred bucks poorer and half the man you used to be. Loser!

Her boyfriend, Mikhail, is this short-fused brat whose parents died on a scenic helicopter ride in Vegas shortly after they had won the Lotto in the amount of $2.5 million. A freak accident involving a collision with a private Cessna aircraft whose pilot was momentarily distracted while enamoring with his brand-new girlfriend over the radio waves and paying little mind to briefing his location. His fractured mindlessness cost four people their lives.

The gangster appeal, for Mikhail, was much more ancient than the final materialization of these aspirations, and the death of his parents, and the money left to him by default, aided simply to crystallize this unbecoming, senseless yearning. First, it was just the gangster persona that he bought, then he purchased his first Austrian semiautomatic handgun—a nice Glock that he was quite impressed with because it can shoot as you hold it under water. Of course the question: when are you going to find yourself in this scenario (fighting someone, shooting at him . . . underwater)—never made it to his consciousness.

Then, he sold his parents' old cars and purchased the Impala—and it was not that he needed at all the money in order to complete this last transaction, but he did want to get rid of those two old pieces of crap that were taking up space in his life and garage.

"You know, you really look good in a tracksuit."

"You're fucking my legs!" He jumps on his seat, surprised, proud.

"No, I mean it; you're real cute in that tracksuit."

"Well—it's comfortable," he started, innocently feigning a sort of laughable modesty. "Practical . . . but, above everything else, it's stylish." Mikhail looked down at himself, momentarily taking his eyes off the road. Then he looked at Tanqueray, who had extended her arm across the back of his seat. "It says: Hey! I'm laid back guy, you know—like to have fun, have money . . . and will shoot you if you fuck with me! Is that right or no?" He laughed and beat the steering wheel violently in front of him, making the car horn go off once.

"Is what right?" She was distracted by a billboard.

"The tracksuit, God damn it, Tank. What it says. It says: I like to party—but don't fuck with me. What the fuck? Am I right or am I right?" He's bummed out by her sudden lack of attention.

"You're right, pumpkin!" She squeezed his cheek and spoke with a goldfish-mouth pout.

He grew serious then. "You treat me like an infidel and then you wonder why I get mean, Tank." His eyebrows pinched.

"Infant, honey—like an infant."

"What did I say?"

"Infidel." She started bouncing from laughter.

"Isn't it the same thing?" Confused.

She came down a bit . . . shaking her pretty head. "Not at all."

"I thought infant was more . . . for animals—you know, like a little baby elephants," he said, looking at her seriously.

"No." She looked to the side and bit the inside of her lip.

There's a canal. A string of boats of all sizes was docked alongside the edge. The water's black, and the lights of the houses at the other side reflected, trickled, and danced on the surface. A sense of anxiety rushed through her and quickly left. It's not unusual for her: unannounced panic that compels her to leave wherever she is. But luckily she's in motion, and so it doesn't last. "Aren't you hungry?" She turned to him.

"Nah—I've been doing coke all night." He turned to her with a slight grin, a curious grin, gauging her. "But I'll take you someplace. What do you want?"

"Anything."

"Okay—so anything. What do you want?" his tone typically intensifying.

"Take me to Pietra; I kinda want that lamb ravioli."

"Anything for my baby cakes." He looked forward, grinning with half his mouth. The light turned yellow half a block ahead and he floored it; running the red.

"Your whore, you mean." She lit another cigarette, grinning nervously. A passing rush of violence darted through her mind. "You mean your whore."

*   *   *

"That waiter's such a weirdo—he has that look, you know, like you can't trust him."

"Mikhail, he's our waiter. What could he possibly do?"

"I don't know, but I'm not letting anything pass."

"The coke has you all paranoid. There's nothing wrong with that man. He's perfectly fine."

"I'm telling you, there's something sinister about him."

"You're a psychopath."

"Would you fuck him?"

"Of course I would fuck him, Mikhail. He's a perfectly fuckable individual. There's nothing wrong with the man. I insist!"

"I can't look at him in the face without a chill going through my vertebrae."

"Mikhail, that's because the man has strabismus. You are an idiot."

"What are you talking about?"

"Strabismus. A wandering eye, Mika. His eyeballs are fucked! That is why you think there's something the matter with the man."

"Oh?"

"You're too impatient. You take no notice of anything. Didn't—"

"I knew there was something terribly askew about the way he looked at us; I just couldn't place my fingers on it. So—"

"Mmm."

"You say he has wonderment eyes?"

"A wandering eye, Mika, please; how many years have you been in the States, now?"

"More than I like to count."

"I'm going to buy you a DVD set of American English."

"You bitch."

"I'm serious."

"You know, Tank, sometimes you make me want to squeeze you by the throat and not let go."

"And this is precisely why I chose you."

"All I can tell you is, I got instincts. If the guy has fucked-up eyes, that's nature's way of telling everyone, 'Hey! Don't trust this guy; he's up to no good . . . look at his eyes.' You know what I'm trying to tell you? This is old, ancient wisdom here, you know. The eyes are the window to the souls, and if he looks like that . . . if a man can't look you in the eye directly with both eyes, he ain't shooting straight!"

"Mika."

"Tank."

"You are making a buffoon out of yourself—more than usual. Look, there are numerous people who have a wandering eye and are famous and influential!" She shrugged and laughed nervously.

"What the fuck do you know about anyone who has any influence, Tank?" He punched the table with a grin.

"I know enough." She took a sip of water and looked to the side, hoping no one was listening to this idiot.

"Who? Name me one cross-eyed motherfucker who's famous."

"Abraham Lincoln."

"Get the fuck out of town!"

"I'm serious."

"You're telling me that Abraham Lincoln was cross-eyed?" He leaned to one side, pulled out his wallet, took out a five, and held it in front of his eyes.

"Not cross-eyed, Mika. Strabismus . . . wandering eye. It's different."

"Whatever. He looks fine in the bill . . ."

"That's not Abraham Lincoln you're holding; that's a bill you're holding."

"Well—this is what I think." He put his wallet back in his pocket. "This is my instinct. That's how I survive out there." He leaned forward and motioned toward the passing cars. "By instinct and—"

"Oh, God . . ." She squeezed her eyes with her fingers and suppressed a laugh.

"Abraham Lincoln is not going to change my mind about this shady bastard."

The food came, and Mikhail regarded the plate with great suspicion. The waiter was enchanting, if slightly distracting, with his chameleonesque ocular organs, which scanned the table like two independent, harmless telescopes. It was hard to know which was indeed the eye that did the seeing, and which one did the wandering, but at least to Tanqueray, this was unimportant; so she looked at both eyes, one first and then the other, giving equal attention to the nomad eye as much as the other one, regardless of who was actually paying attention. For all God's creations need love and attention, she thought sweetly as she regarded the pair of crazy eyes, even those who stray from the straight and narrow path.

Her eyes fluttered in the balmy heat and the steam rising from the lamb ravioli. His name was Fernando, and in fact, there was something in the air that night, and the stars were bright.

*   *   *

"Open the fucking door, Yuri, before I tear this shit down and bust a capsule in your asshole!" Mikhail screamed right into the door, and then he turned back and whispered with a smile, looking wild. "He's such a baby—always sleeping . . . always dragging about."

The door opened a crack. "Hey, whatz up, fellas?" Yuri said through an incredible amount of halitosis. He opened the door just enough for these two to saunter into the living room and scan his pad with a measured amount of disgust. Debris, and the telltale signs of a single man living in the midst of a profound personal irreparability, encroached upon them like an army defeated—the spoils of a war where junk food, liquor, and drug paraphernalia were the conquered in this battle. Little light came into this room, which smelled like old beer, dead smoke, and unsafe sex.

"Can I mix you a drink?" Yuri said, closing the door, bobbing his head above a Lakers basketball jersey that encased his scrawny body. He looked like a malnourished child salvaged from some wreckage, gifted with his savior's article of clothing—too large for him to wear comfortably and naturally, but too cute and heartbreaking for the press to ignore—just the kind of close-call horrors we like seeing on a daily basis to affirm that there's goodness left in the world—in fact, in all of us. Being moved by such a thing is testament that there's some of that collective heart left in humanity out there someplace.

"Cosmopolitan for the faggot—and for you, Tanqueray?" He walked toward the fridge.

"Oh, I'm fine, thank you, Yuri—we just had dinner and . . . I'm okay, thanks."

"Fuck, I'm out of cranberry juice, Mika!" He clenched his eyes tightly, pretending he hadn't known this.

"Don't give me this shit, man! You knew today I would be passing by . . . you know the deal." He laughed, but deep inside he was disappointed. "So what do you have, Yuri?"

"Well, I have the Stoli," he winced, "and the ice."

"Okay, well, Stoli rocks, then, I guess."

"Stoli rocks, special for you! Coming right up." He made a cute face, which appeared very ridiculous to everyone, because he was truly and seriously uncute; in fact, he looked like a smug rat on two feet who provoked nothing but irritation, really.

"Great."

"Name your poisons!" He clapped and rubbed his hands together.

"Give me an eightball and about a thousand bucks of crystal for Tank."

Tank sat down on one of the more acceptable pieces of furniture available. She looked out the window and counted the seconds to when she won't have to be stuck in this place. She looked at her French manicure, which was fresh and perfect . . . the smooth rounded soft claws of a beast made of some kind of unearthly substance. But no drug or poison can contend with her body. It's soft as it's invincible—her youth is defiant against any chemical, any evil at all to be found in any kind of wilderness in this planet, yet. The blocks of ice echo in the tumbler through the filthy apartment, and the vodka falls into the recipient like a reminder of vice and that cold, smoky, and harsh safety. The lamp in the room was yellow and mimicked the sun—the quality was very similar and, for a moment, soothed her considerably.

She escaped, and a bitter pebble of something formed in her throat, which we might call profound sadness: an emotion she can't afford, she thinks, or even deserves. She doesn't know that tonight she will die.

Music started on the stereo—a song by Radiohead she liked. She sang along with the song, called "Nude," although she didn't notice she was doing this. She closed her eyes too and leaned her head back against the filthy armchair—she didn't care anymore. A flock of birds rushed through her mind, and although they are all the same kind of bird, only one of them was blue. She thinks of birds only because, since she's still a woman, the better part of her sex hasn't left her, and it seems it can't be erased—I just found this out about her.

Truly good songs are often too short. She lifted her body from the armchair as if from an outside force—a ghost.

"So what are you guys doing later on? Going to Mango or something stupid like this?" Yuri said with a slimy laugh.

"None of your business," she said flatly, swinging her purse around her shoulder, perfuming the atmosphere.

"Let's get out of here," Mikhail said, handing Tanqueray her bag of meth. She grabbed it and put it in her purse, her eyes following her hands; her eyelids were powdered blue—they sparkled. Yuri took this opportunity to steal a glimpse of her cleavage. Another song started, pulsing and growing. Mikhail's phone vibrated in his pocket as they stepped out of Yuri's apartment.

A huge flock of birds swarmed inside Tanqueray's eyes.

*   *   *

There was a blinding light in the tunnel; she put on her sunglasses even though it's night. Her pupils were dilated like black round plates. She grinned widely, her teeth dry in the rushing wind.

"I feel good! I'm so happy, Mika."

"Good, darling, I'm glad . . . I mean, no, really . . ." He grinned like a hyena—coked up.

The Impala zoomed forward against the hot wind as the water and trees passed violently by undefined . . . a thick, sweet, dark smear. Her hair snapped in the wind, and all was well. Meth rushed through her veins. Orbs of light played along the rim of her dark sunglasses, and she was deep inside her head. No worries, no thoughts—felicity . . . total stillness as the drug kept her safely enveloped, impenetrable!—and assured.

"In and out—you must have done something right. He wants you again," Mikhail said, bringing her down.

"Fuck, Mika—when do I do anything wrong, honey?"

"That's my bitch!"

"So, his apartment—?"

"Yep."

"Fuckin' Godzilla, man . . . He smells weird too." She shook her head a bit and closed her eyes behind the black plastic lenses.

"Don't be a protester, now. You're a pro. What the fuck is wrong with you?"

"You should fuck him. Then tell me what the fuck is wrong with me." She laughed and then ran her tongue over her fangs. The radio played some new lounge shit. Harry Connick, Jr., or some atavistic gramma's boy revivalist anachronism like that! She hated it—but didn't do anything about it, though she did comment, "I did it my way, my ass!" She exhaled and her body trembled underneath her breastplate. "What the fuck is this bullshit—this day and age? Can you believe people still belting out this sort of thing? Broadway, for Christ's sake! What a bunch of crazy clowns, no?" She's someplace between sarcastic and angry.

"Um . . ."

"Certainly!" Her eyes were gleaming—marbles.

"He's gonna fuck you up your butt this time," he said, changing the subject. "I hope you know!" She started laughing, leaned her elbow on the edge of the door, and gripped her forehead.

"Fine, Mika—I hope I feel it. I mean so I know when he's done." She laughed again, then made a face at the radio. Her lip rose; she looked . . . funny—like Billy Idol.

"So what's the deal?" He's confused. "You don't like jazz? Sinatra? What's wrong with you?"

"What, am I supposed to? I didn't know I was obliged."

"Well, no, but I mean . . . I always took you for someone with, you know, with taste."

"And who's to say this shit is tasteful, Mika—you?"

"What are you trying to say?"

"I'm not trying to say anything. I'm saying it. You are one corny, tacky motherfucker, Mika!" She laughed very loud. "Have you taken a good look at yourself lately, man? Besides, how long are we supposed to stretch this lounge bullshit? What are we supposed to be, stuck in an era till the end of time? Is that what it is? Fuck lounge, fuck Sinatra, fuck Harry Connick, Jr., fuck you, fuck Joe Pesci, fuck—"

"Joe Pesci is not a lounge singer." He shook his head and gripped the wheel hard.

"He's not?"

"No." Curt.

"What the fuck. What is he, then?"

"He's an actor. He was in *Goodfellas*."

"Then who am I thinking of?"

"I don't know—Dean Martin?" He shrugged, his feelings hurt.

"Probably."

"Probably . . ." He looked away.

"Yeah, okay . . . Well, fuck Dean Martin!" she said and pointed to an incoming car as he was ready to make a left.

"You're just not cool enough." He shrugged and coughed to suppress a strange discomfort or insecurity, pressed on the gas, made that left. "You don't get it. It's music for the cool," he said. She chuckled.

"That's it, Mika, for the cool—because they're dead!" She laughed a demonic laugh.

"You're an abomination!"

"All I'm saying . . . it doesn't reflect my sensibilities, honey—"

"What sensibilities?" He tried something.

"Ooh! . . . Very funny; but no. I'm serious. I find it ridiculous. I can't relate to the nostalgic melancholies of an eighty-year-old, Mika. That's absurd! I'm not denying old-timers their time machine misfortunate emotional stagnancy. I'm just saying . . . I'm not joining the club, that's all. It's not my place, babe."

"It's called nostalgia, Tank."

"It's called it's over.'"

"You're heartless!"

"I'm honest!"

"You have no . . . sentimentality?" he said, and she belted out laughing.

"Umm, for the past? I don't think so," she said, looking sort of away now . . . looking nowhere.

"You're heartless," he scowled.

She turned her head to him. "Fuck Dean Martin—again!" She regained her strength and pushed what perhaps was an ice-cold stab through the memory of her heart; she laughed into the night like a beautiful devil with jellyfish wings aglow in the night and with stingers the size of islands.

Her hair beat in the night wind like wild fire about to consume it all.

*   *   *

"Her eyes are gone, man, can't you see?" the fat man said. Tank sat on the armchair. "Gone. It's like there's nobody there. Nobody home! There might as well be nobody there!" He yelled this, spitting as he spoke, a spray of saliva sprinkling her thighs. She shuffled her legs slightly.

"Come on, man," Mikhail said, tilting his head with a faint weird grimace.

"She's asking for it! Garbage like her . . . polluting every inch of this planet. A filthy whore like this, Mikhail, what do you expect? You think people want this? To have this kind of thing walking around?"

"What the fuck do you know about anything, Heavy? Shit! And who is people? What the fuck do you owe and what the hell are you to them, may I ask?" Tank yelled right into the barrel of Heavy's snub-nose .357 magnum chrome revolver. "What are you here for—to get some kind of People's Choice Award? Look at yourself. Not ten minutes ago you were fucking this whore up the ass," she punched herself in the chest "—and you're talking to me about morality . . . about what the world out there wants?"

"That's what's wrong precisely!" he hissed through clenched teeth. "People like you that lure good citizens into your . . . vice—your twisted vice and perversion! That's what you teach! What you do!"

"What I teach?" She laughed. "Well, I had no idea I was such an educator, Heavy."

"You do the devil's work, my dear harlot," he said in a typical tone, washing away his involvement in any of these proceedings, assigning all responsibilities so far away from himself. He crossed himself and kissed the fingers of his hand that was not holding the deadly weapon. "And it's because of you I'm going to hell! But not so fast! I'm going to avenge this ill curse! I'm sure as hell going to make sure this won't happen to someone else! Not if I can help it!" He shifted to one side. "Mikhail, if you fucking move again, asshole, I'll make a hellish mess out of your face with this." He nervously shook the gun in his fat hand.

"What the fuck is wrong with you, man?" Mikhail said now, pushing back on the armchair, petrified, horrified. "What the—"

"Mikhail, she's a putrid prostitute," the fat man said through a sweaty grimace. "The worst of the worst! Do you think God wants people like her doing what she does—behaving like she does, going about, carrying on the way she does?" His eyes bulged out of his skull, yellowed and crazed.

"I don't really know what God wants, Heavy, to be honest—I don't know what plan he has in mind, man. But I doubt we'll find it in this apartment. And I don't think we'll find the answer at the end of your revolver," Mikhail said.

"She's a twisted fuck and doesn't deserve to live, Mikhail! This is obvious!" he chuckled, leaning to the side and casting a shadow over Tanqueray. He caressed her thigh weirdly, leaving a wet spot of sweat. "Everyone will be happy to see her gone from this place!"

"I don't know about everyone," Mikhail said, looking now into Tank's eyes. Though they were unmoving, they were set in terror.

"Don't get cute. She's a whore, Mikhail," Heavy said in disgust. "A whore for Christ's sake!" His lip trembled. His gaze hinted at a strange psychosis that straddled the precarious line in his mind between what he has done and what he's about to do. He had enjoyed so much, partaken in such an ultimate pleasure of the flesh with this barely ripe young girl. And now, sitting across from him, are the remnants of this—the body, the evidence of his terrible sin, the form of that temptation . . . the literal embodiment of evil: a girl.

"We know what she is. She knows what she is," Mikhail said under his breath.

"Do you think God wants people like her doing the kinds of things she does?" Heavy sweated, and his hand trembled as he gripped the gun. He was nervous. Behind him, in his kitchen, hung a crucifix that Mikhail glanced at quickly.

"I really couldn't tell you, Heavy," Mikhail said, "but the will of God never includes murder—I wouldn't think. Thou shall not . . . kill, Heavy."

"It's justice, Mikhail. Divine justice. For my soul, for everyone's soul . . . the soul of any . . . any potential victims she might plague. She's a viper, a parasite, an illness, a vermin, a canker."

"She's not. She's not an illness, Heavy. What the fuck is wrong with you? She's not anything else you're spewing here. She's a human being, for Christ's sake. She's a human being—she's my girlfriend, Heavy. I love her. She loves me." Mikhail's eyebrows pinched together, and he closed his eyes. He was very afraid. "Please don't hurt her. I beg you." He folded his hands in a prayer.

"Don't you see the damage she's creating around her? You say you love this thing? She has you trapped in this cycle of perversion and vice, Mikhail. Don't you see? You are an instrument! She's a demon—disgusting, putrid, ugly, perverse. An animal. I hate this skanky bitch so much. I want to strangle her . . . kill her—with all the strength and hatred of my heart! I swear to God." He wiped his forehead with his sleeve as he glanced at a picture of his parents hanging on the opposite wall. He looked at the picture in passing and with apology, as if taking a rightful accusation from it. He took a breath and swelled like a beast. "Even while I was fucking your girlfriend back there, I was consumed with so . . . so much hatred for this ugly bitch. Disgusting how she takes the dick of anyone in the ass. Anyone, Mikhail! That seem normal to you?" He laughed again with a strange, irritating, and terrifying arrogance. "She's a fucking abomination and shouldn't be allowed to roam free to corrode the fiber of society like this! She got me once, but she won't continue; that I assure you."

"You're a washed-out weak simpleton, Heavy. You are a real ugly monster, you know that?" Mikhail said right as Heavy raised the barrel to his cheek and squeezed the trigger once. Mikhail's lifeless frame rolled off the chair and onto the ground like a voiceless object, and Tanqueray was again alone in the world. She did not move or make a sound; her body was covered with her beloved's blood. Tanqueray's blue eyes quivered like gelatin. *This room?* she thought as her face melted into despondency. She closed her eyes and disappeared into paradise—away!

Lions . . . and deer . . . and baby elephants . . . a waterfall and a mountain. Golden light shone from heaven, and the sky was wide and blue. *This is paradise, Tanqueray, just as they've always said it would be,* the voice of an angel murmured close by, and above the elms a flock of bluebirds circled the sun.

She opened her eyes. She saw the fat man approach, and she did not move. She saw a large man consumed by self-loathing that corroded him, directing it all, at her, an easy target, an unvirtuous woman, easy to reproach, so easy to belittle, and to project his false . . . oh so false! . . . sense of loftiness!

He saw this girl as an easy scapegoat. A siphon for his own strange guilt . . . a blameful serpent.

His mind twisted. He can eradicate her and will go unpunished. He can erase her and she'll go unmissed . . . abuse her and only she will bear the blame. He will be celebrated privately and perhaps even publicly as he'll eliminate the vice . . . one of the socially intolerable . . . lowly specimens of our race. And all the suffering she will endure, she has surely earned!

His repressed monstrosity boiled to the surface. Confusion and compulsion both brewed in his mind . . . abominable and large like a rolling mass of smoke. In the midst of castigating his own guilt-riddled acts, he still approached the object onto which he will direct this . . . that brief embodiment, that someone who will need to pay this toll—a guilty party for this aberration of the soul.

And of course there she was! It's evident to him. He wiped the sweat that trickled from his forehead into his eyes, stinging like acid. She was the object of his impure desires, the provocateur of his tremendous lust, the inescapable lure to his libidinous ungodly perdition. That little sneak! His personal serpent in his personal paradise from which he was cast. The instrument of the devil, here reeking of cunt and promises of indeed so much punishable pleasure—unimaginable sin—punishment! You kill the temptress, you destroy the obstacle, the symbol, the embodiment of evil—you do good, oh such good. All the good to redeem yourself by the saintly laws of righteousness, Lord! Your soul washed clean . . . your acts vindicated. This is your personal holy war . . . your exorcism . . . the expatriation of one more demon! Your crusade that so well ascribes the will of the righteous creator to rid the world of such sinful evil and that curse of temptation! Right? Absolutely!

Strangle this perverse whore! The thought was written in his eyes. Kill her and you strangle the former victory over your righteous foundation, my son! You avenge your divine devotion. He will avenge the wrongdoings of this invisible demon, and kill it in that girl now made of flesh and tears and terror. Little Tanqueray Princeton, a soul—just one more, at the end of its day.

Watch her closely; the world departs in an instant for everyone.

Who instilled such incomprehension and poison in the totality of the human spirit? The chaos? Who dropped the cyanide in the well? pondered a ghost, an angel that lingered above her, placing an invisible hand on the girl's head. Who was the first of our *monsters*, the one who placed the pen on our holy chants and prescribed murderous license to those divine aberrations which but approximated his warped and loathsome misogynistic deformities to inject into the many minds of millions of men?—he who wrote hatred and called it holy. Who poisoned the purity of human linkage and compassion?—because I assure you, it's the case. When did we start murdering—literally and poetically—all those possessing of the flipside of our reasoning? When did we stopped letting be?

The ghost has no body and doesn't exist and loves everyone. The angel can't die but would give up its celestial immortality to taste life, that is, at least, a clue, to the value of it.

Through the window, a car that passed by blasted the Beatles' song:

> *And in my hour of darkness,*
> *She is standing right in front of me,*
> *Speaking words of wisdom,*
> *Let it be.*

Suddenly, Tanqueray was lifted up by a force too overpowering for her to contend with. She was turned around. She looked at the ground as two powerful, fleshy, cruel hands wrapped around her throat. She looked at the crucifix across the apartment in the kitchen and thought, *Mary, please help me.*

Her body tensed under the grip of this terrible man.

The light in the room began to dim as she saw the world retreating from her.

Her body rushed with a sudden warmth and peacefulness.

She called out to Mother Mary one last time.

Her eyes pooled with water, and her body relaxed completely. A bluebird flew out of her chest through the walls and into the night unseen.

Tanqueray's body died.

*   *   *

Tanqueray, if only I could have saved you then instead of only watching your death from this lofty, impermeable beyond . . . through the horizontal cages these words draw, and tell your story with no fair ascertaining or proper tribute. Your story, which is so much worthier of mere words, or any other form that I, or anyone else, could recount through any imperfect medium. Or in any depth or through effort attempt to depict with any amount of true substance or unfailing certitude . . . nor in any other conceivable manner of liking, possibly approximate—even in the least, with a semblance of meaning at all—your essence.

But now that the worst is behind you, far gone into the void of moonless remembrances, now that you're gone and pulse-less, I may paint you free and untainted—imperfectly, I'm sure, and clumsily most likely, but if my efforts will succeed but a fraction, they will fashion you the best I may, unencumbered by things we do not wish to curse you with: free of rape, free of exploitations, free of the untimely death of your innocence, free of torments or ill necessities, free of that canker-like corrosion of your spirit, and free of your too youthful—and cruel—passing.

I will be your genie, if not in a bottle, well, at least at this keyboard. I will give you life back, from the beginning, and in the way that you wish. From the start. I will grant each one of your desires. You will have every joy brimming that by right every person, and especially child, can justly expect—free of preoccupations, and of overwhelming and cruel monstrous anxieties and of unjust and strange hardships!

This life will be a pastoral! Hills and a splay of blue skies shining at you, and the days will be filled with the perfect and kindly devotion of mother. A beauty that is possible only in dreams and exuberant clichés. No matter; sometimes a beautiful normality is what we need at the end of things. And here, in this new place, you will start all anew, and have it all. And should you feel lacking, I'll be here waiting. And even if it's only on paper that you may now live and all that I can offer, here you will have everything.

Please never confuse my love, for I love you both, the new and the old. Because both of you are virtuous. Since both are one and the same. Even when in this life you did not believe so, I knew this was the case—even when you were submerged in that poisonous inky well of toxicity and self-destruction and dissatisfaction, I knew you better than you could ever understand yourself from the restless whirlwind of your mind.

Oh, it's easy to be kind to yourself under the right kind of circumstances, you know. This is, too, no doubt, my biased perspective, but I will take the risk should this judgment backfire and I'll take the heat and lashes from those who'll disagree. And it's true—at least to me—that it is the easiest thing in the world to be virtuous when born from a soil of lauded virtue.

But your virtue resided in a place so much deeper, so very much concealed, but so much more true thusly and in so many ways that you, yourself, couldn't even comprehend. Your virtue was atypical, and complex; and too because your heart remained unscathed and pure despite the reality that the fuel of your upbringing was so savage and cruel, to me this made you purer, and the more virtuous . . . more lovable. You became more deserving of this love because of your origins, because and in spite of them! You raised above them. Even unbeknownst to you, you became more desirable as a woman, more worthy for one to surrender to this truest, blindest love, because of this almost-profound understanding, and knowledge of where your spirit resides . . . from where the glow and flame of it blooms.

That bluebird that, hidden, emits and throbs its blue light; in that unreachable and precious obscurity of your dreams and longings—the invisible and tender desires that lay dormant when you lived, which were even to yourself unbeknownst . . . the beauty you never were allowed to experience, perhaps—no, surely!—because it was true you never had the luxury to allow it to surface. But you do now. Your bluebird may rise from its obscurity and take flight upward and out. And a flock of them may swirl all around and make mirrors of your eyes as they swarm among you.

Here you are at last restfully beginning anew . . . stepping into a bright beginning, uncertain and filled with all the promise of the better part of hope—fulfillment at last. And I assure you this, as I type the certainty that will become the absolute happiness of your future: no one will harm you, because this time I will stand vigil through your entire new life. Because I know you, because you've earned this—earned safety, happiness, and freedom.

Your body has taken shape—and your cheeks—life, blood, and color. You eyes glisten, and you are awaking. You flutter your gaze open to orbs of the sun as if for the first time, and I release you unto green pastures. You are seven. And you are free. And I'll now close my eyes, and I will let it be.

"Go play, Tanqueray. I love you!"

Dedication

To all the survivors of abuse and rape and exploitation

To all judged and misunderstood women

Killing the Tooth Faery: Science Fiction

Contemplation

To see a world in a grain of sand,
And a heaven in a wild flower,
Hold infinity in the palm of your hand,
And eternity in an hour.

—William Blake

Camilla Siss woke up at the ding of her doorbell. Her alarm clock showed 2:00 AM. She threw the comforter off to one side. Her eyes were wide and blinded in the blackness. Slowly, her pupils dilated her room into some violet suggestion. Without turning on a light, she went down the stairs, barefoot, the hardwood steps squeaking as she made her way toward the living room. Alarmed and alone, she flipped the light on. On the floor by the door was an envelope. On the front, in large letters, was written: *TOOTH FAERY FILE 1.*

She grabbed the envelope and, with a faint quiver in her chest, rushed back to her living room. She sat in the armchair and turned on the halogen lamp that stood next to it—a long tube-necked black lamp with a small head that looked over her shoulder, shining a warm, seemingly natural light.

Sweeping her eyes quickly over her own shoulder, Camilla inserted her index finger under the side of the envelope's flap and tore upward along the edge. The envelope was of thick bone-color material that resembled paper, but upon opening it, she realized it tore more like a very fine cloth . . . but once she looked closely at the frayed fibers of the rip, even that was inaccurate, since the fraying appeared to look now more like very diminutive fiberglass shards and thorns. She pulled out a translucent acetate sheet the color of milky water. Raised lettering, watermarks, and a holographic seal at the bottom left corner gave the paper an official appearance. The holograph was of a sphere with a thumbprint on its surface.

She scanned the page. The text read:

TOOTH FAERY PROJECT 15-8845-849 FILE 1.
Camilla Siss
Date of Activation: March 28, 1975
Date of Briefing: November 29, 2008
CAMILLA Sonata Deployment—1st movement

Hello Camilla.
Camilla Creation,
Camilla Responsive.
Surroundings, Knowledge, Proposition.
Information.
Immensity.

Hello Camilla.
You have read the words above. These will be the first for you.
This language is for your understanding.
First Plateau.
Commenced.
15-8845-849

Camilla turned the envelope over; there was no return address . . . no other information that would give a clue of why this document had been sent to her or where it had come from. Beyond bizarre . . . since although the document itself looked important, the contents made no sense.

She returned to bed, where she attempted to get some rest for the remainder of the night. Though there were no more strange events—or even any other, even unrelated, disturbances—she spent the night restlessly . . . in shallow sleep and unpleasant dreams.

The next morning, though tired, she followed her routine regardless. Plagued by the strange occurrence of the previous night, Camilla somehow felt it hadn't been a prank—the document was too detailed, too complex in design . . . too good. But what can this odd thing be? She spun her brain fruitlessly on this as she pulled her new towels from a closet adjacent to the bathroom. The sunshine swelled through the small square of her shower's window, igniting the white tiles into a space classically catering to the human pupil and soul. She stepped into the tub and tried her best with hot water to wash herself clean of worry.

When she had looked very closely at the document, she'd noticed how the woven patterns of the watermarks were not continuous lines, but instead, upon close inspection, she had realized they were but minuscule strings of unknown symbology and of an almost-imperceptible diminutiveness! If the symbols are not language, why are they not repeated patterns? If they are language, they are not of any writing she recognized.

Camilla came out her shower and went back to the broad whiteness of her bedroom. She slid aside the large mirrored doors of her closet and pulled out her jogging suit. Once she was dressed, she snapped an elastic into her ponytail, strapped her music player to her biceps, and skipped down the stairs toward the kitchen, where she juiced some beats and carrots, as was her morning routine for weekends. Out in the yard, beyond the sliding doors, beyond the deck, on a branch of the maple tree, she glimpsed a bluejay at the bird feeder. A few mental snapshots of the bird would return as thought fragments during her jog soon after.

Camilla trotted through the yard and around the house onto the street. As she ran, she revisited those scrambled words on the page: Creation, Responsive, Immensity. To her, these had nothing but general resonance—nothing particularly meaningful. There was nothing at all, as a matter of fact, about these words then that had any congruity with her life at present. None. But she tried to remove herself from these thoughts and focus on her run! On the road, and on the fall. An image of the bluejay appeared as she blinked through sweat, and to her right was the gray skyline of New York City across the Hudson.

She loved the fall. Loved it. Especially because of the crisp, new air and that kaleidoscopic transformation of the world into the colorings of melancholy. The fall, to Camilla, had a calming and muting effect—maybe because orange, the color of fall, was her favorite color. Orange is such a cozy, trustworthy color, she thought. Orange means you no harm. "Orange is your friend," she muttered, laughing at herself. There's something introspective about the fall . . . meditative . . . that promotes seclusion. And being, by nature, solitary, the fall was Camilla's season.

Just around the bend from her house, she slowed for her cool-down walk. She had broken a heavy sweat about a mile ago, and she had enjoyed riding that runner's high—there was a palpable buzz all around her. She skipped up the three steps of her house and walked inside. And as soon as she'd made her way in, there it was! This time, a green envelope had been slid under the door: TOOTH FAERY FILE 2 in luminescent lemon-yellow letters across the top.

She immediately grabbed it. *What is this?* she thought, looking once again over her shoulder in a chill. She double-locked the doors behind her immediately and walked into the kitchen. She stood at the counter and ripped this envelope open.

TOOTH FAERY PROJECT 15-8845-849 FILE 2.
Camilla Siss
Date of Activation: March 28, 1975
Date of Briefing: November 29, 2008
CAMILLA Sonata Deployment—2nd movement

Hello Camilla.
Camilla Creation,
Camilla Notified.
Surroundings, Doubts, Prologue.
Information.
Immensity.

Hello Camilla.
You have read the words above. The following information is a primer.

It is fact.
Please absorb.
Everything Creatable. Around you.
Implants by Adaptation.
A success

Please absorb:
Second Plateau.
Continued.
15-8845-849

The document was similar to the one she'd received before—acetate sheet, holograph seal. Only the watermarks here were in a different pattern! The waves were more pronounced, and the symbols were small hieroglyphs. Her own image was on the holograph now! She wandered into the living room and sat on the futon. She opened the envelope from the night before and took out the document. She laid the sheets side by side on the coffee table in front of her. Creation, Responsive, Surroundings, Knowledge, Doubts, Prologue, Adaptation!

What does this all mean? But the words, even by themselves, had a strange impact now. Creation, Responsive, Surroundings, Knowledge, Doubts, Prologue, Adaptation! They were random, but specific! Some kind of religious proposition? Creation, yes . . . but Adaptation—Darwin? She looked for clues but could not link all these words into anything that made any real sense. She leaned back and looked all around. Then she grabbed the pages and got up. "Surroundings . . . surroundings?" she muttered to herself, looking everywhere for a sign, any clue at all—anything slightly out of place. Surroundings, Knowledge—Doubts. Doubts?

She was stumped. This was an impossible riddle. There was nothing she could possibly derive from this bizarre text. There was plenty to observe, plenty to know. Surroundings. But Doubts? There's no doubt without a proper scene to provoke it! What is this? What could she doubt in the absence of any one specific . . . context?

Everything Creatable. Around you. Implants by Adaptation. These words were unsettling. They were not clear, but the combination of words approximated something closer to a puzzle—a very hazy, nebulous hint of something for her to consider.

The rest of the afternoon passed without further developments. She was unable to make any sense of this, and there were no more envelopes. She retired from that incomplete formula.

She cooked herself some sea bass and couscous for dinner. Dried cranberries in the bass gave it a good sweet tang, and the large-grain couscous with shitake and garlic shavings was enough to make it all a nearly perfect improvisation of hers. After supper, she lied down and read some William Blake. Soon after, she passed out. . . .

She woke up to deep blackness in the middle of the night. The only light around then was from the clock on the stove that marked 2:00 AM. She twisted herself off the mattress and staggered her way up the stairs to her bedroom, semiconscious. Once she was almost all the way up, there was a loud and repeated banging at her front door. This jolted her into sudden—and raw—terror! The sound was so harsh that it rattled the entire house. She fell flat on the floor in the darkness just as the banging stopped, and then came that total silence. The silence was worse than the noise. She went into her closet and grabbed her aluminum baseball bat. She went down the stairs slowly, hunched over, looking over the corner of the wall and gripping the base of the bat so tightly that the skin around her knuckles tightened around the bones, making the grip creak like cold leather.

She turned the living room light on, and there, slid under the door, was a red envelope! *TOOTH FAERY FILE 3.*

She ran toward the front door and immediately searched through the peephole, but there was no one and no discernible movement anywhere around. She spun around. The envelope waited. She grabbed it and ran to the kitchen, where she pulled a stool to the counter and ripped the envelope wide open. She pulled out the document. This time it was a smoky black acetate sheet. The raised lettering was silver, and the holograph seal was of herself standing at her front door—as she'd been that very day—in her jogging gear! She could see through the hologram: there was the house, her standing in front of the open door, and on the floor there was clearly yesterday's envelope. This was the image!

TOOTH FAERY PROJECT 15-8845-849 FILE 3.
Camilla Siss
Date of Activation: March 28, 1975
Date of Briefing: November 30, 2008
CAMILLA Sonata Deployment—3rd movement

Hello Camilla.
Camilla Creation,
Camilla Revealed.
Surroundings, Reality, Body.
Information.
Immensity.

Hello Camilla.
You have read the words above. The following information: content.

Hi Camilla

- *Your surroundings are a fabrication for you.*
- *This language is designed and utilized as per the capacity of your inherent intellect.*
- *All the knowledge you possess is your best response to your surroundings.*
- *Today one basic truth is unfolded to you.*
- *Everything around you is creatable at once.*

- *Every ounce of information known and knowable has been created and catered specifically for you.*
- *You are observed.*
- *Everything is from the same place.*
- *Your entire reality is an intricate fabrication.*
- *You live in a pseudo-ecology, in a predesigned environment.*
- *Your mind is a shape-changed metaphor that creates substitute interpretations, placeholder imagery of what is truly happening around you—which you cannot "see."*
- *Look at your books now.*
- *William Blake never existed. Nor anyone else on that shelf.*
- *All accessible sources to any information have been predetermined.*
- *Every discoverable element has been preset for you.*
- *The only thing "real" in this one particular environment is you and your responses.*
- *Laws, the man on the moon, shot presidents, all events: these are all preset—(in-confirmable facts persuasive to you by the hysteria that our capacity can forge to dominate and shape emotion acutely).*
- *All theories and facts have been preset to cater to the specific demands of your intellect's capacity in relation to everything else that surrounds you.*
- *Convincing formats have also been perfectly adjusted so that some things are beyond your comprehension—but not so much that they are beyond the comprehension of your comprehension: that is to say, you understand that you don't understand it, but you accept that someone else does, thus deeming them "true."*
- *You yourself are unable to substantiate or contest anything, since all elements in favor (or against) have been predetermined for you. Both answers in opposite views in every conceivable topic to you are nothing but predetermined persuasions. You could only choose, never decide.*
- *You live in a controlled environment; your most minuscule whim is predicted to a capacity too large for you to believe.*

- *Your most profound thought is our most basic, predictable behavior of you.*
- *As a small example of the scale and potential of us, consider any book on your shelf. We designed and wrote the entire book. We fabricated the author, along with his or her history—and thus all interlocking histories throughout, forward and back to the beginning and end of your "confirmable" time spectrum. We did it in order to form the entire net that is your Worldview.*
- *The entire universe is a handful of oscillating particles that hiss in a predetermined pattern. Because once a particle is determined to behave a certain way, this is inescapable. A grain of sand on your fingertip was meant to land there from the beginning of time.*
- *"Will" doesn't exist. You are only responding, even if you believe you are willing.*
- *Try to will you no longer have will, and that would be true, absolute will.*
- *Nothing ever existed before you. Everything was created at once. History was created at once, but the events that fill it never took place . . . never existed. They exist only in form of record and shock.*
- *All history is confirmable only by what we have provided to you; and since these ways are but what you have lived to know, you are unable to question or dispute. These are your sole available methods of confirmation —to prove any certainty.*
- *All possible interactions for you have been determined.*
- *Surroundings. Knowledge. Doubt. These are trigger words, and now that you have your surroundings, and your knowledge of your surroundings, this new added information will give you the tools to question further. Although you already have the answer—or at least a larger portion of the question.*
- *Now ponder on our capacity again.*
- *Second reiteration.*
- *Second reiteration.*
- *Branding:*

- *Consider the work of Mozart or all the plays of Shakespeare. All that and everything else is us. We created their writings as well as their lives (second reiteration) as well as everything else that is connected to anything that is confirmable by you and you alone—although the illusion of hidden confirmations and knowledge of others is a necessary tool for completing the world as you see it.*
- *Your world.*
- *All reality is nothing but a grand persuasion.*
- *It all happens in stages, so that you can become familiar with the concepts of fantasy, and the destruction of these into a different reality when you open your eyes to broader and newer truths.*
- *When you realized for the first time there was no Tooth Faery.*
- *When you learned there was no God, and now when you find out there's only you—and not only that, but that there is an us!*
- *We created this vision of the universe for you, which is so much smaller than you have been trained to believe.*
- *Your most extreme complexity is of unfathomable simplicity to us.*
- *Your most profound revelation is as effortless to us and evident as seeing is to you.*
- *The reason that we can never come in contact with you in the traditional sense is that it is physically impossible, but even this is unexplainable to you.*
- *We can tell you that we have, but that would be meaningless to you and impossible for you to understand.*
- *We are so different that you cannot comprehend our existence.*
- *If we came in contact with you, you would not be able to see us, hear us, or feel us. We call this comprehension.*
- *It is not at all like seeing what we have presented to you—say a dog or a snail or a cow.*
- *We exist beyond any of your senses, but the truth remains that we exist, as sure as light exists beyond a blind man's capacity to experience it. We exist in a range that the instruments of your*

body cannot reach—our mere "existence" is even beyond your intellect.

- *We cannot acquire a form that would be comprehensible and perceptible to you, and the only way we can exist to you is through the fabrication of these documents and the usefulness of this language we designed and implanted and you acquired by adaptation.*
- *To give you a comparison of this—and, abysmally, not even a close comparison—and with full knowledge of running the risk of sounding patronizing, but we promise, it is not how we mean this: just as you understand the basic necessity of keeping a goldfish, what with a tank that you procure and food that you supply it with daily, we have devised a controlled, full environment to nurture each of your own demands. In essence: what someone like you would fully need to be and believe in his natural environment, just as a goldfish cannot grasp the concept of being in essence "trapped" in a tank.*
- *And all the science and the literature in your world is part of this perfect illusion we have created, to accommodate the inevitable interactions that will form, given the present elements, in comprehensive and reflective forms that will indubitably birth curiosities in you. Science explains these events to you. Art comments (intellectually and emotionally) on these events in a series of configurations.*
- *And so it is fair that you are made aware of this truth, now.*
- *It is time for us to, in essence, kill the Tooth Faery once again for you, so that you may have yet a broader view of the total picture.*
- *Question further—into where? Not hard to say—but though impossible for you to comprehend even a fraction of the picture, it is, in essence, that we tell you that the scale will forever remain away from reach even to us who could never come to grasp the definition of ourselves—there is no truth to be found for you, as there will never be an untruth in your enlightenment.*
- *Camilla, you and you alone are the epicenter of the universe's Love. It is the greatest manifestation of the universe that there is*

no beauty to be possessed. Instead, it is to be given unaccounted for. Life—Love, is the improvable existence, except for the crude object whereby we approximate its position.

- *You are perfect because you have the capacity to fail. That makes you priceless . . . beautiful.*
- *You are perfect because you know so little—your innocence makes you the best among all in the universe.*
- *The purpose of intelligent life—to call it something—is to be kind and to observe. Life is the opposite of what is not. And what it is not is cruel and thoughtlessly reactionary—like gasses, heat, and violence. It's that simple.*
- *But instead, with life you have the power to choose things, to guide your reactions above the behavior of mere particles without choices.*
- *Life is unexplainable in a unifying manner—that is to round up the accident of life with the purpose of it.*
- *Meaning is an invention—like automobiles in your world. Things sometimes simply "are" without having to have a profound justification for being other than the pure wonderment of themselves.*
- *And thus is life . . . wonderful. Your life. The meaning of it is not to be found outside of it, but within it. The meaning of life is itself, nothing else.*

More to come in the future.
Or as we've now both come to know it . . .
After Death.
Much love.
Us.

Third Plateau. Concluded. 15-8845-849

"What is the meaning of human life, or, for that matter, of the life of any creature? To know the answer to this question means to be religious. You ask: Does it make sense, then, to pose this question?

I answer: The man who regards his own life and that of his fellow creatures as meaningless is not merely unhappy but hardly fit for life."

—Albert Einstein
Ideas and Opinions

Out of Body

No place, indeed, should murder sanctuarize;
Revenge should have no bounds.
—William Shakespeare
Hamlet, Act 4, Scene 7

Revenge is a dish best served cold.
—Quentin Tarantino
The film *Kill Bill*

Prologue

She tasted metal. Her mouth and nostrils hissed with foam, and there was a puddle of thin phlegm under her face. She'd come to consciousness slowly, and the room fuzzily came into view . . . sideways, as she felt the moist hardwood floor against her cheek. She looked all around, still down there on the floor, and recognized nothing. She was disoriented and in a state of dreamy detachment akin to coming off anesthesia.

She began to get up, her muscles quivering, protesting under her weight. Her body was unusually heavy and unfamiliar, with a thick layer of numbness throughout. The clouding in her eyes began slowly clearing as she scoped the room: a closed door, a counter, a sink—she was in a kitchen. A second door off to the side was open to a small bathroom with a small square grimy window that let in the sun mellowly. There was one window in the kitchen as well—and a barber's razor two feet away from her on the floor. In front of her, there were double doors leading to a dark room. The door was ajar, and she could see through an open band of light into the hazy ambiguity. She craned her neck forward, sharpened her eyes, and saw a large bed. On the bed, there seemed to be someone . . . someone asleep. Her eyes went in and out of focus; her sight, giving out.

She was weak but seemed to be gaining strength. She tightened her muscles once again and pushed herself up to her knees . . . and then to her feet. A rush went through her head and her ears began ringing. She felt faint but stayed in place until it passed.

She started to step heavily toward the partially open bedroom door. She pushed the door aside and stepped into the room. On the bed—sheet-less and stained—there was a woman . . . . in the nude and stretched out like an X. She walked closer toward her—toward the side of he bed. As the hardwood moaned under her heels, the woman began to wake up. Oh!—a horrific scene. The woman lifted her head and with wild and terrified eyes looked right up into the eyes of the woman standing beside the bed—the eyes now pooling with salt water and beads of sweat covered her. The woman on the bed was gagged, and her arms and body were garnished with thin burgundy cuts. The blood from a deep gash on her thigh was streaking onto the mattress. The woman beside the bed stared, the blur of her eyes finally dissipating completely. She lowered her face close to the woman—who looked at her now with disbelieving terror. The woman beside the bed narrowed her eyes and, in disbelief, realized she was looking down into her own eyes!

Suddenly, she remembered everything!

She turned around and ran to the kitchen for the barber's blade.

*   *   *

Her blood was coagulating and already sticking to the mattress, pulling at her arm hairs, and she could see the man flashing by the small crack left by the slightly open doors. It was horrendously hot in the room even though she wore no clothes at all, and the beads of sweat that mixed with the sticky blood steamed with a rusty wet smell. She had been superficially cut with a fine instrument on her forearms and other parts of her body. She was cuffed by all four limbs to the metal frame of the bed. She knew she had been raped because there was blood and semen and pain. She was gagged with leather cording but was not blindfolded, which suggested this man would make sure she would not live to identify him.

The man paced back and forth in the outer room, and through the cracks, she could faintly make out his features and discern part of his jumbled rant. The man was at imprecise and dysfunctional odds with himself—insecure, tormented, anxiously psychotic. She was witnessing the workings of an obsessive and infirm mind—shallow, contrived, juvenile, indecisive, but unsympathetic and terrifying! He grew increasingly nervous and worked himself into a grotesque and hesitant, unreasoned fury . . . the beginning of an irreversible and final compulsion!

She watched his pacing through the space left by the ajar door. He was nude and holding a barber's razor. He moved closer to the door . . . then away again. Then came the sound of him searching though the crowded drawers. Her eyeballs panned around the room, sweat rushing from her brown hair onto her eyes, down her cheeks onto her lips—a ceiling fan, a closet, one stool, and a small TV set. A barren room . . . violet . . . black molding. Wooden venetian blinds at the windows let in bright bars of sun that revealed the dust in the room, suspended in midair. It was an empty room, lonely and harsh. Sounds that signaled luckier lives crept into the room: voices and cars and children. She tugged at her cuffs. The iron grip of the rings only made her wrists more tender. She thrashed about, and the small slices on her forearms opened and closed like small gaping mouths filled with crimson wells of blood.

The door to the bedroom suddenly slammed shut with a thunder and a wobble, and there was no more sound.

One tries to picture, with no accurate approximation, the degree of raw terror this unfriendly and impossibly unreasonable presence may cause. The physical pain of a kind, terrible and prolonged like no pain one has ever had to endure. One tries to imagine the futile attempts to postpone in one's mind the dreadful event by perhaps processing each passing instant faster and faster to try and lengthen the time we remain unharmed—to prolong a second toward infinity!—but all the while knowing the moment will inevitably come. To know that, not far in the future, one's life will be gone, and that this going will be very painful—with no pity or considerations to any of one's pleadings—at—all. It is by no stretch a possible thing to deal with. It's a pointless and desperate terror. Seeing someone deriving pleasure, or worse, showing indifference to, one's misery is the most hopeless, strangest, and most inconceivable feeling one could ever be forced to endure. Where there is no escape, and once one has gone beyond those empty attempts of reasoning with this unyielding and strange presence, the realization that this horror is unrelenting, is an unbelievable and uselessly unacceptable reality to behold! Anger, disgust, hatred, and sheer panic are what result. The present is never as present as then—it becomes the absolute *now*. One is overcome by loathing and disbelief and fear. An anxiety so tremendous one's senses are heightened to where life is insisting by any means to remain! The harsh, crude idea of becoming a mere object of blood and meat reduces one to a breaking point of total and absolute desperation. One sees oneself as possibly becoming . . . a thing—a thing like any other, and nothing more. A thing that exists still and unencumbered, unknowing of the world and unaffected all around.

"Corpses that fill the markets; we live in carnage!" came rushing in singsong through the door as the blade clanked on the floor when the phone rang. Of course one would do anything to survive, but that is a respite that didn't exist here because living was not a possibility.

She could see the blade gleaming in the sun. The handle was made of hard brass, and the blade was of shiny stainless steel. It was sharpened to a paper-thin edge. She could hear him on the phone on the other side now.

"Yes . . . yes . . . yeah, it should be all okay by tomorrow. I'm in the waiting room right now . . . yes . . . yeah . . . tell Barbara thank you—and thank you for relaying the message. All right?"

He laughed. "Okay . . . okay, thanks . . . all right . . . see you tomorrow, God willing . . . all right." He hung up. Tomorrow. Tomorrow. Tomorrow. This word rang over and over again in her head. Tomorrow was nothing. Now was all there was left.

She saw his shadow flick by and then saw him bend down toward the floor. He walked away from the slit, and she could no longer see him or the blade. There was a short moment in total silence. And she momentarily went away; she escaped for the seconds she could gather, through the venetian blinds, somewhere far, somewhere far and safe.

She heard a fridge open and other indistinct sounds. Smacking sounds, cutting, then liquid pouring.

With a loud bang, one of the doors to the bedroom swung open and she jolted, tensing all four cuffs. He walked in with a sandwich on a plate and a glass of milk. He was sweating and trembled with a repulsive, indiscernible motivation—impossible to understand . . . to place in context to anything ever witnessed, let alone to relate. On his body, there were fingerprinted blotches of her dried blood. She drew from him such an alien, disparate goulash of emotions. It was as if he was stopped suddenly by a troubling suggestion in his own mind, where he would be both repelled by, and at the same time compelled to do, these things. He was apparently confronted by a monumental struggle within his own reasoning. As if suddenly he had a moral brain, but the other, monstrous side of it castigated and overpowered the ethical self, violating it, and forcing it to witness what he could not stop! His face!—he was in horror of himself, yet he was pushed to bear witness to the unforgivable. He both wanted to do, and was repelled by, what he was about to do.

He looked at her with the unyielding look of resolution, and it was much worse than a look of threat now: compassion is inconsequential, indifference is part of the pleasure, cruelty is limitless. All this was written in his gaze.

He sunk his heavy body at the foot of the bed. He looked into her. She trembled, and tears of terror welled up in her eyes while he dug his teeth into his sandwich . . . and chewed.

"I don't know. I don't know exactly what I'm going to do with you," he said, pointing to her face with his index finger, holding the sandwich, shifting his weight on the bed. He put the plate in the v-shaped space between her spread legs. Her head felt as if it weighed a ton, and she looked down at her mutilated body, at her ankles gripped tightly by the bloodied metal cuffs.

"I just don't—know. I'm going to kill you at the end; I know that much. I have to! I mean—I have no choice," he said, and he took another bite before he continued speaking through a muffled mouthful of rye and roast beef. "To tell you the truth, I don't even know how this happened." He looked around the room and chuckled. "The point is, I couldn't control myself, and I know you'll forgive me. You have to understand," he said as he poked at her stomach with his finger—still holding the rest of the sandwich. "It wasn't my fault, you see. I didn't plan this. But you were flirting with me! What do you expect? What do you take me for? Don't you show respect? Weren't you taught to show respect?" He took a big gulp from his glass of milk and then got up. He grabbed the plate and placed it on the stool in the corner of the room. "You're sweating like a damn pig! And that's because you are a damn pig. I hate pigs sweating on my bed. Why are you making such a mess of my bed? Manners, pig!" he said, hitting the metal frame with his thighs. "You see what I mean? There you go once again! I guess you weren't taught that sweating on stranger's bed is bad manners." He walked to the wall and flipped a switch. The ceiling fan began to revolve. "There! I hope this helps, cause you stink!" He lifted the glass to his face, took a few gulps, and finished the milk. "Ah! That was good. That was really good. Is there anything I can do to make you a bit more comfortable? Here . . ." He walked to the right corner of the room and grabbed the remote. He turned the TV on and flipped the channels. "Let's see, let's see . . . you look like you probably like cartoons. You're young and dumb, so we'll find . . . you . . . some . . . Ah! Here we go. SpongeBob SquarePants! This guy is hilarious! Check it out," he said, putting the remote next to her, sucking debris from his teeth. "I'm going to go take a shower, and I'll be right back. Don't get impatient; I won't be long.

Don't go anywhere." He walked away, and moments later she heard the shower come on.

He had left the door to the bedroom open; she could see steam from the shower quickly form and roll into the kitchen from the right side. The TV's volume was very high. Above her, the fan swung left and right as the blades spun, and the pull chain dinged at the light bulb, making a sound like a crystal bell. She heard the shower squeak off. After a brief moment, she heard soft, wet footsteps approach from the bathroom. He made his way into the room—his form large, irritating, and horrible. He stood there soaking wet, holding the barber's blade. He opened it and closed it, opened it and closed it as he walked around the bedroom to the rhythm of the metallic beats. He then got close enough that she could feel the heat of his soaking thighs.

"You know . . . if I could only explain to you this sensation . . . if I could only put it well into words, I think this would catch on. The pleasure is quite weird, I must admit, and I'm a bit guilty. But it feels good. I don't know why. It gives me . . . peace. Like everything is going to be all right—like it's my turn, you know? You know what I'm trying to say?" he said. Her eyes begun rolling back, and she started fading into unconsciousness. But he wouldn't let that happen. He grabbed her jaw and slapped her twice into awareness. "Listen to what I have to say! It's important. This . . . it excites me, and I don't want it to end. But I understand it has to. It's not like I can keep you here for the rest of our lives, you know. I'm sorry, but it's the truth."

Her heart was beating so strongly it was visible through her ribcage. Her jugular and aorta veins were straining from the sides of her neck. Her eyes were open wide, as she looked feverishly around the room, as if with her sight she could escape that horrible prison. But she was in hopeless restraints, in her final, cruel constriction. She began to cry. She cried so desperately—for herself, for her mother, her sisters . . . for the insurmountable, horrid pain that her body would be exposed to. She looked then to the side. That putrid human form came toward her and sat on her body. His weight on her was insupportable. There was not a sufficient amount of oxygen coming into her—her ribcage was being crushed by his great mass, and there was next to no room for her lungs to expand. She grew dizzy, lightheaded, and eventually semiconscious. He finally rose off her and she gasped. Turning around, he bent down, close to her face. The hot steam from his nostrils dried her eyes.

"Do you know what this is?" He put the barber's blade fractions of an inch in front of her face. "This is . . . how can I put this . . . well, you know, strangely enough . . . this right here . . . this simple instrument—the very same you are looking at right now—is going to be the thing that will end your life. This here . . . is death. Your own personal death. Weird, huh? Say hello to it. Say hello to it! Oh, right. You're gagged. You can't speak. That's okay, I'll take your look of terror as a hello. I think I have figured out what I'm going to do to you. When I was taking a shower, it came to me, but I'm not going to spoil it for you. I'm tired, so I need a nap after my lunch. I'll just do all that I need to do, then kill you when I'm finished."

He went to the closet and grabbed a blanket. He crawled into bed with her and got comfortable. "Now, don't wake me up. Don't move too much, and don't bother me! I'll make it hurt more, I'll make it last longer, and I'll pour hot oil into your eyes, okay? Okay . . . I'll see you in an hour."

She tried to stop her body from trembling by holding her breath and tensing up for moments at a time—abandoning her mind and forcing it to go somewhere else. His naked body was disgusting—pressed against her like a lump of hot, hairy meat . . . a demonic overture to her death.

He woke up, as she knew he would. The light had dimmed outside—clouds had blotted out the sun, foretelling rain. He had slept for an hour. The television was still blaring in the room. "Fucking TV!" He grabbed the remote, shut the set off, and flung the remote across the room. He took a deep breath and sat up in bed . . . looked through the doors into the light of the kitchen.

"Oh, man. That was sweet. Shit, I had a dream that I kidnapped some slut, tied her to my bed, and was about to cut her up and eat her in small pieces while she watched! Uh . . . wait! I wasn't dreaming . . . There you are! I hope you slept well; I slept like a baby." He got up and stretched next to her. "Fuck, did you hear me? I think you heard me. Did you hear me? Shake your head yes or no. Dang, I ruined the surprise? Well, yeah, you heard right. I'm going to heat up some olive oil over there, then I'm going to cut strips from you—because you're a pig, and I just love bacon! How lucky for both of us. So, yeah, that's it! I'm going to fry strips of your delicious bacon, and I'm going to eat them here, with you . . . while you watch me. And I'll put some television on too so you don't get bored."

She suddenly felt the sensation of a million ants crawling inside her head. Her fear and her now-definite knowledge of her doom was so immense that her body began to shake and convulse. There was a horrible noise ringing in her ears, and her heart beat with a low booming pulse in her throat. Her eyes grew hot and swollen, and her body grew so heated that the beads of sweat turned into streams that ran down her sides. The mattress was soaked in her salty fluids, and he came closer. He drew the barber's blade open, and she heard the metallic swipe of the blade coming unsheathed with a fine and crystalline echo—a cold and perilous sound. He grabbed her thigh with his left hand and squeezed it; the flesh turned white as his grip cut off the circulation. He then dug the tip of the blade into the flesh, popping open the fatty layer—an initial puncture, a slight but deep cut. Blood began to pool around the tip of the blade. Her eyes drew back not only from the sensation, but from the horrendous idea of what would come next. Before she lost consciousness, she noticed that the man had stopped cutting into her and had gotten up.

*   *   *

Suddenly, his nerves began to falter at the sight of muscle and tissue exposed underneath the first spongy layer of skin. There was an electric sensation running through his body, like a jackhammer running up and down his insides. This grew in intensity, and he staggered out to the kitchen, where he felt these strong hammering, repeated pulsations beating on the inside of the back of his head!

There was bile now rising in his esophagus, and his mouth began to foam. He dropped the barber's blade and fell to his knees. His vision blurred with an electrical panic, and there was a feeling of needles in his eyes before he lost consciousness.

There was an uncomfortable wind blowing on his face. He regained consciousness and felt sticky and covered in sweat. He was weak . . . disoriented. He opened his eyes to slivers of light. His eyes were painfully sensitive, and everything was a blotchy blur. He heard the slight creak of a door and barefoot steps getting closer. He opened his eyes a little bit. Then he opened them a little wider. He lifted his head. The figure was there in front of him—and there standing over him, staring down, looking close and deep into his eyes . . . he saw himself!

There he was, his own shape staring down into him, looking into his eyes, now frozen in terror. What was his body ran out of the bedroom into the kitchen.

But when he, himself, looked down, he saw, shackled to the bed, the body of a woman. And he remembered. The thoughts all rushed to the forefront of his mind! He looked at the foot of the bed; and there was his body, staring right at him, opening and closing the barber's blade.

She . . . was in him. He, in her.

The woman was opening and closing the barber's blade, looking at him. Knowing. She looked down at herself now. At this hairy male body she inhabited. She looked beyond her chest and saw that penis—the same one that had raped her some moments before. She then looked back up at him and ran the blade against the metal frame of the foot of the bed, screeching, making him cringe.

It had happened, and she was not questioning . . . somehow she just knew. She knew something, and she suspected he knew now too well, and so she began.

"So, isn't this exciting?" she said in that alien baritone voice. He thrashed about in a cowardly, disbelieving panic . . . looking at his victimized, mutilated female form . . . light, fragile, vulnerable.

It was so painful to him! The cuts were burning—each individual one was a hell to bear. The incision on the thigh was fresh, yielding a substantial amount of blood, which the mattress drank greedily. Already, an island of blood was forming next to the leg. "You know . . ." She ran the blade along his girly chin. "This pleasure is quite weird, I must admit; but I have no guilt at all. It doesn't excite me. I don't know why. But it gives me peace . . . like everything is going to be all right—like it's my turn, you know? You know what I'm trying to say? Do you know what this is?" She put the barber's blade in front of his eyes. The hairs on her hairy arm waved in the breeze cast by the ceiling fan. "This here is death. Your own personal death. Say hello to it. That's okay. I'll take your look of terror as a hello. Now, you were playing a game before. Remember that game? Well, I'm going to play a game of my own here too. I have a feeling that mine is going to be better. But there's only one way to find out if it's really going to be better. You wanna play? What am I saying? You have no choice! First I need the keys . . . to the cuffs. Where are they?" He looked into her/his eyes, wide and horrified. "Come on, where are the keys? You see, part of my game is that I'm going to free you!" He was frozen, mute, unable to utter a word. "It doesn't matter; I have time. Don't go anywhere." She put the blade on the plate on the stool, took a bite out of the partially eaten sandwich, and stepped out of the room into the kitchen area. After a moment, she returned, holding the keys between her thumb and index finger. She jiggled them in the air. "Here. I found them."

He was shaking uncontrollably. She came close and put her face right in front of his and said, "If you in the least move or try anything, I will empty your eye sockets with a spoon, you understand that?" She grabbed his wrist and unlocked the first cuff. He let out a hum through the gag. "Don't . . . fucking . . . move!" She walked around to the other side of the bed and unlocked the other cuff. Both hands were now free. "Sit up, you faggot!"

He sat up. His hair was covered with sweat; his body sticky with blood and fluids—a miserable sight to behold . . . abused, used, mutilated, worn, tired. She then walked around and stood at the foot of the bed in front of him, staring at her own body in this sad state of disrepair, and looked into his eyes. She spoke: "This . . . is not right . . . what you do! It is not right. What you do is unforgivable." She stood there and threw the keys on the mattress. "Open the cuffs." He reached for the key . . . grabbed it. Before he went to unshackle his ankle, she spoke again.

"Look at me! I don't think you heard me well enough!" As she said this, she opened the barber's blade with a resonant *ring*! She raised her head to the ceiling, lifted the steel blade to his throat, and with one deep, strong, sharp slice, cut open the throat of his body in a wide, red splurging gash.

*   *   *

Wind was blowing on her face. She regained consciousness . . . although she would not dare open her eyes for some moments. When she did open them, it was to a blur of light and motion. After her eyes adjusted, she found herself staring directly at the ceiling fan—the blades spinning and spinning and spinning, the chain dinging on the light bulb like a crystal bell.

She lifted her head, looked down at her body . . . and saw the cuts, the blood, and the sweat. She pulled her arms forward, and her hands came in front of her face, free and painful. She took the heinous gag from around her face and sat up on the mattress. By her legs were the keys. She unshackled both ankles and stayed there for a moment, still, slumped.

She pushed down on the mattress with her feeble, shaking arms and swiped her legs sideways. She put her swollen bare feet on the floor and pushed herself up until she was standing. She then walked.

At the foot of the bed there lay that *sickness* . . . lifeless and in a growing pool of blood. Next to his body was the barber's blade—the steel so completely covered in burgundy liquid not a hint of silver was visible anymore.

Epilogue

Her naked, bloody body was wrapped by the graying light and wind of the day outside, and soon after, by the pouring rain that washed her clean.

Oh, the cool rain! . . . She'd seen so much. She'd been so brave!

Bent

His shadow puppet figure cut a pitiful outline indeed, descending against the silver of the building's brick facade. The fire escape lowered him to the ground with a rattled noise like a drum roll on metal trays.

He was almost gone then. He must have weighed no more than a hundred pounds, but he kept doing it to himself. Daily. The alleyway was deep and tall and rectangular, and looking through it from its mouth to the hollows beyond, he walked in our direction—an upright shadow without identity, his shoulders raising and lowering and growing as he moved closer and closer. A streak of his form was slapped on the ground by the silvery trumpeting of the light behind him as it cast a shadow sharp as a razor threatening to stab—forward and forward and forward. A rendezvous of cats was broken up as he kicked a bottle into a trash bag he couldn't see: a typical scene of one of those nights that seem somehow so familiar, so the dark side of the soul.

He came beyond the two walls—a next-in-line man ready to receive, to cash in, to walk into the open. A lamp afar smeared his face diagonally in cool, informal, careless light. His face was wan and long and gray, and his sockets so deep there was no evidence of eyes there at all. His forehead displayed a y-shaped vein with no other distinction of color apart from the pallor of his chalky, dry skin . . . so arid. His face looked as if it would crack like a cast if he frowned. He panned his occult eyes through the black and silver assortment of architecture, sky, and wire and mumbled to himself how everything was getting so much better. But of course that was a lie.

*   *   *

The green apartment. He had come across it by sheer miracle about a week and a half earlier. Samantha. She brought him in. Almost nightly now. She brought him in that first night when the fat men were chasing after him to break him. He had no choice but to fling himself out the window and down the fire escape. They knocked on his door. They knocked very hard the second time—loud enough to raise him from his slumber. And he then knew. He knew needed to get out of there . . . in a hurry.

It wasn't funny any more, and his slippery ways and excuses were no longer going to buy him any more time. The fat men kicked the door in to a wide and breathy darkness, where there was a rising ribbon of smoke snitching him out as he slithered out the window toward his escape. Two curtains billowed into the alleyway outside and clung to the black steel bar above. He scurried down the metal steps, grabbing onto the sharp railing, swinging down the angular spiral. Two floors down, once he landed, it happened! As soon as his shoes thundered on the metal, two long arms reached out, grabbed him, and pulled him into the green apartment. Although I should say it was black—pitch black when he was pulled into it that first time.

Long fingers gripped across his mouth. Cold, long, feminine fingers pressed against the taut and irregular topography of his bony face. He heard his own heart beating against his eardrums. His hot, agitated breath, coming out of his nostrils, thawed her chilled hand, the mist making it human again.

The fat men thumped like wild beasts down the fire escape, rolling down in metallic rattles that bounced off the building across the alley's groove. Once they passed and nothing of them could be heard, the room slowly swelled into an emerald green light. She let go of his mouth slowly, peeling each digit off like an opening fan and slowly backing away. He spun around on one heel, his back curved like a frightened animal and his eyes transfixed in a wild stare that quivered and shifted from side to side. His birdcage of a body expanded and deflated under his breath, which, if it weren't for the hint of jerky flesh and muscle that there remained, would have creaked. His head, too heavy for his neck, slumped forward as his mandible weighed down, slinging his mouth agape like a fish out of water. His eyes were wide and bewildered like silver dollars and just as gray. Surprise and relief then came to him, as she was not at all what he had expected. She was . . . well, she was a *she* for starters, and then, very pretty . . . beautiful even!

She had very curly, golden hair and the greenest eyes, and wore, too, all kinds of green things. The lace on her skirt was an olive green, and her sweater too was of alternating horizontal striping in the faintest of greens. Her shoes were also green, and made of wood!

She was odd, sure, but very easy on the eyes. The kind of odd that breaks the norm, makes one feel one has been given a glimpse into how things would be if they weren't how they are—she was of a sort of mysticism that's just enough . . . because it remains . . . I suppose . . . because it remains earthbound.

She looked at him then and tilted her head to one side. A hoop earring showed underneath the jungle of golden locks. She squinted at him, the bottom of one cheek pushed up slightly against the bottom of her eye. *I don't know about you,* she thought to herself—playfully. She sighed in his direction, and he fell into a seat.

"Would you like some tea?" she asked with curious, comforting sweetness.

"Yes, please," he answered, hesitantly and bashful, but somehow compelled to accept nonetheless.

"I have peppermint," she said, opening her cupboard.

"Peppermint is great, thank you. You're very kind," he said to her simply, and a little self-consciously.

"No problem." She lit the fire under her teakettle and set the teapot on the counter. "It's always good to have some—company, you know. I don't get very many visitors at all," she smirked.

She sat on a small stool—green also—decorated with insects and things, hand-painted and carved onto the wood.

She looked at his arms. She saw the marks then but said nothing about them. He noticed, too, as she glanced and tried to hide them—embarrassed, or ashamed.

She looked closely at his face . . . and liked it—there was, in fact, something about his face that she liked. "You have a very . . . handsome face," she said blankly and with no other meaning than what it was—which was the fact that his face was truly handsome in some form.

"Oh," he said, jumping slightly in surprise. "Thank you. You are . . . very—sweet." He raised his hand to his cheek strangely and with a surge of joy and smiling a very kind, but strengthless, smile.

"Although," she said, slumping forward, his eyebrows pinching at the center at her tone, "I *do* find you a little bit lean." She paused and he tilted his head. And just maybe, or likely, in fact— he *knew* this to be true.

"Huh?" He was surprised if somewhat disarmed by her directness, but then there was the cadence in her voice to make this all okay.

"Yes. I find you very lean. I don't think you should be this thin. There should be a little . . . a little *more* to you—don't you feel? You need to take a little better care of yourself it seems," she said to him. She had a voice with a cadence like honey; she could *say* anything. "Who were those men?"

"They were—friends," he responded.

The teakettle began whistling lowly now, and she got up. As she walked to her small kitchenette, she said, "Some *friends* you have. Do you think you should get better friends then?" But he just twisted his lip . . . making such a pitiful wrinkle at the corner.

She brought two china teacups; the cups were as odd as she—*the type only grandmas would have,* he thought. And they were very fine; the material was thin—white, with gold-leaf rim and dragonfly-shaped handles.

"Thank you." He grabbed the teacup with both hands. "I never saw you in the building before," he said with a rush of courage and before taking a small sip.

"Well, we have never bumped into each other, but here we are," she said, raising her cup slightly.

"Here we are," he said, lowering his head onto the teacup, taking a sip.

She was sweet, charming—the sort of people who are unabundant in this world, but the sort one bumps into once in a blue moon and where time is not a factor in order to form interpersonal ease, and as far as he knew from tea . . . she had the best!

"What is your name?" she asked him, batting her green eyes as some of the steam rose to her face, and somewhere the brevity of that was magic.

"Bent. Sam Bent. But most people call me just Bent. Well, not most people, but people I know . . . and that really isn't very many," he said, then with something faint, resembling an eager spirit, "You?"

"I'm Samantha. But most people call me Sam."

"Sam and Sam! How about that! Well . . . but you call me Bent, so we don't get . . . confused."

"Too funny, Bent! How would we get confused?"

"Oh . . . yeah, I guess you're right," he said, looking around now and noticing how the light in the apartment seemed to have no source. It just happened. The faint throb of green simply was, pulsing like a shallow breath—like being in the inside of a giant firefly.

There was a brief moment of silence during which some far-off sounds made their way into the apartment—cars and voices, and there's always a siren, and the hum—the hum of the world.

Bent was ready to go on along.

"Well . . . I must go. They must be miles away by now," he said with a weak chuckle, pressing his thin lips together—forming creases at the corners of his mouth. He got up and thanked her for the tea . . . and for saving his life!—which she would have probably found amusing, if it hadn't been true.

"Okay, but you have to come back," she said to him, taking the teacup from his lean hand and setting it on the small counter behind her. "Will you come back?"

"Oh, yes, yes! Of course. I would love to come back."

"All right then!" she said with a slight nod. "But only on the condition—that you come here through the fire escape. Just like this time," she said. He found this odd, but then everything about her was odd.

"I promise," he said, contorting his tall, lanky body through and out the window; becoming a marionette and then a shadow once the blackness of the alley erased all definition.

Inside, the light throbbed and Samantha stood in the glowing green, still and pretty as a fairy. He turned around and continued to climb down. Before he took the first step, as he gripped the steel bars, she saw again his arms and his face . . . the pathetic malnourished wrinkle that forms just by his mouth, such a small thing disclosing so much more. If there was anything she could have done then, she would have. He made his way down the wall, down the side of the building like a hardened, dried bug. From below, he looked up at the pulsing green glow up high near the center of the side of the building.

*   *   *

Not very many nights later, he found himself out again . . . but he had not yet stopped by her apartment. He had crawled by but hadn't been able do it then. These days it was risky taking any chances, leaving the building through the front door, risk being seen—being caught by them! God only knows what "the fats" would do. He cringed at this thought. He stood there at the mouth of the alley for a moment, cut right. His shoes crushed the little pebbles, scratched the ground below him with his pointy leather shoes. His arms swayed beside him as if made of rubber, his hands pale and long with those bony metacarpals, the knobs on his fingers like knots on the branches of a tree. His nose protruded from his face like a sharp shard of limestone. Black shoes, black socks, black pants, so tight they showed off in detail those tubular and frail thin legs. Black shirt, black hair. Black! He preferred to pass inconspicuously—disappearing below the black telephone poles and wires against the metallic gray of the building behind them—puppet sticks and strings.

He was getting closer, and his hunger was more intense as he grew more and more tense. The pasty white skin on his temples yielded beads of sweat, and an intermittent chattering of teeth began in his mouth. A black cat walked by in the opposite direction—casual, almost familiar. Then a fat lady went by, and then a car with its tires shushing across the wet pavement. His reflection walked on through the large lagoon of a puddle along the curb in the middle of the city. Briefly, in this water, formed in perfect symmetry, a colossal dragonfly's image.

The buildings blurred by him as he got closer; the closer he got, the faster he walked. *It's so empty tonight. Clack, click, ssschip, click, click, catlap*—the sound of his footsteps filled the air with anxiety. Finally, *Click, clap, click, sssshhhhpt.* He arrived. *Clok, clok, pooom . . . pooom!*—he knocked on the large metal door at the entrance—twice with his knuckles, twice with the fleshier under-fist. There was a brief wait. Then a narrow slat slid open with a sharp slice first, then a locking sound. Bulging eyes widened behind the great black door, brown and yellowed where they should be white.

"Bent!" The slat closed swiftly, and he heard the sounds of locks quickly turning: First lock, second lock, third—fourth! "Get in."

He stepped inside. He took one step at first—crossing the line between the street and the inside—stepping literally into another atmosphere, another place altogether. He stood there for a moment and rolled his eyes through the place as if for the first time. Only this was not the first time. Not at all. He knew this place quite well by this point. And through the door, there was a long hall, dark and dank, and there were pipes in the ceiling, pipes of all lengths and girths, going in many directions and turning in whimsical corners like roads . . . like the trajectory of travelers—going here, going somewhere.

Facial expressions . . . well, those were difficult to estimate here. It was very dark, but faces were really unnecessary here. He heard a laugh—a woman's laugh—coming from far away that echoed metallically down the hall, vibrating inside the larger pipes until it disappeared like a haunting yelp.

Clack, click, ssschip, click, click, catlap—he walked down the long snake belly of this dungeon, until he got to the room—to the right rear at the very end. There was a dim light there—red—coming from a lamp on a round table standing small in the corner, flush against where the two walls met. The lampshade was crimson. Red jewels hung in a fringe along the bottom like drops of blood. Next to this there was a large, high-backed velvet armchair, burgundy and comfortable, where the man sat.

Ox. That's how they knew him. He was large, with a penumbral and ominously hot presence. He sat between the red light and the shadow in a place where neither of the two completely touched him. His hands rested heavily on the arms of his armchair; a large gargoyle silver ring strangled his pinky finger. Different sized rubies adorned that ring, the largest of which made up the eyes of the gargoyle, which grinned demonically.

Ox was in the field of procurements—illicit procurements of any kind that would be of great benefit to himself. In front of him was a medium-sized cedar box placed on top of a low oak coffee table. It was a tiered jewelry box that contained what Bent was there for. The product was sorted into the tiers of the box by quality and, therefore, by price. The higher the tier, the higher the quality.

"Take a seat," Ox told Bent, pointing to the small chair at the other side of the coffee table. Bent sat, his knees pointed forward like rifles and his hands clasped together as if in prayer. The large mass of man leaned forward, turning the open box sideways so they could both look at the display. He pointed his chubby finger at the levels . . . sequentially running his meaty hand upward as on a small and invisible escalator. His deep barrel voice rang out: "One—two—three—four, and five."

Bent fluttered one of his knees like a soundless jackhammer. He knew what he wanted, but he also very well knew what he could afford, and after looking at tier five for a considerable length of time, he finally said, "Two."

"Very well . . . two it is." Ox motioned to the man who was standing at the doorway, looked at the box, and raised his index and middle fingers. The man approached, closed the box, and retreated for a moment. Ox leaned back into the darkness with a leathery scrunching sound reminiscent of saddles.

*   *   *

No one had seen him going into his building. He had been careful. He'd looked around for at least five minutes before slinking in. As soon as he dared, he ran up the marble steps in long strides, holding his key in his hand. The front pocket of his pants was bulging new once again, and he was content, even though his wallet was depleted once again. He walked fast to the end of the hallway, his clacking heels echoing through the building.

It was a very beautiful old building that had been nothing shy of magnificent back in its day. The melancholy presence of old things, that confessed that *it had been* while still being, made the place all the more endearing. Art nouveau wrought iron lamps like luminous exoskeletal creatures of another world bracketed the hallways. The woodwork around the doors promised to host again and again the entrance of ghosts of that long-ago era. The moldings throughout and around the ceilings were the last frosted details of a cake of ambrosia. Finally he reached the cage elevator, cast iron and wood with its oily mechanics that had persisted through time.

He stepped into the lift, closed the collapsible frame gate, and pressed nine. He could, at that moment, have been a prisoner in a spider's web—the latest of one black widow's prey pulled by her long silky string awaiting to be devoured. The elevator arrived with a harsh, inconsiderate clunk, unusual in modern machines but so true to character to the unambiguous and unyieldingly austere temperament of all machines from the past.

He walked down the hallway to his apartment and inserted the key smoothly; he could sense the spring bearings inside the lock lift with a small roll inside the keyhole, then twist. Nine H. He walked into the gloom where the residual light from the alley seeped into his apartment. The image of the fat men flashed once in his mind's eye, and so he was compelled to leave things as they were in there—dark . . . and noiseless.

He put his key in the bowl—one single key strung with a thin chain onto a small brass globe reminiscent of a tiny wrecking ball that rested perfectly at the center of his palm when he held the key in his thumb and forefinger. He went into the bathroom to grab his instruments. He then thought of Sam and the green apartment. He was suddenly overcome with guilt, as he had promised he would go by to see her—today. But he just couldn't. He had business to attend to. This was important!

He was behind on his rent, and he would need to do something about that sooner than later. It was the fourth of the month, and anxiety knocked on his chest as he couldn't hide from the fact that this was becoming a pattern. Oh no, no. He had promised himself that, regardless of anything else, he could never let things get out of control—get to a point where he couldn't manage things! *Miss rent?—this is important! A conscience—okay, I still have that.* He would deal with this tomorrow. *Tomorrow's another day. And tonight's tonight. Tonight is good.*

Before he sat in his armchair, he reached into his bulging pocket, pulled out the contents by one corner of the waxy paper, and put it on his coffee table in front of him. *Number two. That's okay. Someday, we'll be able to afford . . . number five! Yup.* Next to this, he placed the leather pouch he'd brought from the bathroom. This he opened and spread out like a rectangular butterfly: the spoon, the water, the syringe, the burner, the cotton, the rubber tubing, and matches. He opened the paper bag and scooped a small amount of powder with the spoon, poured some water into it, and lit the burner. The clay substance bubbled in the liquid and dissolved into a murky, thin fluid. *This is going to be so good for me, tonight.* The syringe drank all of it from the spoon, and he clamped it between his teeth. He tied and tightened the rubber tubing around his arm, above his elbow, as his long, white limb extended from him. His vein swelled and lifted, strangled. He grabbed the syringe from his mouth and pressed the needle against the vessel. He punctured his flesh. A brief plume of blood rushed into the syringe and courted with the fluid inside just before he pushed the glass piston, thrusting the mixture into the bloody, fleshy branch. Number two then mixed in with his cells and quickly took over, traveling throughout his body like a runaway train: his arms, his legs, his neck, his back, his brain, and every small vein of his eyeballs—his eyes rolled back in an unfortunate and tragic pleasure. His large fish mouth opened and let out a breath and a moan. His thin lips framed the hollow blackness in his throat. His eyebrows pinched at the middle while he hovered there, somewhere in an unreachable limbo between agony and ecstasy. He pushed back into his armchair and melted into it. "Damiana." He whispered this. And, in his fading thoughts, alone in the fog of an endless and arid, nameless land, he knelt with withered violets in front of a very small grave plate. Dried-up vines claimed the stone in his dream as he ran his bony digits over the arid surface of it: *Damiana. In loving memory. Dad.*

His body contorted into an unlikely rest. His frame, angular and contradictory, stayed this way.

*   *   *

When she looked through the window, she saw death, and she let him in. He had rapped on the glass slightly, making a noise that she first mistook for a bug crawling on leaves. He was crouching down looking at her, attempting to smile.

"Bent!" she said in surprise, hiding her alarm at his wan and troubling semblance. "Get in." He twisted his long body through the window and stepped inside.

"Well, this is a good moment to come visit," she said and kissed him on his cheekbone. "I'm making supper."

"Oh good!" he rasped, then—after a pause: "Sam . . . I'm sorry I haven't come by to visit; it's just—"

"Don't worry," she said, not wanting him to have to excuse himself. "You're here now, and that's a good thing. That's a great thing. It's great to have you here, Bent." She grinned widely and turned her head toward the stove.

"Thank you, Sam. It's always good—great!—coming here . . . to see you . . . and spend some time," he said, still standing there, not quite sure how to fill the silences.

"Take a seat. Make yourself comfortable, for Pete's . . . I'm making rabbit stew," she said then and grabbed a fat wooden spoon from a porcelain vase.

"Rabbit stew? My mother made the best rabbit stew!" he jolted, then calmed down some. "I haven't had it since she passed away," he said then.

"Well, I hope it's as good as your mom's, although I won't be offended if you say it isn't. It's never as good as Mom's, right?" she said to him with a wink. A tender little smile ambushed her face, dimpling one of her cheeks. This brought about a faint blush to his face—and gratitude.

"Did you learn this from your mom?" he asked.

"Well, no. I've always liked to cook," she said stirring in the pot. "It's so much fun mixing up things, you know, and so I pick up from here and there as I go."

"How about your family? Do they live nearby?" he asked, leaning forward on the armchair, his eyes silver and round and now coming into view with the light of the kitchen.

"My family. Well," she said with a chuckle, "I haven't had a family for some time now, Bent. I'm on my own. Have been. But it's okay. It's how it goes."

"Oh," he said.

But before he could say anything else, she gathered up utensils and handed them to him. "Here. Help me set these on the table. We can start soon."

He placed the two settings down: forks, knives, spoons, dessert spoons, napkins. The utensils were garden-themed, and they were all different! Not one had a partner. Flowers and insects were shaped on the handles. The napkins were made of fine linen and were all hand-embroidered with tulips and bees and other icons of nature.

"Here we go!" She came in with a large porcelain pot, and with a fine steel spoon tucked into it. The spoon's handle was green and made of chiseled marble. "You just sit, and I'll bring the rest. Just sit tight." She brought back a vegetable tray—sweet potatoes, carrots, and cauliflower . . . pear juice.

"This is just—great, Sam." He exhaled, looking at all the food. "Thank you. Wow! I can't remember the last time I had a meal like this!" He was excited, confused, guilty, afraid, grateful, joyous.

"Well, let's enjoy it. A meal is always more enjoyable with nice company, no?" she said, smiling—that dimple forming again.

His fragile, long fingers rested on the table, and he was certainly glad to be there, if a little shy and conscious of himself. His semblance was anemic and was for the most part very introverted, but though he was at times moribund, his innate natural kindness remained evident and vital somehow, even through his deathly pallor.

She served the steaming rabbit stew, and he didn't question how this had come about—what he had done to warrant such kindhearted attention, because had he done that, pondered on this, he feared he would not let himself stay. Sam stood, unaware of his faint stare. And Bent thought she was likely a saint . . . the pulsing green backdrop behind her throbbing like an emerald heart.

The stew was perfect! The sauce was of a flawless consistency—not too thin, not too thick, and the pinch of salt, nuanced to perfection. The vegetables were as God intended. Perfect. Discussions . . . conversations were rendered unimportant; what was happening on their plates was all that mattered then. And that silent company was the unspoken and only necessary topic.

Once they finished, she took the dinnerware away to make some tea—peppermint again. When she was gone, he panned around the small apartment—kitchen, small dining room with only two seats, small bookshelf. She had an old phonograph and a shelf full of old records, and that was the only music she had, it seemed. In a corner of the room, an empty rectangular glass box, the type to keep things away from dust. There was a small closet, and a small bed. And that was it. In one small area was all her home, all she had and needed.

She brought the tea in on a tray and placed it on the table—she noticed how he never leaned his back on the seat . . . and unbeknownst to her, this was because, somehow, and for some inexplicable reason, to him this felt wrong: perhaps the neurosis of some lingering hidden memory of a since-past discipline of a sort. He took the teacup and saucer, extending his long white arm like a crane. Thin and ghostly shadows crawled upward, ominously haunting his veins.

"Bent?" she said, looking straight at him. Her eyes were like green emerald marbles trapped in a sphere of glass. He noticed them, and they seemed—like the apartment—to be glowing now. "I know what you do," she said. He took the teacup from his lips and raised his brow to her. Bent became . . . very vulnerable. "I know what you do to yourself."

He said nothing as he deflated slightly into his seat. He felt a shard of shame pierce his body, and he looked to his side . . . toward the window—maybe to an escape?

She noticed the vein on his neck was pulsing. "No," she said to him. "No." She grabbed his hand, and with her pink, moist thumb, caressed the palm and shook her head a little. She lifted his hand and kissed his long fingers. If he had any moisture in him, he would have perhaps wept.

*　　*　　*

"Sam . . . Sam . . . Bent!"

He jolted to consciousness to a bunch of wildflowers and a window.

"Oh . . . what is this?" He opened his eyes and sat up. He found himself in a bed in a strange and bright place. "What is this?"

"It's, ah . . . it's your wake-up call! Isn't this great?" she said.

"Sam!" he said with all the strength that he could gather. A smile widened across his brick of a head . . . he wrinkled the sides of his mouth almost to the point of snapping. "What is this place? How did I get here?"

"I brought you here. You're in the hospital," she said, putting the flowers aside.

"Oh . . . ?"

She had found him two nights earlier. He had never made it back to his apartment. He had barely even made it to the fire escape. She had found him in the alley lying on a pile of garbage. There was blood in his arm. His skin seemed to be made of papier-mâché; it barely clung to his bones. He looked like a bundle of bones and clothes, barely a living thing. He was dying, fast.

"I found you in the alleyway. You—overdosed, Bent. But the medics came quickly. You have been here for a couple of days," she said to him. She grabbed his hand, and there was a hint of cushioning now on his fingers. Living flesh. Grateful hands. There was a light coming from behind her. Her curls were lit like an apparition aflame. Her eyes, despite the brilliance of the sun behind, intensified in a green glow. Ablaze along the sun behind her.

"Thank heaven for you, Sam."

"When you are released in a couple of days, you are coming with me," she said to him definitely . . . and gently. "Something is going to change."

The night she found him had been terrible. He'd scraped all the money he had to the last cent and gone to see Ox. "Number five!" he'd said to Ox and wouldn't wait. He couldn't. He had waited beyond what his body could endure . . . beyond endurance and into desperation.

With his prize, he ran fast to his building. *The fats!* The fats waited at the building's steps. Inconspicuously. They figured he had to return at some point. *They look like putrid boars!* he'd thought. Through the shadows, he went two blocks past them and came around the building on the other side and into the alley behind. He was shaking; there was a sharp and cold pain shooting up his spine. His clothes were soaked in his sweat, and his teeth rattled like a strange overture of death's castanets. In his trembling vision, the alley shook from side to side—an earthquake? *I need to do this!* He would never make it up the fire escape; he would lose his grip . . . he would fall.

He ran halfway into the alley. Behind a large metal garbage container, he sat on a black plastic trash bag. There, he did it. He took off his shirt and tied it around his biceps into a tourniquet. He shot up. And his pupils widened, each one like a black hole swallowing a sea of stars around it. He faded away . . . so much closer to death then that she stood next to him. Oh, death carried her own breeze; he felt her invisible blackness bracing against him. A hot strange breath, alluring and terrible. The fabric of her dress like a bride against his hand.

She beckoned him with the sure promise of that black, indifferent void—where life doesn't only *not* exist, but where *it* no longer matters. And *to matter*, being the reason those that stay behind, grieve: not so much because those who have passed don't have *it*, but because we understand that *we* do, and when you love, you want your loved ones to have all that *you* have—and most certainly, life. As much life as they possibly can.

He crashed then in that alleyway. Pounds of human wreckage. One of God's sorrows who almost then tasted infinity.

*   *   *

The day was harsh on his eyes. It was hot. And his black clothes absorbed all the heat of the sun and clung to his body. He looked very unnatural—misplaced in the daylight, like a bat at the beach. He hunched and walked forward as if hiding from the sun, as if the light would destroy him, reduce him to cinders. He squinted involuntarily, his eyes fearful the light would penetrate them, melt his brain. He hugged himself and crossed the streets in a strange panic, skipping with those outstretched, inflexible legs.

It was a harsh break into the broad blue sky, sure, but he was released, and that was surely freeing. And, as he looked up, the trees and the green and the blue reminded him of something he thought he'd lost under the murk.

Damiana flashed inside his eyes in a pastoral scene, and she walked beside him now, invisible and telling him secrets . . . and pouring gold into him. Damiana. He looked in midair and looked into nothing, where she clearly was! And she held her father's hand, and she'd never let go, and he knew this now, finally.

There was color surrounding him! *Odd. Very odd.* He felt lost and confused in this element. "No. Not at all!" Damiana said to her dad. "Keep walking; it's . . . well, it's great!"

People's faces bore a strange an unfamiliar glow . . . they wore strange expressions so uncommon to him. Bright and wide—content!

He'd forgotten about all this; he'd forgotten it was all right. *The park. Hmm.* He looked down at the glass silhouette of Damiana as she pulled him toward a dirt path. He walked and walked for most of that day, listening to the sounds, reacquainting again with the colors of the world.

He sat on the bench made of worn green wood. And it was okay. Damiana then left to play. And she was everywhere.

Bent got up and walked and felt a bulge in his back pocket . . . bulkier than usual, and he pulled it out. There was money in his wallet. *Huh?* Brand new bills and a note.

= *Trust.*
Sam

Hmm! Equals, trust. A small but very special feeling permeated through him. He bought a hot dog and, later, an ice cream.

He walked some more as the day turned into twilight, into night. He walked all the way home, where he came to face the old and too familiar picture. He looked all the way into that long, dark, and rectangular alley. It was like a large stone grave fit for demons. The fire escape hung there, lean and cold, a grotesque skeleton perched on the side of the building.

He walked on and went in through the front door of the building. Once he closed the elevator gate, he noticed a burst of unfamiliar strength in his pull. He unlocked his apartment and turned the light on. It struck him all at once as he looked into the space with certain amount of disbelief. A square and disheveled gray space. Not a centimeter was without a layer of dust—all except for his armchair and coffee table, the only two things in this place that seemed to get any use. There was an envelope on the coffee table. He sat on his chair and opened it.

> *Hi Bent—*
> *The money in your wallet is a loan for your rent. Pay your*
> *landlady tomorrow.*
> *Come when you get this.*
> *Sam*
> *P.S. I came in through the window—of course.*

He was about to make his way out the window when he heard a loud banging on his door. *Oh, God! Really?* He quickly rushed down the fire escape, leaping onto the landing of Sam's floor; she pulled him inside once again, in the dark, as the fat men crawled down the fire escape—big balls of blubber and leather rushing and huffing into the night.

"Welcome back, Bent. It's so good to see you," she said to him, cradling his lanky anatomy, which hung on her like clothing on a tree branch. "They won't give up that easily, it seems."

"If at all," he said. "I got your envelope. Thank you . . . but you didn't—"

"It's a loan, Bent. And you return it when you can. It's the least I could do."

"The least you could do? You have done so—"

"Sh-sh-sh-sh—" She pushed him back onto the armchair slowly and with both hands. "Rest. The doctors all said you needed to rest. And you have your regimen to follow after this. Correct?"

"Correct. I mean, yes. I have all the . . . paperwork. I still have it all in my pocket. See?" He took it out and unfolded it. There it was . . . the address of the place and—all the information about what he would need to do. The change had happened in him. Sam could see it, but best of all, she could feel it.

"You're no longer a caterpillar," she said with a smirk. "You are a pupa, now, Bent!"

"Huh?"

"Um . . . pupas rest," she put a hand on her chest. "They rest as they . . . become." "Become—what?"

"Well, what you were *always* meant to become."

210

"It's been hollow, Sam," he said as he scrunched his sweater in the middle of his chest.

Sam said nothing.

Damiana floated outside her window—a crystal ghost.

"I'm so tired," he muttered.

"You are supposed to be. You need to sleep now, and then you need to sleep a little more. You take it a day at a time. Lie on my bed." He raised his body from the chair and walked to her bed, took off his shoes, and placed them neatly at the foot of the bed. She tucked him in.

"Bent?"

"Yeah?" He looked her way with his large, gray eyes, his brow bending upward in the middle.

"Did you know . . . you are special to me?" she said. He shook his head, which rustled against the pillow with a sound like hay.

"Just imagine what you are to me, Sam." She kissed his pasty forehead, and he went to sleep, peacefully, as he had so long ago.

The green glow dimmed all throughout. The small crease by the side of his mouth upturned, and Sam kissed it.

*   *   *

He woke right up. It was morning . . . the next day, and the light shone in his eyes. It was pink, hot inside his eyelids, and once he opened his eyes, his pupils squeezed to a point. He lifted his heavy head and realized he'd woken up in his own apartment! His shoes rested neatly next to his bed, and the money was clamped underneath his alarm clock—which read ten o'clock.

Using his large head like a sling and for momentum, he flung it toward his feet until his entire body became vertical. He sat on the mattress this way for a few moments until the blood flowed naturally again and the little scurrying starts disappeared.

He took a shower, put on a clean set of clothes, unclenched the fold of bills from underneath the clock, and ran down to the ground floor toward Mrs. Dobbs's apartment. He took the stairs down rather than the elevator. An electricity, a new vitality, brewed inside of him. He skidded on the mosaic tiles on the floor at the bottom of the stairs. Mrs. Dobbs opened the door not long after his rapid knocking.

"Good morning, Mrs. Dobbs. Here's the rent," he said to her nervously.

"All of it?" She took the payment without taking her eyes off of him, noticing this—new radiance.

"Yes. All of it. And I'm very sorry I have been late these last couple of months," he said briskly. She almost wanted to slow him down, though this new "thing" he had going, this bug that had bit him . . . had done him good. "Thank you, Mrs. Dobbs, and please say hi to Mr. Dobbs for me."

"Mr. Dobbs has been dead for six years, Bent."

"Oh . . . well, send him my regards anyhow . . . um . . . wherever he may be, Mrs. Dobbs."

"Bent?"

"Yes, Mrs.—?"

"Excuse me for being nosey—or forward—and it's just out of curiosity, really, but it's just odd that you pay me in cash—you usually give me a check. Any reason for that?"

"Well, okay . . ." He looked down at his shoes. "I must be honest. This is a loan, Mrs. Dobbs, from Sam. But I *will* pay it back!"

"I'm sorry, Bent. Sam?"

"Yes, Sam. From Six G. Ms. Greene. Samantha Greene?"

"Mr. Bent, are you all right?"

"Well, I'm better than all right. I'm *great*, as a matter of fact . . . thanks for asking, too!" His eyes gleamed, wide and silver.

"Okay, but, well . . . Mr. Bent, I must tell you then, Samantha Greene has not lived here in more than fifty years," she said.

Bent froze.

"But . . . she . . . her apartment . . . also—her *mailbox*!"

"Mr. Bent," she said, "Ms. Greene was the former owner of this building . . . many, many moons ago. She bequeathed the building to our family long ago . . . and with the only condition that her apartment would never be rented out, and that it would be left untouched. And—that is the way it has been ever since."

Bent thawed. "Mrs. Dobbs . . . can I . . . could you . . . would it be too much to ask if I can see Ms. Greene's old apartment?"

"Sure, Mr. Bent." Mrs. Dobbs said with a gregarious chuckle. "In all these years, believe me, you are the first one to ask that. I'll be right out with the key."

She retreated inside and the door closed behind her. When she came back out, Mrs. Dobbs and Bent went up the cage elevator all the way to the sixth floor. Slowly, catering to Mrs. Dobbs's pace, they made it to the apartment: Six G. It was an old brass key, and already corroded . . . blackened with time and tarnish. The key turned with a chalky resistance, and the door opened into a bright apartment. Light flooded every inch of it. Sunny. Dust particles filled the empty spaces, floating like bits of gold leaf in a vintage snow globe. Bent stepped inside. Yes, it was definitely the same green apartment. Everything was as he had seen it the night just past. Only everything here all bore the wear of time. Of many decades upon it! Everything was faded by the years . . . years of exposure to light, to air, and to dust. Everything green was faded and subdued . . . quiet, as if dormant, and holding great and strange secrets.

The teakettle! His heart thumped once; he took a closer look at it: part of the kettle was rusted, some of the paint chipped away. The dragonfly teacups were all covered in a gray film of dust—the skin of time—the painted flowers hardly visible on them. Dust also dulled the embroidered napkins resting in the crystal cabinet by the yellowed box of peppermint tea.

The wildflowers she had picked and taken to him were here! Only withered and wilted and preserved in that glass rectangular box in the corner—sealed away from dust. On the wall—something he had not noticed before in the room—was a picture, a framed picture by the door. He got close and could see nothing but a fog. With his forearm, he wiped the dust off the glass . . . and saw her!

"That was Ms. Greene," Mrs. Dobbs said to Bent from the doorway, holding the key with both hands. "Wasn't she lovely?"

The reflection of his eyes scanned up and down the likeness.

"Oh yes! She is . . . *absolutely* beautiful," he said, looking at her spiraling curls, her striped sweater, and her handful of wildflowers—the same in the glass box behind him—only here fresh and vibrant. The dimple on her cheek was immortalized in the sepia roughness of the old photo. He looked all around one last time and beyond the window through which he'd climbed so many times, as he then turned around, leaving the green apartment behind.

"Thank you, Mrs. Dobbs. Thank you very much," he said as he walked past the frame of the doorway.

"You're very welcome, son, of course."

He knew now and stood there for a brief moment while Mrs. Dobbs looked at him, pondering, waiting. "Okay," he said, digging into his pocket and taking out the key to his apartment. "Here is my key, Mrs. Dobbs. I won't need this now. Thank you so much! I'll leave now . . . you may keep my deposit. I'll leave my apartment as is. There is a little furniture in there, and it's practically unused." His face was lit by a broad, fine grin, and Mrs. Dobbs stroke his arm, almost as if knowing something. Or at least recognizing it.

"Well, it was good having you here, Bent. Please know you'll always have a home here."

"Thank you, Mrs. Dobbs."

Bent walked out of the building and into the open, crystal clear night.

There was a crisp, cool breeze blowing from the north to where he headed. And Damiana followed with him.

* * *

Not very long afterward, a lanky hunched figure—pale, wan, and stale—walked into his new apartment: Nine H.

"And this is your key, Mr. Worn," said Mrs. Dobbs, dropping the little brass globe attached to it by the small chain into his palm. "Rent is due the first of each month—but you have until the fifth, really." The door closed, leaving her in the hallway, and him in the penumbral breath of his apartment.

A few nights later, on a black and silver cold evening, lit by a large and round blue moon, and as one looked high but not too far up, through one of the building's square windows, beginning to grow, one could see a pulsing and throbbing green glow.

The Beach Girl

Live in the sunshine, swim the sea, drink the wild air.
—Ralph Waldo Emerson

Early in the morning. Dawn, and the first golden strip of sunlight sits on the horizon. The sky is swelling into a placid and rusted blue, and there's barely any sound at all. The clouds smear throughout like yogurt, and I'm already here. I feel the breeze on my back; so early—earliest. I've caught the dawn of her for the first time. *I love you.* I've loved her ever since I met my beach for the first time. Today the ocean is flat and still, and the water graces my feet gently . . . cold and small and in secrecy. Later on the sun will shine through my eyelashes and I'll see golden orbs. A vapor will radiate from my body—an invisible glow in the afternoons.

I've spent the whole night here. I guess I had no choice—and my best friends came and visited, or else I dreamed it. *Should I tell you?* The Witch and the Pumpkin Patch Man. They're both made of cloth. They're stuffed. My grandmother made them. She's gone now. She sewed them, stuffed them, and gave them to me; left them on me when I was still asleep.

The Witch is green and wears black and burgundy, and the Pumpkin Patch Man is the colors of fall. I was lying on the sand when they came, and the sand was cold and moist where I was—it didn't bother me. The sky was black and the stars were out—like spilt salt on deep blue velvet. They came waltzing down, and I heard their small feet in the sand—*crush, crush.* The Witch came and sat on a wad of seaweed, and the Pumpkin Man leaped onto my back.

216

To me, they were not a problem because I've known them for so long now. They've kept me company, especially through so many scary nights growing up. They sit on my bookcase next to my favorite trophies. The trophies are all from swimming competitions. But last night they came all the way here. The Witch stuck her broom in the sand and asked me, "Well—aren't you cold?"

"I am but it's okay."

The Pumpkin Patch Man stroked my back, and it tickled. I tried to swat him, but he slid further back.

"You've always been hardheaded, River," the Witch said, and the Pumpkin Man nodded.

"It's the beach. We love each other."

"Well—we miss you. We have missed you."

"I'm sorry. I'm so sorry," I said.

"You know, they are looking for you."

"Are they?"

"Yes!" she said at once, and the Pumpkin Man nodded again—this time shaking the skin on my back.

The Pumpkin Man doesn't talk—but he pantomimes sometimes. He's always been good with that, and he makes us laugh . . . his pantomimes and his dances. They wake up at night. Every night. He has a butt sewn onto his body. He makes prints with it on the windowpanes in winter. He's made of sackcloth, and his details are outlined in black pick-stitch. His body is filled with cotton, and his legs with sawdust. The Witch is made of linen and cotton and buttons. They always know things. They know how to make things well again.

The night was a still jewel, and when they appeared, time stopped and the ocean turned to glass, the sand to marble, and the air to platinum. The Witch straddled her broom and flew toward the water; the Pumpkin Man jumped up and walked down my body—down my back, my thighs, my calves, and jumped into the crystallized sand. Above us there was a blue seagull, frozen there in midair; far off was the lighthouse. The lighthouse shone a beam of light in our direction, making a spot of light precisely where the Witch now walked. I got up and made my way to the crystal water;

I stepped into the slippery surface. It was smooth—so smooth and translucent and black! The beam of light shone all the way through, making a spotlight on the sand below the glass where there, frozen in place, was a school of small yellow fish just about to make a swift turn. I breathed the wild air, and the stars fought for my eyes. I sat on the large fist of water—surf, like a multitude of glass marbles.

"Are you coming back?" The Witch flew around me and then perched next to me. The Pumpkin Man came close, taking clumsy, puffy steps. He sat on a smaller wave.

"I can't, I'm sorry. Not tonight."

"River."

"I can't." I put my hand on her linen cheek . . . ran my thumb across her button eyes.

"Well—they're looking for you! And they're going to find you."

"Okay," I said. I slid down the cold wave and got up again, digging my heels on the glass of the water. The hard water boomed like thunder under my weight, and a flock of startled angels flew through the clouds. The two followed behind me, and I walked toward my spot in the sand and lay down.

"It's so cold out here, River, and it's dark." A small diamond tear came out from underneath one of her button eyes, slid down her linen cheek, and dropped to the sand—breaking into a hundred pieces. A second diamond was about to fall when I caught it in the air and swallowed it like a pill. The Pumpkin Man came close and, with his sewn lips of yarn, kissed me. The sounds of the beach returned, the blue seagull flew across the sky, the thick beam of the lighthouse spun around slicing once, freeing the sky. The Witch and the Pumpkin Man walked away, crunching in their small ways in the sand. They walked away from me, beyond the sea grass and beyond all that blackness.

* * *

The beach. My sister—my twin! Couldn't do without her. And in the summer she makes my hair golden! My eyebrows . . . my eyelashes are all golden, and my skin is the color of honey—warm, velvet, and joy. In the morning, there's peace, the opportunity to find the secrets. The afternoons sizzle, and the old peace returns again at dusk. A day is a life. That warm air booming against my face—my cheeks push under my eyes—the calm, the sound of my feet digging into the sand. The large wave coming in—then a run . . . a few shallow splashes. And a plunge! Silence—silence then all around. Then I come out to the surface to a wide-open gasp, and I swallow the world. There's a sharp blade of water that expands toward infinity. Night—the fire in the sand and the smell of burned salty wood, embers, and orange flames.

Now the water pushes against my side, lightly, and I swivel like a boat. The water is cold this early; I feel the rhythms . . . slow . . . and the waves whisper at me. My legs dig into the sand as the waves retreat. I will stay here again. Wouldn't it be perfect if things didn't change at all? Freeze a single moment for all infinity—now for instance.

Wild violets are growing beyond the sea grass. Are they supposed to grow out here? None of my friends have come to find me, and the sun is already yellow. And they know I haven't returned. Do they think I'm hardheaded too—is that why? The Witch told me they were looking for me—I'll wait the rest of the day for them, and then I'll leave. But not before that. Not now.

*　　*　　*

You should have seen me last week. I was on fire! We broke for summer just three weeks ago. They want to have first picks on me to play for their team because I'm as good as if not better sometimes than the guys. I scored the most points last week and had very few mess-ups. At one point I made two in a row right on my serve.

My surfing is fine, but that's about it—just fine. What I'm really good at, and what I love, is swimming! Breaststroke. At that I'm undefeated! So far. I must have been around three years old when I sensed it first. I just knew there was something about the water—I felt it; I loved it. I remember my father dunking me in and out of the water, and there was a joy there unlike anywhere else. I dreamed about it. Still very small, I learned how to swim—and very well. I was around five when I stated racing against bigger kids and winning the races. There was nothing better. Nothing more fun—it was as if I was born in the water! I said one day I would swim, touch the horizon, and swim back.

And *nothing* beats racing in the ocean. Because the ocean is alive! This water has not been domesticated. I come early, then the guys start pouring in slowly. Sometimes they spend most of the day here too. I'm usually the first to get here and the last one to leave. I like my time alone with my beach. They wouldn't understand that. They would think I was strange for it. Two days ago, I wrote something for the sand. It goes like this:

sands as far as I can see them stretch ahead of me.

beyond the air I breathe sitting at the bottom of my pupils wide and gray.

there are flat waves coming toward me.

I can see them.

their rolls are long and small, and I can hear their hissing.

speaking to me?

neither can I understand the wind in my ear, and I've known them for so long!

I'm sorry.

I notice there's a sky above the water.

I've been so preoccupied.

it looks just the same but the clouds don't move.

they're frozen.

where am I?

white and flat like razors.

there is no sun, and the day is broad.

her figure passed far, but she could have been here just the same.

she could have been anywhere.

I see her; she's me.

her heels pressed into the sands and displaced the picture.

the sand moaned.

but quiet.

it looked at itself imprinted.
present.
her heels were long gone.
three seconds ago when the water hissed over.
her form now deformed.
again and again, the water.
smoothed over the print.
if it wasn't for the rocks there would be nothing else.
thank you.
the water comes farther at night but that's all.
and nobody can see it.
not even I.
the night comes in and the days are long breaths.
so long!
what is it like to live for so long? a day is a breath.
breath is life and so is a day.
how many breaths in a day?
anything that lives that long is dead.
not quite. life and death are one; inseparable.
who tells the sands that she's lived so long?
she's been so many places. she's everywhere.
you know her voice.
she's in my hand and slips through my fingers.
she knows you; she knows all of us.
she's seen the loss of you so many times.
have you heard her beckoning?
have you heard her weep with the throat of the ocean?
that's why I'm here.
caressing her. loving her as she loves me.
she will keep losing us all till the day she'll lose us completely.
but we'll keep coming and dying.
we'll keep coming back to her every day.
if we only knew. she's seen so much.
she's felt your heels.
she's felt our heels till she'll feel them no more.

People find the beach unusual at night—especially to swim. I don't. I never have. At night she speaks a different language. She changes, becomes even more feminine. I plunge into the inky waves and open my eyes as I swim in that empty, cool space, looking into that black liquid infinity so unequally haunting.

Today I won't move from here. I'm hers! I'll spend the rest of the day with her *just* like this—feeling her around me. The sun is waking now, stretching and growing hot. Soon I will feel the heat of it on my back . . . my arms and my legs. Soon it's going to *burn* and turn my hair just a little lighter. I just tasted the salt water, and the rough sand cradles around the contours of my curves, pushing against my body. I don't want to move from here; I want her to move *me* where she wants. The sun is high and gold now. A faint coolness comes over me when the clouds sail over and obscure the sun. The seagull comes to visit. She's curious of me. But no people today. Not here—I have the beach all to myself. Quiet—and time is passing, but it's not.

The tips of my fingers and toes are pruned. The coconut trees rustle not too far away, and, after the sun peaks and starts falling down in the west, the shadows will come and lie on me. Then the golden threads of sun will dance though the leaves made of ribbons.

I can feel them. I now sense them. It's time to go home—getting closer. I will have no choice.

"They are close, River . . ." the Witch's voice sings in my ear. But I don't see her. They're nowhere, but they're close. I'm going home. *Oh, the sea. My beach. When again?*

A tingle of foam forms between my toes, and the far-off rumble of a boat comes and goes. The day is swelling, and now the laughter of children pours into open space. The wind is cheerful, and I drink the wild air. The waves beckon me. The sea cries high . . . lifts me to the zenith of a wave—a vessel this much closer to the sun, and once it sighs, it brings me forward and lays me on the sand once again—an offering, or a surrender.

Oh, my beach. When again?

There are heels that dig in the sand; they approach me. Behind me—closer now.

"River." I hear the Witch's voice before it closes like a disk and an angel peeks behind a cloud.

The boot heels dig behind me and stop.

"We found you."

"You found me."

"Yes."

"I'm going home."

"Yes—yes, sir, I'm sure. Female around eighteen years. Yes—she's been here in the sand for around two days now. Drowned. Yes. Silver necklace . . . Name's River."

*　　*　　*

River drowned just as she made her swim back from the horizon.

She went back home.

River's ashes were scattered on the deep sea, and the sea spread her through the beach just before dusk fell on them both and the night turned to glass.

> *For life and death are one, even as the river and the sea*
> *are one.*

—Kahlil Gibran

In Search of the Bluebird

Blue skies smiling at me
Nothing but blue skies do I see
Bluebirds singing a song
Nothing but bluebirds all day long

—Irving Berlin from the song "Blue Skies"

Prologue

The blood ran down the driveway: a purple snake slithering and glistening in the light of the moon, which was perched on the night's velvet cloak like a silver button. The moon—the only witness as one blue feather rode the serpent of blood down the pavement, riding the grooves of that slant, the rough glittery black terrain, the final incline. The feather like silk, so deep, so blue! So blue and unusual it would make one ponder—stall. Wish? There was something about that blue: something true, transcendent, unreachable by the understanding! If you can believe it, all the answers simplified to the singularity of color. A yearning beyond riches forged upon one look of it. One. That blue! One look—and everything else around washed away and left nothing but that *one* thing: that one and only thing that truly mattered up until this moment; that is *right*—infallible, pure, complete!

The streak of blood rode to the shoulder along the curb; it moved quickly, and the feather sailed on upon the neck of the purple snake. All the way down, down they went. All the way until she and the feather plummeted into the gutters of town to share their new history among the damp, lightless, and obscure walls of oblivion. And the moon hung high . . . the sole, silver, and silent witness.

*   *   *

Saturday 11:55 PM

"ID?"

"Samantha Infante, twenty-two years old. She's a well-known prostitute in this area. Priors for soliciting and possession. Last place of residence: Motel Azul. Two gunshot wounds to the chest, one to the face. No witnesses to the homicide. Casings found for a .38 caliber. Victim was found face down and was clenching in her fists a handful of blue feathers."

She lay face down in the middle of the driveway, her head toward the street. Both glittered sneakers pointed to the left. Her hands and arms were tensely tucked and held against her belly under her small, limp, and lifeless young body. Her hands held tightly and reluctantly a fistful of blue feathers. She wore tight denim pants and a denim jacket. Her curly, dyed-blonde hair fell on her restful face, and her open eyes shone still as if seeing, looking toward her own soul as it departed.

*   *   *

Sunday

The body of Samantha Infante was stowed away in the morgue's locker. Death had been almost instantaneous; two of the gunshot wounds out of the three would have been fatal on their own. One to the chest went through the heart and lodged on a rib: fatal. One through the sternum missed the heart, punctured the right lung: not fatal. One below the left eye, through the cheekbone, with no exit wound: fatal. There seemed to be no sign of struggle at the scene; no other bruises or contusions found on the body. Bullets

225

were extracted and sent to the lab for ballistics testing. Clothes were sent to the lab for fiber and particulate analysis. And the seven feathers were sent to the lab as evidence.

Several calls were placed to pertinent subjects after reviewing her case record. They had been summoned to the station for interviews.

Monday 9:00 AM
Interview with Trevor "Money" Brown

Trevor is a john; he'd been known to patronize several of the working girls of the area. He had been a client of Samantha's. As well, he had been indirectly connected to third-party people of interest. When he had been called in, he had appeared without hesitation or delay. However, he seemed tense upon arrival at the station. He was withdrawn—his body turned inward and his gaze evasive.

Detective Ramirez opened the door for him, and they stepped into the room. It was a small interrogation room with a camera in one corner of the ceiling, recording every nuance, and a small one-way mirror on the wall opposite the door. Ramirez brought in a cup of coffee and set it on the table. He placed his file down, took out a pen, and began, "Hi, Trevor."

"Hi."

"Well, we both know what this is about, so why don't you just start telling me what you know?"

"I don't know nothing, officer!"

"Anything, *detective*"

"Whah . . . ?"

"Anything . . . you don't know *anything*—and detective . . . not officer."

"Whatever."

"Okay," Ramirez said, "let's start like *this* . . . what can you tell me about a guy known as Pretty Face."

Trevor let out a laugh. "*Baby* Face, dude, not Pretty Face."

"First: don't call me dude. I'm not your *dude*. You call me Ramirez or Detective, but I'm not your dude, all right?"

"All right, man."

"So?"

"Chill out . . ."

"What can you tell me about Baby Face?"

"Why the hell do you want to know about—"

"Because we have to, Trevor! We have to ask about everything. We know Samantha lived with Face, and we have to know about him, and that means through people. And people means *you*!"

"Shiyet! Man . . . well, you're barking at the wrong dick here . . . me and him . . . I mean, me and him we chill from time to time, 'cause we have mutuals, but we really ain't that tight! I know he's a hustler, but that's about all I can tell you about him."

"What do you know about Samantha Infante?"

"Samantha who?"

"Samantha Infante, Trevor! Sammy Torch . . . aka Skippy . . . Sambooka?"

"Oooh . . . right, yeah . . . yeah, yeah . . . Skippy! Man. Yeah. Well, shit . . . I didn't know that was her name. Fuck . . . sue me! Well, somebody capped her, bro."

"Well, thank you for the enlightenment, Trevor, but what can you tell me about her? Anything you know. Anything that was happening . . . anything that you've seen that might be—"

"Here's the deal, Ramirez. I was her client—from time to time—you know? And that's as far as our affiliation went. For real. We weren't exactly telling each other secrets, then, okay? I mean, it's messed up, man, yes! But like I said, I don't know *shit* about this business. I was her *client*. In and out—so to speak."

Monday 2:00 PM
Interview with Monica "Sweets" Gonzalez

Monica was one of Samantha's closest associates among the people from the streets. She was a working girl like Samantha, but she had been in the life for much longer. She was a bit older and had a lot more mileage. She was a large-framed, generous, pretty girl of about thirty-two with luscious onyx hair and tanned skin. She had called the station as soon as she heard about what had happened in the streets; she had been a good friend of the murder victim. When she came in, she was shaking like a wet cat—in shock and grief. Ramirez led her into the interview room and immediately handed her a glass of cold water. He left the room for a moment and came back with a small box of tissues.

"Hi, Monica—I'm Detective Ramirez. Please take your time. Just tell me what you want to tell me . . . I'm sure anything will be of help," he said as Monica looked straight into the floor, her glassy eyes shaking under her eyelids.

"Okay . . . well, me and Bookies were close . . . Umm . . . we used to look out for each other." She choked up and took a moment to recuperate. "We'd tell each other who to look out for, you know—who had a bad reputation with the other girls, who was shady or who was a dick to the girls. We'd warn each other about things." She nodded, her eyes still fixed on the ground. Ramirez leaned forward, his elbows on his knees, his fingers locked together.

"Do you know who would want to get rid of her?"

"No . . . I mean—well, she was around so many people. I was close to her. So many other circles we ran with, too, you see? I mean, she was always going here and there . . . for jobs, you know. When things are slow up at the strip, we all go in different directions. It depends. It's—"

"Yeah, I understand, but does anyone in particular stand out to you . . . anyone, in any way? Or any event?"

"Umm . . . well, she had this fight with Nelson over some money—or something? I never found out exactly, but I know it got nasty! He punched her, and they fought, and then Cedric came and kicked the shit out of him—"

"You say this kid's name is what?"

"Nelson."

"Nelson—?"

"Yeah, Nelson!"

"Nelson what?"

"Oh . . ." She chuckled through her stuffed nose and gleaming tearful eyes. She looked up finally at him—sniffled. "I don't know;

they call him Nelson Mandela, but that's just a nickname they gave him to fuck with him. I . . . I don't know his last name."

"When was the last time you saw Samantha?" he asked.

Monica remained silent for a while, recollections painting Samantha in her memory . . . alive, vital. "I saw her at Friskies . . . it's this pub we go to sometimes—it's—"

"Yeah, I know Friskies."

"It was about Tuesday or Wednesday . . . and we were just shootin' the shit . . . just, you know . . . and she looked real good, then. Real good! So I don't . . . I mean . . . I just don't know." She shook her head, looked down, and poured a string of tears onto her shoes.

"Monica, is there anything else you wish to tell us?"

"No—I mean . . . no. That's all I can tell you now . . . but if I hear of anything else I . . . you know that I will call you, but . . . I mean this is . . . oh, my God . . ." She crumbled in her chair. Ramirez got up and went to her. He bent over and put his arms around Monica.

"She was twenty-two, twenty-three, something like that, you know . . ." Monica said—muffled—into the detective's jacket.

*   *   *

Tuesday 11:00 AM
Interview with Nelson "Mandela" Johnson

Nelson was a dealer. A good portion of his clientele was made up of the prostitutes at the strip where he was often seen. He had already been locked up for dealing but continued after his release despite the punishment, because at this point dealing was the only thing he knew and the only way he could ever survive. He was a lanky, tall man with bug-yellow eyes. He was very dark skinned and had sharp, thin lips, purpled from chain smoking.

He sat down nervously. His eyes shifted around the room. He looked like a trapped fly looking for an escape. He fixed his jacket unnecessarily, trying clumsily to divert attention away from himself.

"Hi, Nelson."

"Hi, officer."

"So, for the record, your name please."

"Nelson Johnson Jr."

"Okay . . . so what do you know about Samantha?"

"Oh . . . shit!"

"Oh, shit?"

"Nah, nah . . . not *this*, man! Listen . . . I have *no-thing* to do with this shit, man. I wadn' even here when this shit happened. Don't—"

"Nelson, Nelson . . . calm down. Nobody is accusing you of anything . . . we just want to ask you a few questions. You are one of the people who knew her. It's procedure for this investigation. We have to follow procedure . . . you're here for that . . . let's talk. You want some water or . . . ?" The detective leaned forward, slapped the table lightly, motioned to Nelson with an upturned palm.

"Yeah, yeah . . . I want some water," he said, and Ramirez stepped outside. He came back with a plastic cup of water, which Nelson gulped down quickly."

"Okay." Ramirez sat down, adjusted his jacket, and made a circular motion with his shoulders, smoothed his lapel. "So tell me . . . what do you know about Samantha?"

"Well . . . she was a working girl, officer."

"We know that," Ramirez scoffed.

"Umm . . . well, she used to hang with my peeps, and that's how I knew her," he said with a feeble shrug as Ramirez locked eyes with him. The dealer bit at the corner of his bottom lip. Ramirez drummed on the desk with his ballpoint pen.

"So, what's this I hear about a fight you two had that got pretty heated?"

"Oh, shit, not this, man, come on . . . it was just a scuffle we had, t'sall—"

"A scuffle."

"Yeah, a scuffle, man. She started coming at me with all this stuff, then came wailing her arms at me. I had to defend myself, so when I tried grabbing her by the wrists to control her, other people jumped in . . ."

"What people?"

"Like her boyfriend and stuff. He jumped, and a couple other dudes too. And then the boyfriend started kicking at me and all this *shit*!"

"Then what?"

"Then nothing, man, that's *it*! Last time I saw her was when I was getting the shit kicked out of me *because* of her . . . but that's it, man. It was about money she was owing me for something and that's it! I didn't have no *grudge* or anything else with her, man."

"Money? Come on, Nelson, you can do better than that."

"Money, man, money!"

"Nelson, we know you were her dealer! We have people that—"

"Okay, okay . . . okay but you're . . . I can't entrap myself here, man, it's—"

"Nelson, we work homicide . . . narcotics is another thing—a whole other ballgame. We are trying to solve *this* case. For now. Now, we can be very forthcoming with narcotics, too, if you wish."

"Come on, Ramirez, man. I'm telling you the truth. Okay, she owed me some *favors,* all right, for some stuff I hooked her up with *free of charge* . . . and she never hooked *me* back up! So the argument started, and it escalated. And that's the truth, Ruth! I ain't gonna kill no one for a couple a' blowjobs, man."

Tuesday 2:30 PM
Interview with Carmen Cecile Oiseaux

Carmen was a young prostitute. She had been Samantha's best friend. She had been the murdered woman's confidant, and each had loved the other like the sister she had never had. Carmen had come on Tuesday morning and waited until Ramirez could speak with her. She hadn't been well enough to come in to talk before then. And when she walked into the interview room, she just sat, wan and weightless, in front of the detective. Slowly, as the interview progressed, her strength returned, somewhat.

"Carmen Cecile, is it?"

"Yes, sir," she said, staring forward, her eyes staring into space with a shaded buzz.

"Please, say what you must. I will just listen. Is that okay?"

"Yes."

"Okay . . . tell me about this."

"This is just *fucked up* is all I gotta say . . . fucked up!" Her eyes were tearing, but her voice was unwavering. She took a moment and then continued, "She was precious—you don't . . . nobody knew her . . . Nobody knew her like I knew that girl." A crease formed on her brow. She was filled with anger, powerlessness, and terrible anguish. Her emotions alternated between fury and disbelief—nothing seemed quite real: a strange, cruel, savage nightmare.

"Tell me, Carmen, what happened here? Anything you know—"

"Ramirez, she was an angel . . . she was a gift—miracles . . . miracles were in conspiracy in her favor. But I guess too late . . . she was getting so much better!" Her eyes looked up, glistening, recollecting. "She really was. You should have seen her . . . she was on her way, and I was so proud . . . so proud of her, you know. It was really something! In the beginning, when she ran away from where she lived, you should have seen Sammie, then. A wreck! Disheveled, desperate, a rag of a person! Lost. Totally lost. And what do you expect when you know nothing else? And she'd told no one. No one but me at this point. The rapes . . . the violation of trust!—all that . . . yeah, all that. And so she came busting out. Like a storm and running . . . running—anywhere! But then—oof!—then she got into all that junk and that made it even worse for her then . . . she fell into the trap . . . into the life. She didn't stand a chance. What the heck did she know about anything? She thought she had her taste of freedom, away from that strange, maddening hell she'd come from! But little did she know. Oh, they got her right away! Who could miss her? I mean . . . she was an apparition, Ramirez. But the sweet-talkers, man—they'll get you! That's how it all happens. They treat you good . . . give you all this. The world is *yours*! You got it made. But slowly, all that starts to change. The ugliness creeps in. And next thing you know, you open your eyes, wondering how the hell you ended up here! You're sitting at some diner at two in the morning with three hundred stinking dollars in your purse, wondering where the fuck your soul is. She was pure, Ramirez! She *was*. She was, even underneath all that poison. She didn't belong here. If anyone didn't belong here, it was Sammie." Carmen broke down crying. She slapped the table twice, gathered herself again, and continued. "This is *bullshit*! Murdering Sammie like that—like an animal, in the middle of the sidewalk—disposed of . . . like a pile of shit! She was just here, and now she's nowhere. I can't . . . is it possible that she's nowhere?" She sat still. Quiet.

"You must understand," she continued, "how sweet and kind this person was. She was the fairest person you will know—*naive*, even! Well. One time she was out there. It was early. She was working. The sun was still out, and a bird . . ." She chuckled. " . . . shat on her shoulder. She was so—pissed! Her jacket was brand new. Expensive. So she started cussing at the bird and grabbed these rocks . . . started flinging them at him, and flinging them until—one finally hit him! Oh, the poor thing fell straight down to the ground! 'Oh no!' she yelled. She never thought she would actually get him, you know. 'Oh, crap!' she said, and ran—I mean, quick!—to where he had fallen . . . and there he was—mangled and bloody. Mmm . . . It was this gorgeous bluebird—the most gorgeous, beautiful thing you could ever in your life imagine. A bird fit for an angel, Ramirez! And she called herself all kinds of names for doing such a thing. And there he lay, fragile and helpless, and Sammie—she began to cry. But not just cry. These were sincere tears of regret, detective—wails! She was begging for forgiveness! From God. She took her jacket off immediately and wrapped her bird in it. She rushed the wounded bird in the bloodied jacket to the motel room. And . . . can you believe, she nursed that bluebird back to health? Every morning, she fed it. Every morning and evening, she put antibiotics on his wound. She bought a special heat lamp for him and a perch. And at night, this bird was her heart! She—*loved* it. And so the day he was healthy enough to fly and be on his own, she freed him into the trees—the same trees he had fallen from. That same night, as she came back to her room, just as she was about to close the door behind her, the bird flew right in and onto his perch! It was almost comical. The bird became *her* caretaker. He'd follow her around. Wherever she would drive to, wherever she would go, whenever she'd turn around, there he was. She told me that the bird *spoke* to her, and that's when I thought for sure she had lost it." Carmen chuckled, shallow tears pooling in her eyes. "Of course he didn't *speak*, but he had given her a message . . . a message that she *understood*. She *saw* things in him, in his feathers. Something she'd been searching for so long! She had found it. The bird would grant her a wish, she'd said. And *that's* what she believed. She asked him for freedom—and happiness. Soon after that, she told me she would be leaving soon, that she was *really* going to do it. She looked ready. She did. And this was two days before she was murdered . . . only two days before." She stroked her chin, nodding. Suddenly, her tongue pushed to the inside of her cheek, and she broke down.

*　　*　　*

Wednesday 11:00 AM
Interview with Antonio Grave

Antonio was a big bear of a man with a deep, smooth voice and a slow, premeditated way. It was common knowledge that was he was a pimp and a dealer who had a history with Cedric Mills—Baby Face, who had been the last person with whom Samantha lived. He was her former boyfriend . . . a person of interest with prior criminal records. Antonio and Cedric had kept their distance after Antonio was imprisoned, but police learned they had been seen together recently.

Antonio leaned back heavily in his seat and continued, "and that's about what *I* know about her, man. I seen her around, but never had no contact *with* her—or none of his girlfriends, man."

"Okay, so tell me about him, then."

"What do you want me to tell you about him?"

"Just tell me about Cedric, Antonio."

"Well, me and him were partners—like you already know . . . ancient history, Ramirez. But then I got locked up. We went our separate ways and Face went straight."

"Yeah?"

"Yeah, man, straight up. He got that legit job at Blockbuster Video." He laughed. "He don't need to be doing nothin' else."

"That's not what I hear."

"What do you hear?"

"Different things . . ."

"What kinda things?"

"Come on, Antonio, man! Everybody knows he's got two or three girls *working* for him! Everybody knows this. It's not hard doing the math here either. He's not too bright or discrete now, is he? Flaunting all that bling . . . a convertible! Now tell me something more about Cedric, Antonio. We know you've seen him recently—you've been seen with him." Ramirez dug his index finger into the wood of the table. "I want to know how he lives. I want to know about the last time you saw him . . . how he's *behaving*. Anything that comes to mind. Don't *fuck* with me, Antonio. I can make shit *real hard* for you. You *know* this."

"Okay, okay . . . hold up! I got nothing to hide here, man." He paused . . . sighed. "I just don't need no aggravation. I don't need to get in a place where it's . . . where it's not too good out there for me. You gotta understand. I don't wanna run my mouth in the wrong direction. This is the streets, *papi*! Shit's no game out there."

"All I need are simple descriptions. Details."

"Okay . . . you're right, he's got good things, man." He shrugged. "He's got nice threads, you know, likes to show stuff off . . . that's how he is. He's a *businessman*. Ostentatious, you know. It makes for good business."

"When was the last time you saw him?" Ramirez prompted.

"Umm . . . last time I saw Cedric musta been . . ." He looked up, stalling. Then, "About a week . . . week and a half. He called me up in my cell 'cause he was having a party up in his spot, and so I went there."

"Okay. Who else was there?"

"He was up there with a bunch of dudes I didn't know . . . well, some I *did* know. Mandela was there. Money was there . . . one of his girls—Pokemon. And his main girl Samantha was there too."

"Okay, so what can you tell me about that night—how was Samantha . . . acting?"

"*Acting?*" Holding back a laugh. "Well, she was fine, man . . . she was drinking some gin-and-tonics. People were getting blunted and high, but she wasn't. I heard she'd stopped doing any of that. She was just thinking *a lot* that night—*that*, I noticed. Like she was a little uncomfortable with the people around her or something, right?—the party and whatnot. She sure wasn't like she was a while back. Before, she'd be partying it up and all over Cedric. Cedric was a little frustrated that she was so *cold* with him, but nothing . . . nothing *extreme* or anything like that happened. That's what I would say. That's what it looked like to me . . . from the outside, you know."

"Mhm . . ."

"Yeah, well, she left early too. Looked like Cedric didn't want to make a big thing of it then and there, but you could tell he wasn't pleased . . ."

"Has he been violent in the past?"

"Well, you know that, man!" Antonio leaned back with a grin, self-satisfied for some reason. "Come on, Ramirez . . . why are you asking me? He's got a record. He should be answering that question, no?"

"Anything else?"

"No, that's it. Now that's really it."

Wednesday 3:00 PM
Interview with Akiko "Pokemon" Yamaguchi

Akiko was one of Cedric's girls. She had an extremely pretty face—young, Japanese, athletic build, middle stature—and was one more of those unfortunate women who had fallen into the treacherous abyss of prostitution. She was the product of grossly unfit foster-care, drugs, toxic environments, and a violent and warped, hostile worldview. She walked in with that typically harsh and somewhat vexed, compensative air prevalent in so many women of the profession; she was edgy in a way that immediately suggested cocaine. She was confused, sad, and angry. But most of all, she seemed desperately concerned for her own safety now . . . a concern born of a drug-induced paranoia enhanced by a very appropriate dose of reality.

"Hi, Akiko . . . I understand you knew Samantha fairly well?"

"Yes, I do . . . um . . . I did, yes."

"Okay."

"So . . ."

"Tell us anything for now . . ."

"Okay, so I work the streets . . ." She moistened her lips, and her eyes buzzed; she stalled on a blink, trapped in an indecipherable thought—perhaps searching for judgment in Ramirez's eyes. Then: "We met in the life . . . we became friends there."

"Okay, can you tell me anything about Samantha? In particular about the last few times you saw her." Ramirez took a sip of his coffee and grabbed his pen.

"Well . . . she, in truth, was doing real well . . . real well the last couple of weeks. Let me explain to you before anything that we never got into any . . . *specific* details about our lives, me and her, but you can always tell things about all the girls around, you know. You can just tell certain things . . . from how they behave . . . their habits and stuff like that. We tell each other certain things, you know; it's a tough business. Can I smoke here?" she asked and grabbed her purse, pulling out a pack of Marlboro Reds before Ramirez answered.

"Sure, go ahead," he muttered. "Do you know about her and Cedric?"

"Yeah, I know about her and Cedric." She rolled her eyes, slightly, as if she found the question inane.

"Can you tell me something about it?" Ramirez chuckled involuntarily at his own clumsiness.

"Well." She sighed before she started to speak, looking at him . . . giving Ramirez a chance, as he squinted in the smoke. "He was the one who got her into this, as soon as she first got here, we know that. He had been doing this already for a while by that time, though. Anyways—he had a couple of girls working for him already, and when she came in, he zeroed in on her right off; you know how that goes." She took a drag and batted her eyes, reinforcing the evident nature of the statement to come. "Took her to all these places, treating her to new things, showing off his place, turned her into his girlfriend, basically. But . . . all that changes sooner or later." She grinned with irony, blew smoke, and flicked ash into an empty coffee cup that Ramirez slid toward her. "That's when she started spiraling out of control. It started with her just partying at first. Fun, fun, fun . . . fun and games, yeah. Liberated! Free—she thought. The damn illusion." She arched her brow, stretching out the *u* sound in *illusion*. "It's a bitch! I'm telling you. Then, just like that, and before she knew it, the whole thing flipped on its back—like a dying cockroach! Can't move or go anywhere. She was in there. All the way in there . . . in here. She was the best girl—still had that unjaded freshness of all the newbies. Cedric's snow bunny. Those are hard to come by. But that don't last. They turn into ragged things real quick—used . . . dragged. But!" She shook her index finger. "There was something in her that wasn't going to let her be pulled down that way. Not all the way like that. She saw herself. That was the turning point because . . . because many of these critters out there, well . . . the transformation is too slow for them to notice, I suppose. Like all lengthy things, 'all lengthy things are difficult to see, to see in their entirety.' Who said that? Nietzsche, I think. But it's true. She saw . . . she saw what she was turning into. She caught herself just in time, and that's when she stopped with all that garbage. Immediately! She quit putting all that stuff into herself—the coke and then the heroin and all that. It's hard. Oh, it's hard from the inside, my man, believe it. The splendor!" She belted a sad, strange laugh that seemed to catch her by surprise. "That was coming back to her. It was *blooming* . . . slowly, but it was coming. I'm telling you now, about two weeks ago, she was looking as fabulous as when she walked into this place for the first time. She had been wanting to come off Cedric real bad. But that's not as easy as it sounds. It's not like dumping your boyfriend—okay? But she had some guts, man." She coughed, nodded, and swallowed. "Excuse me. And she really was about to leave." She took a last drag and blew the smoke to the side. Clipping the cigarette between her middle and index fingers, she waved her fingers forward—slowly. "Cedric was growing nervous. Anxious. He was very agitated one night, very aggressive. She told me—he was about to beat her that night. That same night she told me this, Cedric had a party at his place. I was at the bar, talking to her, and that's when she told me she was definitely going soon! She left early, and Cedric was not happy about that at all. The next day, he left his place. That's when she rented the room at Motel Azul. It was in the morning at the diner on the strip, she told me. She gave me a tight hug, and she just looked radiant! She really did—a little happy sun. She just said it. She said she was going . . . that night she was going to leave! And, of course, that was the night she was shot."

*　　*　　*

Thursday 9:00 AM
Interview with Cedric "Baby Face" Mills

Cedric "Baby Face" Mills. Pimp. Priors included possession with intent, robbery, aggravated assault, assault with a deadly weapon. Cedric walked into the interview room, dragging his feet. Shoulders swaying side to side—big and brown like an elephant—he wasn't that large a man, but somehow he carried his weight like one who was. He was a calculating conman who feared and resented the world for not giving him anyone to trust, because how could he ever trust a world he was trying to cheat?

He sat in his seat, leaning on the back of the chair, his hands folded in his lap, his chin lifted. He was clearly irritated and attempting to impress with an annoying kind of defiance. His eyes were insincerely restful—calm by force—looking at the detective from beyond an irksome slant, and a phony air of superiority that immediately confessed a laughable affectation of very much the opposite.

"How are you, Cedric?"

"How are *you?*"

"Cedric, do you know why you're here?"

"Yeah."

"Can you tell me anything about it?"

"No."

"Nothing?"

"No."

"Well, let's begin with—what was your relationship with Samantha Infante?"

"She was my girlfriend."

"Girlfriend?"

"Yes, sir."

"So—do you know of any reason why anyone would want to murder her?"

"No, I don't."

"No, *sir.* Okay, when was the last time you saw her?"

"I saw her . . . um . . . I seen her last in her motel room about Friday . . . we had broken up."

"Mhm . . . and how did that go?"

"Umm . . . she said that she was going to New Jersey—to stay with her grandparents."

"And what did you tell her?"

"Umm . . . nothing, I mean . . . I didn't want her to *go,* if that's what you mean."

"I don't mean anything at all, Cedric. I *ask.* Don't worry about what I'd like to hear."

"Okay, well, I wanted to fix it."

"Fix it?"

"Yes."

"Yes, *sir,*" Ramirez emphasized. "Cedric, do you know that we have information that substantiates the allegations that you were a little more than just her boyfriend, that you were *pimping* Samantha in the streets?"

"Umm . . . well, *that* happened, but only because we were out of money, and that was only—"

"Cedric . . . we know this was an ongoing thing. We also know you have other girls that work for you. You see why we can't ignore this, don't you? I can't ignore how you are evading all this. This is important, wouldn't you say?"

"This is not true, detective. I don't have nothing to hide from you! I've—"

"Where do you work, Cedric?"

"I work at Blockbuster Video."

"Mhm. And how do you afford all the gold on your each one of your fingers and in your teeth? How can you afford the convertible you drove here today on a video rental store salary, if I may ask?

"Umm . . . well, it's not like that," he said, shaking his hand, dismissing all of it, "because my grandfather left me money when he died, so . . ."

"That so?"

"That's so."

"Some people tell me of a party you had about a week ago . . . said Sam left the party prematurely, looking very . . . unhappy? They tell me *you* weren't looking too pleased about it all yourself. Do you mind telling me about that night?"

"Well, would *you* be pleased? She was telling me she wanted to break up—and she picked *that* moment to tell me? Bad time to tell me."

"Very well." The detective wrote the last lines of his notes and put down the pen. "One thing that strikes me as *odd* here, Cedric, is that you seem to be very defensive with all these questions . . . but not at all distraught or even affected in the least about the death of your girlfriend! Don't you find that strange at all? 'Cause *I* do—I mean maybe it's only *me*, but if it had been *my* girlfriend who had been found shot dead on that driveway, I would be the *first* one to run here, and try to find out who did this to her. Thank you very much, Cedric. We'll be in touch."

*   *   *

Friday 9:00 AM
Interview with Jermaine "Gums" Wilson

Jermaine was an errand boy for Cedric—though he was far from a boy. But he was cheap and would do most anything for Cedric, from walking his dogs, to taking his car to the carwash, to buying his groceries. He was a skinny, ridiculous-looking guy with a strangled, nervous little voice. He had a learning disability, due to a vehicular accident in his teens. After the crash, he'd developed some cognitive problems, though it must be said he had never been particularly bright even before that.

"So, they tell me you run errands for Cedric?"

"Yeah, I just do things for him, and he pays me. Things have been real difficult finding a steady job out there, so . . . you gotta look for it somewhere."

"Okay, so exactly what do you *do* for him?"

"Well, just small things, you know . . . get his groceries . . . bring him lunch, sometimes . . . his dry cleaning. Basically I'm around and I chill with him—in case he needs help with something."

"So you're like a secretary, kind of." Ramirez smiled and looked down at his notes.

"Well, like a personal assistant, yes."

"So, tell me, when was the last time you saw Cedric?"

"Last time was yesterday . . . I see him every day, almost . . . and I will see him again today." He nodded.

"Did you see him the day of the events?"

"Umm, no . . . well, yeah . . . during the morning and part of the afternoon—but that was a Saturday, and I like to have the weekends mostly for me—for me and Grace."

"Grace?"

"Never mind." He bit his nails. Grace was his shih tzu.

"Okay, so how was he looking then?"

"Looking? Umm . . . well, he was just fine, I mean . . . he was a bit edgy, but nothing out of the ordinary for him. We went to the diner by Frisky's, had breakfast there. We came back, played some Xbox, and I left around one, one thirty. There was nothing—"

"Were you at that party the week before?"

"No. I didn't go to *that*. He didn't invite me. I borrowed one of his cars that day, though. Made sure he had liquor for the thing that night. He gave me a whole list of all the stuff he wanted there. He usually keeps his cabinet full, but there were going to be a lot of people there that night, so . . ."

"Lately . . . precisely, after the murder . . . how has he been acting?"

"Well, he's real distraught, of course—his girlfriend, you know! On top of that, he's been real anxious. And just yesterday he almost didn't get up from his chair the whole day. He was just crying and crying and wiping his eyes and looking at that bird in the cage—the whole day almost! That's all he did."

"What bird in what cage?" Ramirez's eyes widened.

"He's got this bird . . . he has animals . . . he has an expensive saltwater fish tank too and an anaconda, and now also this exotic bird. It's beautiful . . . beautiful! And he was just looking at this bluebird and looking at it. The bird hardly moved at all. And he just cried all day!"

*   *   *

Saturday 10:00 AM

The detective stood in front of Cedric's apartment door. He'd come to ask some questions and had brought with him one of the seven feathers that had been found with Samantha's body. He was just about to knock on the door when he realized it was ajar. A draft came through the open door that blew and flapped his shirt collar. He pushed the door open and stepped into the light of the living room. There, next to the bar, was an open window. Sheer curtains swayed with the cool air that came in. Next to it there was a small cage. And Cedric stood next to it, his face gleaming with tears. He was gently gripping the bluebird in his hands. The bird was not scared, not thrashing about or trying to escape . . . it just sat there, tranquil. Cedric turned around slowly and, facing the window, let the bird go. The soft, airy flapping of the bluebird's wings could be heard as he flew free out of sight. The detective didn't make a sound when Cedric got to his knees and placed his hands behind his back.

*　　*　　*

Next Saturday 10:00 AM

The narrow casket was lowered into the ground. Inside, rested the small frame of Samantha Infante, aka Sammy Torch, Sammie, Bookie, Sambooka, Skippy—twenty-two years old. The only people attending the funeral were Carmen, Detective Ramirez, Monica, and Akiko.

Samantha was buried in a beautiful blue velvet gown Carmen had given her as a farewell gift. And buried with her was a small handful of blue feathers.

The service had been brief, and they all went their separate ways.

Carmen walked all the way back to the Motel Azul. The day was a pale gray, and there was a mist erasing the horizon. And the horizon could have been anything—even anything she wanted.

When Carmen walked into the room, the clouds parted and the sky grew golden. As she sat on the bed, she heard the distinct sounds of wings. In front of her, the bluebird flew back to his perch! She grabbed a packet of seeds from Samantha's drawer and fed him. She sat up in bed all day and all night . . . all night long until dawn.

In the morning, they left together. And the bluebird would never leave her.

Epilogue

Carmen Cecile Oiseaux was buried at the age of ninety, surrounded by her great-grandchildren, grandchildren, and children.

She was buried in a white velvet gown with her bluebird at her breast.

One New Year's Day, several years before her death, at the break of dawn, Carmen Cecile Oiseaux had sat on the grassy pastoral of a masterless valley. At her feet, gathered all seven of her great-granddaughters, who told *my* great-granddaughter what she'd said: "If one is ever so lucky to find her bluebird—better still, if one is so lucky that her bluebird finds *her*—every day take time to care for him . . . and follow him wherever he sends your heart, because it's your *heart* what he looks after in return for your care . . . and your reward will be completeness—it will be your happiness!"

Today I Found a Bluebird: An Autobiographical Fantasy

Thirty years have passed since I first came to behold the bluebird—and it took me completing this little book of horror/love stories to realize that what had planted the initial seed for it had been that film I had watched when but a snot-nosed little pup.

My Lord in heaven! Is it at all possible that a movie can touch someone so profoundly—and at so tender an age—to stay in the back of one's brain for so long, and so ineradicably, as to so strongly branch out the head and ears to be the so-called inspiration and source for *this* entire thing in some form?

Yes.

And I'm not only affirming that but am also surprised—or something even greater—because of how both distantly and immediately memories can inhabit your mind! And I'll explain why I say that.

After I wrote "The Bluebird and I" (sort of the second introduction to the book, which I actually wrote *after* the book was all done), I started looking into the movie I mentioned, to see if I could find it somehow. The movie had been poking at me too incessantly, and the obsessive part of me couldn't let it go. I wanted to see it, make sure my memory was not a mere hallucination or a dream of some kind.

I remember three things in the movie: the bluebird (of course), the jewel in the boy's hat, and the separation—two kids were holding hands, and some old fool broke them apart, sending one of the two away without any compassion at all. What a sad little face on the boy! Oh, I remember his face. He looked torn and had circles under his eyes. How urgent and desperate those last seconds were before the other boy was led out of sight forever. What a cruel old fool! He looked like a warlock of some sort, like Gandalf from *The Hobbit*, but mean—like a mean-spirited old teacher, the old-fashioned type of schooling where they whacked children with wooden rulers for speaking in class.

I was whacked like that in the first grade, for speaking in the lunchroom, for Christ's sake—I'll never forget that. I'll never forget the fear more than the pain. Everyone feared that teacher. She was a crazy old witch, but in retrospect she could have been no older than twenty-five, but to a first-grader, that was ancient! I remember her face. She was pale and freckly. She milky soft skin like an angel, but to me she was a demon! She loved whacking the kids and would use any chance she could get to whack us. Hard! It made a sound all the way to the back of the class like a whip on a horse. It was both terrifying *and* humiliating. What a Nazi! I remember thinking, *Boy, I hope that never happens to me*, looking at those poor kids on their tiptoes flapping their hands, clenching their teeth, crying. What a spectacle, until one day *my* nose was an inch away from that blackboard. WHACK!

These days, they give you something like five years in prison for whacking a kid like that. My grandmother was a whacker when she was a mother, but by the point she turned into a grandmother, she was already a saint. Something happens to people in their old age that for the most part makes them pure and kind and understanding and all sorts of great stuff. My grandmother's name was Ofelia—it's a Shakespearean name, which always aroused my curiosity since they were simple country folk who knew *nothing* of Shakespeare.

But before my grandmother was sanctified by the long years trudging through her life, she was a whacker! And my mother told me that she was beaten with a rod every single day; the beatings were savage and ruthless, and one day she was in such terror that she tearfully crawled underneath the bed, where Ofelia mercilessly stabbed at her with the rod like it was a bayonet.

My mom came out defeated and in agony, with bruises and bumps and scrapes all over the place. What a beast! My God! My little sweet *flan*-making gramma was a monster? I won't accept it! You look at pictures of my dear old gramma—rest her soul—now and you'd scream bloody blasphemy that such a diminutive old lady was capable of such cruelty in her youthful years of early motherhood. They'd give you the chair in Texas for a thing like that, I'm sure!

My mother—on the other hand—never beat me with a rod. She was always a flip-flop woman herself, and that's why I'm spoiled: because she spared the rod. Her father, by contrast, never beat her. Ever. And my father never beat me anywhere except in the heart.

But pain taught me the first lessons on how to write. And that art was about taking thorns out—slowly. So you could write with blood on their tips. Like this.

Perhaps *that* would be a good place for psychoanalysts to dig—or philosophers or whomever is in charge of this department. Parents and our beatings. Perhaps war is nothing more than the revenge *we* seek for our beatings, and since we can't kill our parents (because we love them—in some cases with the same kind of love that some have for God, in that they are too terrified *not* to love him), we kill someone else. Not a bad theory at all, but anyhow . . .

I also vividly remember the beginning and end of the film, which showed these Russian letters, large, fat, colorful letters alongside these bright, blocky drawings.

I called my friend Gigi and asked her to do a bit of research for me since I was busy like hell with this large, profound novel I was trying to put together to impress myself.

I asked her to look for a Slavic movie under the title *The Blue Bird*; it was a movie from the seventies—most likely, since I saw it in 1980. After much insistence, she agreed to help me.

She called me up not many hours after that phone conversation and said I'd be receiving the movie in the mail soon. *Wow!*

I nearly shat my pants with joy and immediately looked out the window—toward the sky and then the ocean about two blocks from my apartment.

"It's from 1976," said Gigi's voice on the other end of the line. And I could hear chewing and the rustling of paper—like she was rummaging inside a paper bag. I know she was most likely eating fries, and I was interrupting her snack or lunch or whatever the heck she was ingesting at this ambiguous hour of the *early* afternoon. "And it's got Russian letters—all over it!"

"That's it!" I said. "That's *gotta* be it."

"Yeah, it's gotta be it!" she said. Then, "Because there were 180 *The Blue Birds,* and that was the only one from the seventies. The rest were from mid—to late eighties and nineties." She was golden and I loved her!

"Gigi! I lov—" But before I could finish my expression of gratitude (or better yet, my effort at *hinting* at my underlying true feelings for her—we often can't help ourselves but *pretend* to say, "I love you," casually when, in fact, meaning it), she hung the phone up sharply without saying good-bye.

She's a great girl, but she wears black-and-gray stripes and owns a black cat that is old and half-blind. That should explain some things to you.

She's not the mushy type, except in secret, I bet. *Everyone* is mushy, damn it! Everyone! Even Mussolini, I bet, when he was alone in bed with someone, right?

Check this out: It's a riddle—or something.

Gigi's both the love and acceptance I yearn for, and the rejection and misunderstanding I get. Without her, I would have neither motivation nor purpose nor drive nor spirit. My soul would be stagnant.

Gigi—a dark muse? . . . Perhaps. She's the challenger and necessity to all true art-making.

Art is rebellion. For the discontent, for the true. For the lover of things for their own sake. Not so much the art to *please*—no, no, no. But the art to *reach*. To reach those in whose lunacy resides the power to change the world! Why? I have no clue. But someone once told me—I think it was a rat, and I was half asleep—that if you give people what they *want,* they will be content. "Thank you very much, dear artist man," they will say. But if you give them what they don't expect; they will be empowered. And they will not know what to say, for the gift is new—*Voila!*

And *this* is what the rat gave me as advice for art in my slumber, friends. Not bad, huh?

"Empowered, *why?*" I asked the rat—and he said, "Empowered because this means things can be changed, you fool!" and he ran away on two legs with one of my shoes in his hands.

Gigi is the obscure fairy, with wings of black lace—and instead of glitter, it's glittered ashes, where deep within each particle of black dust, there's one tiny little shiny diamond.

I'll never tell her, though. Never! She'll abandon all responsibility at once if she ever knew this.

But the truth of the matter is, you need a jewel to see this type of stuff—of *truth!*—since in reality she would *insist* she's but a person.

Okay, I don't press, for what more enchantment could there be that in the enchantment of the *enchanted,* who can not "see" this in herself?

Her greatest magic is her ignorance of it.

But anyhow . . .

A couple of days later—it was a Saturday, not that it matters—I got the box in the mail. Holy *shit!* I felt a strange surge of melancholy through my body. Something that watered my eyes and made me feel like an *idiot*—but I was happy. I ran upstairs and ripped the cardboards and pulled this thing out. A blue DVD box with a little blonde girl with a bluebird perched on her hand. *God Almighty, this is tremendous!* I thought to myself—or to God—and had to sit down.

There were Russian letters all over this thing. I could understand nothing at all. And then, I saw Elizabeth Taylor toward the top of the box, dressed like some kind of fairy, and that's when I understood even less.

What the hell *is this? What the crap is Elizabeth Taylor doing here?* I thought.

The Russian letters and Elizabeth Taylor were a tremendous curve ball to me that chiseled away at my rock of joy. "Damn," I whispered. "Damn," again.

Maybe it's not *Elizabeth Taylor,* I thought to myself; *maybe it's someone who just looks like Elizabeth Taylor.*

I held the box close, very close to my eyes—*RUSCICO was* on the bottom of the DVD box there. *Okay, okay, Russian Cinema Council,* in what looked to be a Greek Pantheon-type of logo, you know, with the columns and the triangular top and all that. *Very good. Lenfilm. Yeah, this is definitely Russian of some kind!* I nodded in place, furrowing my brow. I began to take the plastic wrapping away—with great purpose, turning it around.

Then, *20th Century Fox! What the* crap *is this? What's going on?* I almost cried. This was the most confusing box ever imaginable! *Damn!* I was really hoping hard-core by this point, but the 20th Century Fox and the Elizabeth Taylor look-alike were throwing everything off kilter. "Nonsense!" I said out loud and ran to the bedroom, opened the DVD player's tray, put the disk in, and pushed Play.

I felt like I have not felt in thirty years. I felt like a child! I closed the curtains and rushed back to the couch, sat there with *such* expectations, boy. My feet tingled—needles and pins, folks, needles and pins—I had butterflies in my stomach, and I bounced on the cushion, then I stopped. I dared not move!

Some sounds came out of the speakers that sounded like twentieth-century Russian music. Sounded like Stravinsky's *L'Oiseau du Feu* (The Firebird), a ballet, or something very similar. It was just the presentation music for the Pantheon production logo. Pretty good, though. Good music.

I waited for the first frames of the film to show—okay, okay, when the title of the film showed in Russian, English, *and* French—*L'Oiseau Bleu,* so similar to Stravinsky's ballet. Only Stravinsky's bird was of Fire. I guess, the antithesis of this one? Ah . . .

Suddenly a girl and a boy appeared in what seemed to be a cloud of blue.

The boy had on a hat. And on the hat? The jewel. *Oh—Lord and gravy.* He *had* the jewel!

There it was! Right in front of me. Without question. This *was* the film! She found it. Gigi had found it!

I was motionless. Enchanted and in a frame of time of true and absolute beauty. And I was grateful that I allowed myself to feel this way. This *was* a gift. A true gift of fate. A gift from whom? I do not know. But it was a *gift* that this movie had flown on its own force and current all the way through the galaxies of time and into my hands.

The movie started: a bunch of Russian credits—but it had English subtitles, thankfully.

Then, starring Elizabeth Taylor! *What the hell?*

. . . and Jane Fonda!

Wow! This is getting weirder and weirder. Okay.

Ava Gardner, for Christ's sake! What the fuck is going on?

Okay, so the film—turned out—had been a coproduction of American *and* Russian efforts combined for a single piece of art. In the seventies! *Holy shit!* I thought. *These folk were cats and dogs in the seventies, weren't they?* Aahh—yes, yes, but these are *artist,* my friends. And there are *no* frontiers in that field. The film was directed by George Cukor and was based on the play by Maurice Maeterlinck. So it turned out that Elizabeth Taylor is the Mom and the Light Fairy and the Witch and Love, all at once!—same woman, different people. Much like Sam in my book, who's all the same man and different people.

Ava Gardner is Luxury. A weird scene of laziness and excess of all sorts and abhorrent narcissism and human waste and all that stuff. Vanity and all things repugnant by instinct.

And then it flashed through my eyes clear as crystal. A response to this scene thirty years buried in the subskull is at the very *end* of the first story of the first volume of *In Search of the Bluebird* ("Three Irreversible Psychopaths").

The paragraph says:

As he looked at the images on the screen, a shadow cast over his face, his eyes turned gray, and his chest sank deeply. He saw hunger and famine. Through the glass he saw poverty, saw cruelty. He saw then how we treated each other—with triviality and greed. He saw despicable flamboyance, and then people who were never satisfied with material obsessions even as things replaced identity. He saw the pursuit of things as the very goal—the synonym of triumph. People were reduced to flesh alone. He saw inflation and the celebration of valueless, ephemeral things where real beauty struggles, slipping away unnoticed through the cracks of the hardwood of lauded vanity.

Jane Fonda is Night, and she's really hot in this movie, but aside from all that, what is curious is that in her catacomb of terrors, all the way below and hidden underneath the light—as Maximillian of "Three Irreversible Psychopaths" from the first volume lived all his life—she (Night) keeps all the horrors and dooms and catastrophes of the word behind different doors. Wars ("A Savior's Prophecy," "The Bluebird and I," and "Three Irreversible Psychopaths") and ghosts ("A Demon Wants Your Shadow," "Ghost of Carmen's Past," and "The Two Deaths of Tanqueray") and murder and death ("Zombies of the Enchanted Garden," "seven splinters," "The Beach Girl," and "The Two Deaths of Tanqueray") all prance around in a scene in this catacomb.

Of course, the Enchanted Garden itself is nothing but the garden where the flock of bluebirds is—behind one of the doors Night tried fruitlessly to dissuade the children from entering, from seeing the beauty within, the beauty within the eyes of Sam in Zombies of the Enchanted Garden that he was insisting his girlfriend come join, to come see. That story is nothing but an amalgamation of fairy tale, death, and beauty inhabiting the same fantastic realm—and where Russian ballerina Nadezhda Paplova plays the Bluebird herself! The only scene where the bluebird is in flock! ("The Two Deaths of Tanqueray" is the only story here where the bluebird is in flock.) Not to mention the only scene in the film where once the children each take a bluebird from this garden, the birds die.

A clown in the film, played by a famous Russian clown by the name of Oleg Popov, takes me immediately to the first story in this book ("Regarding Wine, Clowns . . ."). In the film, he too holds in his hand, a bluebird, albeit a rooster, but nevertheless, a bird! And nevertheless—blue.

Once they came onto the screen, I recognized the children at once. There was no longer a question in my mind, and everything took such bizarre sharp focus that the images on the screen were *so* familiar to me that they seemed almost now a remembered, or even other, *identity*—a former past that I'd forgotten (In volume 1, "Sam's Trinity.")

And it was the essence of these very things that to my own surprise began to link this film of youth to the tales in the two books I had just written. The book does *variations* many times on the themes scorched in me somewhere, as the film does at times too, atonements to things that had been buried in my subconscious for three decades, and that somehow needed justice to be finalized to them.

"Clara and Sam's Return" from volume 1, for example, is nothing but returning, giving back the union—the union that they had lost!—to the two children who had been forcefully separated by the old man (time).

The scene in the film is set in a heavenward plane where all the children of the *future* are awaiting to be called to be born down here on earth.

These two kids have been together up there for thousands of years, when suddenly a number comes up and this is why they must be separated—so that he is born. Forcing to break away the love and the thousand-year bond of these two spirits!

This is tragic, marvelous stuff! *All* from the movie. Now—*this* stayed in my head for three decades, and I, of course, had no clue. So one day, I woke up. It was November, and I wrote "Clara and Sam's Return." Which unbeknownst to me was where this "necessity" came from, suspended in filmmaking limbo. This unreal-but-essential place to me.

"Clara and Sam's Return" ends like this:

Together, they rose weightlessly into an inexistent place where they for some moments lingered, and where they would later become infinitely entangled. They rose to and through the galaxies of heaven—to where they had both been formed and from where they had been birthed . . . where they had once been separated and where they now have, finally, returned.

I mean, this is crazy stuff, that these two snot-nosed fools *needed* to be back with one another! It was an injustice not to be tolerated. And not time, or *anyone*, was going to achieve this act of cruelty against them ultimately. *We* were victorious! And they got their wish! They won against ill-will and inhumanity.

The film itself coming back to the forefront and fiber of my brain is the exact same effect as it was for Sam in "Sam's Trinity," when he meets back with Mary! It was as if a past life was suddenly remembered, known again! It was surreal how familiar all the images were to me—the kids and that dog and the cat and sugar and water and all that crazy stuff that goes on there. A lifetime in between, and they had remained as fresh and completely undistorted as when last left them behind when I exited Cine Candido not half a block away from my own house that balmy afternoon.

I would see the film only once.

The scenes were *part* of me. No doubt. Like that strange childhood song that lingers with no sense to the lyrics nor need but that it is indeed somehow so *important,* so essential to you that it's become but a piece of the puzzle without which who you *are* would not be wholly complete. That song of youth that you know and perhaps once in a while sing for no reason at all, even if to seemingly mock it, you are in all essence effortlessly remembering or recalling to surface that distant ghost of where you came from. An emotional knickknack from the array of things in your gallery of personal nostalgia that you can access any day while you transit those red and purple and gold halls of your memory's labyrinth. Where the pictures hang and where in the mirrors you are many ages at once.

The songs that bring you the comedy of who you were. How precious, how senseless, and how perfect.

The film was in English—to my surprise. I mean after all those rolls of cascading Russian letters for English to suddenly jump in the scene is both weird and magical.

I think in many ways the effort in this film *was* (is) a plea for peace.

It's a *symbol*, if nothing else.

Russians and Americans in the seventies? Deadly enemies? But together in the construction of beauty, huh. This reveals finally the truth inside the heart of people, often brutally hidden behind the lies that are the warped fabrications of conflicting political ideals. And there's your canker, folks. No ideal is primarily at fault to cause evil, yet not one of these ideals has been proven *not* to cause it in one form or the next. All of them. Communist *or* capitalist—because it is by the weakness of man's self-centered proclivities that none are completely possible without corruption. To judge a man by the way he differs from you, in how he thinks things should run, is to judge him badly. Simply because he has not lived his (faulty) ideal put to practice does not make him a bad man. Maybe misinformed, misguided, romantic—but certainly not evil by any stretch. And so as I've lived in the flesh that communism simply does not run well, I'm not going to hate the fool who's been duped to believe otherwise. Instead I'll like (or dislike) him for his personal virtues (or lack thereof).

Only through the reflection of someone's personal choices and how he carries himself as an individual may we offer the only fair way of judgment upon a person's character—not because of his opinions, his religious beliefs, nor on those large-scale matters that are beyond the reality of anyone's true capacity to encircle with their minds as an ethical totality.

But hopefully there's *always* film, and literature, and sports, and science, and music, and humanist philosophy—to remind us of what we are, and what we want, and what we can *do* and achieve when we get together for a singular purpose.

The movie perhaps could seem as no big deal, but the soul of it transcends to the point where today, as I watched it with my adult eyes, I was equally moved by it, and once again—and I'm not ashamed to admit it—I wept with a bunch of medicated blue-dyed pigeons.

The message of it is of an essential and fundamental purity that is hard for anyone to accomplish in communicating in any art form, and this I will have to attribute primarily to Nobel Prize winner Maurice Maeterlinck and his beautiful and delicate fable.

The film got horrid reviews once it came out, and it was primarily because many critics were looking at it with the wrong kind of eyes, in my estimation. It's a playful little film with a *huge* soul. It's their loss and not ours. It's not supposed to be a masterpiece of filmmaking, even though it *was* directed by a master—Cukor. But the difficulties in the set made this impossible. Language barriers and bad weather and inedible food and so on. But who cares, anyhow? Who cares about technical perfection when you have others who have nothing to say?—which is the case too often. And where only those fools are in tune to. And who wants to join them? Not I—that's for sure!

What is the use in *telling* a lot and *saying* nothing? Displays of perfectionism can only reach so far—little shallow sewing machines that'll do pretty little numbers for you and me. They're too fast; but in their haste, they *miss* more than what they cover.

Elizabeth Taylor got dysentery and was pooping blood for most of the filming. Jane Fonda was in relentless pursuit of political discussions with the Russians on the set, which Cukor opposed—rightly! But all that caused a bit of trouble, anyhow, and the chick who played the cat, Cicely Tyson, was casting voodoo spells on the set—as reported by Cukor himself!

Crazy stuff—I'm telling you.

But look at all that! Despite all *this*. Despite dysentery and voodoo and political upheavals, the film made it!

Let me tell you: the *disappointment* in the children in those two scenes were the most truly crushing things that I found throughout.

One was once the children found the enchanted forest of bluebirds and brought back a few; at the first sight of *reality*, both bluebirds died.

> *Girl: "They're dead."*
> *Boy: "Why have they died? What did we do to them?"*
> *Light (Elizabeth Taylor): "They are not real birds, Tyltyl (boy)—can't you see that?"*
> *Girl: "But, they were flying. We saw them. They were so beautiful!"*
> *Light: "They're just dream-birds, darling; they're not real. Come. Leave them here; they'll disappear in the sunlight."*

Oh great lord!—this is poetry of the kind one could only dream one day to find in oneself! It's of a tragic beauty I could never express how much I appreciate.

The film is (by today's standards) rudimentary, clumsy, and of course dated—fine. But thankfully, these are *not* the virtues of this great fantasy, which trump and render all these completely inconsequential.

The film—or rather Maeterlinck's play—takes a detour from reality in order to see it more clearly. And this is, in essence, the soul of my own *Bluebird*—both a fantasy and true.

Unbeknownst to me, he'd been with me the whole time—he had *never* left me to begin. And today, I found him again. I did.

I found my Bluebird.